P9-DGD-515

HOOD COUNTY LIBRARY

DEAD
ROOTS

A Bad Hair Day Mystery

DEAD ROOTS

Nancy J. Cohen

KENSINGTON BOOKS
www.kensingtonbooks.com

KENSINGTON BOOKS are published by

Kensington Publishing Corp.
850 Third Avenue
New York, NY 10022

Copyright © 2005 by Nancy J. Cohen

All rights reserved. No part of this book may be reproduced in any form or by any means without the prior written consent of the Publisher, excepting brief quotes used in reviews.

All Kensington titles, imprints, and distributed lines are available at special quantity discounts for bulk purchases for sales promotion, premiums, fund-raising, educational, or institutional use.

Special book excerpts or customized printings can also be created to fit specific needs. For details, write or phone the office of the Kensington Special Sales Manager: Attn. Special Sales Department. Kensington Publishing Corp., 850 Third Avenue, New York, NY 10022. Phone: 1-800-221-2647.

Kensington and the K logo Reg. U.S. Pat. & TM Off.

Library of Congress Card Catalogue Number: 2005924282
ISBN 0-7582-0658-5

First Printing: December 2005
10 9 8 7 6 5 4 3 2 1

Printed in the United States of America

Marla's family tree is based on my own extensive ancestry, so this book is dedicated to my maternal family roots.

Great-great grandparents: Abe and Yetta Sheinbloom.

Great grandparents: Itzrok Miodeck and Zipah Sheinbloom. They had six children, including Goldie, my grandmother.

Grandparents: Goldie, born in Poland, married Max Krizelman. They had eight children, including my mother, Minnie, born in Denver, Colorado.

(My father's parents, Rose and Joseph, had four children, including my father, Harry, born in Russia.)

Parents: Minnie and Harry Heller, who raised me to value the important things in life: love, honesty, loyalty, integrity, service to others, and the sanctity of marriage.

Brother: Charles, an intrepid spelunker who explores places I dare to go only in my imagination.

Husband: Richard, a devoted father and a wonderful husband who is the man of my dreams.

Children: Paul and Sara, to whom I pass on this legacy with all my love.

And to families everywhere: Value your relationships, because this is what really counts in life.

DEAD
ROOTS

Chapter One

"**M**aybe I shouldn't have come," Detective Dalton Vail said to hairstylist Marla Shore while they drove north on I-75 along Florida's west coast. "Your family is holding its first reunion. They may resent having an outsider present."

"You're my fiancé, not an outsider."

"How many people do you expect?"

Marla swept a strand of chestnut hair behind her ear. "I have a gazillion relatives. Some of us will be meeting each other for the first time. We're from all over the country."

Keeping his hands on the wheel, Vail gave her a disquieted glance. "I'd rather have you all to myself."

"We'll have our own room. You're not nervous, are you?"

His broad shoulders stiffened. "Nothing bothers me, sweet-cakes; you know that."

"Right," she murmured, her lips curving in a smile. *I might have believed that before we grew close, but not now.*

When they first met, she'd never suspected the gruff lieutenant could have a soft side. Memories flitted through her mind of their initial encounter. He'd been investigating a murder case where she was the prime suspect. His onslaught of questions had made her quake in her shoes. Later, when they started solving crimes together, her reaction changed to another sort of trembling under his skilled touch. Even now, Marla marveled that the lonely widower and his thirteen-year-old daughter included her as a special person in their lives.

She gazed at him fondly, absorbing the pleasing sight of his ebony hair streaked with silver, sharp, angular features, and tall, powerful frame. Too bad they couldn't steal away for longer.

"I've never heard of Sugar Crest," he commented.

"The resort isn't widely advertised. Out-of-state tourists usually go to places like Naples and Sarasota."

"What was that crack your Aunt Polly made? Something about being prepared for stormy waters?"

Her brow wrinkled. "I don't understand what she meant. Hurricane season is over, and we're supposed to have clear skies this weekend. It should be perfect for Thanksgiving."

"Fireworks often happen when families get together."

"She could be afraid of ghosts." Marla grinned. "The resort is listed in my guidebook under 'Haunted Florida Hotels.' It dates to the 1800s and was a sugar plantation until new owners took over in 1924. I'm sorry Brianna couldn't come. Your daughter would have had fun exploring the buildings."

"My folks haven't seen Brie in a long time. She was excited about visiting them in Maine. It'll be good for her to be with her grandparents for a change." Vail's gray eyes darkened to slate. "So it's just you and me. This can be sort of a pre-honeymoon. What shall we say if your family asks what date we've set?"

"We're still coordinating our schedules." Marla swung her gaze to the window. They'd just passed the Peace River near Punta Gorda. Fingering the amethyst ring on her right hand, she considered their options. Delaying the date for their nuptials had been her idea. "It's only been three weeks since Wilda's salon closed its doors in the same shopping strip as my place. We've been getting an influx of new customers as a result, and it's all I can do to handle the extra business. I must have been nuts to consider Wilda's offer to buy her shop."

"You can't do everything." He patted her arm. "I like your idea of adding spa services to Cut 'N Dye instead."

"Yeah, well, we're not supposed to discuss work on this trip."
Leaving the salon made her edgy. She'd had to assign her clients
to someone else and ask Nicole to take over as manager in her
absence. The other stylist didn't mind; she was always exhorting
Marla to take time off, but being the owner usually didn't allow
such luxuries.

"I can't wait to see the plantation," Marla said. "Ma told me
she'd be arriving early. She's supposed to bring Aunt Polly. I
wouldn't want to drive in their car, the way those two argue."

"You've told me so much about Aunt Polly that I'm curious to
meet her," Vail said, smiling.

"You may be sorry. She's quite a character." Marla hoped her
eccentric relatives wouldn't turn him off about marrying her.
Maybe that's why Vail hadn't given her a diamond engagement
ring yet as he'd promised: he wanted to check out her bloodlines.

"Isn't your Aunt Polly the one who came up with the idea of
holding a reunion at this resort?"

"That's right, although Cynthia made the arrangements." Dalton
had met her cousin while investigating the murder of a board
member for Cynthia's favorite volunteer organization. "She said
there's a lot to do in the area. I believe the resort alone covers
over two hundred acres, and if that doesn't keep us occupied, we
can drive to Sarasota or visit Solomon's Castle. Four days probably won't be enough, especially with the social events planned."

Vail's lips tightened. "What do you mean?"

"Cynthia was working with the social director at the hotel to
provide some mixers for our group. I know there's a cocktail
party tonight. We'll get a schedule when we arrive. I just want
enough time to enjoy the beach."

"If I can look at you in a swimsuit, I'll agree."

Her eyebrows lifted, but she didn't respond to his innuendo.
"You should like the restaurants, although Cynthia may have secured us a private banquet hall."

"I was hoping we'd have free rein during the day and would
just meet your clan for dinner." He gave a resigned sigh.
"Whatever makes you happy."

"Oh, I don't know—after an extended weekend with my cousins, I might go home screaming. I'm more curious about Aunt Polly's motives. I think she may have her own agenda for bringing us together."

Vail glanced at her. "You're not thinking about that psychic's prediction, are you?"

"What, that someone close to me will die during an upcoming trip?" She laughed. "Wilda just used that as an excuse to get me to solve Carolyn Sutton's murder."

"I thought you said another medium in Cassadaga confirmed her reading."

"I'm not worried. We both need a break from work. Let's try to relax." The psychics had also advised her to devote more energy to herself. She intended to have fun this weekend, and that meant casting off her misgivings. "Look, there's the sign. Turn here."

The drive into the estate took them down a bumpy segment of road. According to her guidebook, the road was constructed from an early form of concrete called tabby: a mixture of lime, sand, oyster shells, and water. Their route wound through fields that had once yielded cotton, sugarcane, and citrus. Sunlight gave way to shade when they entered a wooded area where Spanish moss draped overhanging live oaks. In the distance, Marla spotted stately queen palms dotting the grounds, which were splashed with pink and red hibiscus and other perennial flowers.

Her attention shifted to various buildings looming within range, but nothing prepared her for the sight of the main hotel. The road segued into a paved brick driveway that ended in a circular swath. Their car slowed in front of an immense palatial structure.

As Vail pulled up to a section marked FOR GUESTS ONLY, she gaped at the grand entrance. "Oh my gosh. I didn't expect anything so magnificent."

Vail slid the keys out of the ignition. "This doesn't look like a plantation manor to me. I was expecting some quaint old cracker residence." Disappointment edged his tone.

"Cynthia didn't tell me the renovations were this extensive. It must be a well-guarded secret. I'll bet this rivals the Breakers in Palm Beach. The only thing like it on this coast is the Don Cesar Beach Resort in St. Petersburg."

She gazed at the French Renaissance design, craning her neck to regard the central tower, which stood higher than ten stories. The main portion appeared as a rectangle, with four offshoots sprouting like an X-Wing fighter.

After Vail hit the UNLOCK button, Marla stepped into the balmy November air. She'd brought mostly casual clothes, appropriate for a beach house, not for this opulence. When she pushed beyond the massive double doors, she noted that time seemed frozen in the 1920s-era lobby. Crystal chandeliers, wood-paneled walls, and hunter green upholstered furnishings decorated an expanse intersected by a wide, carpeted stairway that climbed to a mezzanine level. The air didn't have the modern smell of air-conditioned purity; rather, it carried a faint mustiness with a tinge of lemon oil.

"Marla, I've been waiting for you!"

She whirled to see her mother bearing down on them. "Ma, you didn't tell me this place was so fancy. I didn't bring the right clothes."

Anita kissed her and gave Vail a brief hug. "Don't worry about it. I'm a bit overwhelmed myself. Did you tell the porter to get your luggage? They still have old-fashioned keys here, none of that plastic card nonsense. Wait until you see the rooms. They're enormous."

Marla and Dalton followed Anita to the registration desk, a wide mahogany counter. Here a concession to modernity appeared: computer stations manned by uniformed clerks. Marla's astounded glance lifted to the far wall where miniature wood cubicles were emblazoned with each guest's room number on shiny brass plates. *Past meets present,* she thought, eager to explore.

"Marla gave me the impression this hotel was built on the site of an old plantation house," Vail said after giving their names to a fresh-faced young man. "I expected southern-style comfort—you know, ceiling fans, wraparound porches."

"You'll find that at Planter's House, a separate building from the main hotel. It's the original residence, built in 1844, when the plantation was established," the clerk explained. "When Andrew Marks took over in the 1920s, he constructed this hotel and converted the property to a resort. Planter's House was renovated and is now reserved for our concierge-level guests. You can tour some of the other early buildings, though."

"Didn't slaves work the fields?" Marla asked.

"Yes ma'am." He handed Vail a form to sign.

"How many of the original structures survived?"

"The sugar mill, some tabby cabins, the old barn, and the stable," Anita cut in. "I'd hoped our family would have exclusive run of the resort this weekend, but we're not the only group here, since it's a holiday. A team of paranormal researchers are staying at the hotel to conduct experiments. I met some of them already. They're looking for ghosts."

Turning to Vail, Marla gave him a seductive glance. "Maybe you'd like to hunt spooks with me."

"You left your poodle with the vet, remember?" he replied, eyes twinkling.

"Leave Spooks out of this. I'm not talking about my dog."

"Oh no? Some of those psychics you've met could be considered animals of an unusual variety."

"You'll see. I'll bet some of the ghost stories are real. Maybe Aunt Polly knows more about them. She's the one who chose this place. Where is she?" Marla asked her mother.

"Polly is getting settled in her room. If I had to stay in her company for one more minute, I'd *plotz.*"

"Ma, that's not nice."

"You should have heard her on the drive over. She wouldn't shut up about Roger and me." Lifting her chin, Anita thrust slender fingers tipped with red nail polish through her white layered hair.

Marla was grateful Anita had not brought her boyfriend. This was a family retreat, after all. It was also her fiancé's first chance to meet the entire clan. She hoped he wouldn't have to listen to arguments the whole time.

"There's talk of converting the property into a Florida living-history experience as a new tourist attraction," Anita said.

"Just what we need in Florida, another theme park," Vail drawled.

Anita snorted her displeasure. "City council members are meeting to discuss the issue. If you ask me, the hotel shouldn't have booked so many groups for one weekend. At least Cynthia reserved early enough to get the prime space. You'll have to get a schedule, angel. Oh, there's the social director." Anita flagged down a lady just coming off the elevator.

Completing the room arrangements, Vail handed Marla a key. "I'll go up with the luggage. You can join me when you're ready." He sped off, clearly anxious to avoid further entanglement.

A woman with hair like spun gold, ocean blue eyes, and a smiling mouth approached them. "Hello, I'm Champagne Glass, the social events coordinator." She held out a firm hand for Marla to shake.

"Marla Shore, my daughter," Anita said, beaming.

Marla felt like Gulliver as she took the petite blond woman's hand. With her shorts outfit, socks, and running shoes, the social director looked like a preppie camp counselor, even down to her ponytail tied with a navy scrunchie.

"We're so *delighted* to have your family with us this weekend." Champagne pulled a stack of papers from her portfolio. "I've designed a schedule of activities for you to meet and greet each other. Most are casual affairs, except for Thanksgiving dinner tomorrow, and a dance party on Saturday night before everyone leaves. You're just going to *love* this place. If I can help you in any way, my extension is on this card. Otherwise, I'll be around to make sure everyone is having a *super* time."

Forced fun was never Marla's favorite sport. "After I unpack, I'd like to explore the grounds. What time is the tour? Seeing the original buildings is a highlight on my list."

Champagne's smile dazzled like sunbeams on the ocean. "I'm leading a group at two o'clock. You're *so* welcome to join us. Um, there's one thing I *must* mention. The hotel is in various stages of repair. We ask that you not go near the northwest wing."

"Why is that?" Marla's natural nosiness compelled her to ask.

"Oleander Hall is unsafe. Termites, you see, and there's some question about whether it'll be torn down or renovated. In the meantime, it is *imperative* you don't venture into that area."

"Okay." Odd that only a portion of the place would be affected by termites. Wouldn't they have to clear out the entire hotel to fumigate it with poison gas? Or maybe you only did that with houses.

"Is the beach far, and is there a charge for chair rentals?" Marla asked. Changing into a swimsuit and lazing under the sun seemed an appealing prospect for later.

"If you head down the Grand Terrace in the rear," said Champagne, "past the pool, you'll come to the beach. Chairs are free, and you can rent cabanas."

"Wait, Marla, here comes Polly. You talk to her," Anita urged. "I want to ask Champagne about our cocktail party."

Before Marla could protest, Anita hustled away with Champagne in a huddled conversation. *Oh great,* Marla thought, Aunt Polly had spotted her. Now she was stuck, while Vail waited upstairs. He must be wondering what was keeping her.

"Aunt Polly, how good to see you," she said, catching the elderly lady's frail shoulders in a quick embrace. Was it her imagination, or had Polly grown thinner since their last visit? Marla had begun helping her aunt with financial affairs at home, and she'd just seen her two weeks ago. She hadn't remembered Polly's bones being so prominent. It gave her face a hollow appearance and her wrinkled skin a sallow cast.

"It's about time you got here," her aunt scolded, waggling a gnarled finger. "I have something for you to do." She peered at

Marla through new glasses, thanks to Barry Gold, an optometrist who kept up his pursuit of Marla even though her affection was engaged elsewhere. Now if only Marla could get Polly to shop for new clothes. Her aunt's shirtwaist dress was clean, with the hem in place, but the style dated back to the fifties. Knowing Polly, Marla figured the garment might be that old.

"What can I help you with?" she asked her aunt, wishing Polly would listen to reason. The older woman saved money by eschewing air-conditioning, recycling trash, saving junk-mail envelopes, and doing her laundry by hand. Rejecting Anita's offer of assistance, Polly had allowed Marla into her frugal life but refused to change her ways.

"It's a long story. We'll need to sit down."

"Then I'll need time to listen. I'm here with my fiancé," Marla explained. "Can we meet later? Dalton is waiting for me, and I have to unpack."

"Whassat? Something wrong with your back?"

Why don't you get a set of hearing aids already? "I've got to go," she said in a loud voice, moving away from a laughing couple in tennis outfits.

"We all have to go sometime. Did you know your granddaddy passed away in this place?"

"What?" Startled, Marla glanced into Polly's rheumy eyes, but they held intelligence, not senility.

"Yep. We used to live here when I was young. Those were the days when everything was golden, mind you. By the time I was old enough to spell my name, Papa had moved us out of the antebellum mansion and into this grand hotel. He had vision, Papa did. That's your granddaddy Andrew."

Marla put her handbag on a lamp table to give her shoulder a rest. "How long ago was this? Ma never said anything about your living here."

"You don't remember your grandma, do you? She took on the place after Papa died."

"Do you mean they managed the resort?"

"Oh no, dear. They owned it."

Marla's jaw dropped. Anita had alluded to some lost wealth in her past but never indicated they'd owned property this extensive. "What happened?"

"Eh? Speak up." Polly cupped her ear, a motion that nearly knocked the red felt hat off her head, exposing scraggly gray hair with self-shorn ends.

"I said, what happened?" Marla shouted. Several guests glanced in their direction. She wondered if any of them were cousins she hadn't met. Her mother had seven siblings, and all but two of them had produced children. A large contingent lived in Colorado. Some resided in Canada, and still others remained in Israel and Russia. She'd met most of her relatives from the Northeast and South, but their family tree was so expansive that mapping it took seven landscape-formatted sheets of paper placed end to end.

"Ruth, that's my mama, sold the resort in the 1960s," Polly explained.

"I never really knew her. She died in 1973, five years after I was born."

"You're too warm? Why don't you take off that blazer? You're on vacation, dear. You shouldn't be so dressed up. Go to your room and get changed."

"That's a good idea. I'll dash off right now." Grateful for the excuse, Marla snatched her purse from its resting place.

"Come see me later, child," Polly ordered. Paling suddenly, the old woman swayed.

Marla felt a jolt of alarm. "Aunt Polly, are you okay? Shall I take you to your room?" She grabbed her aunt's elbow.

"I'll be fine," Polly said, shaking her off, "but only if you'll agree to help me with my search. Where are you staying?"

Marla glanced at her key. "Room 407 in Hibiscus Hall. Where are you?"

"I have a suite in the tower, but I don't sleep there. Too many memories. The tower is where . . . Well, I'll tell you more about it next time." She snorted. "Your cousin Cynthia wouldn't demean herself to stay in the main building. She and Bruce reserved the entire top floor of Planter's House along with that no-good brother of hers. It's time she kicked him out. It's the only way he'll learn to stand on his own two feet."

Give him a break. Corbin just got out of jail. "Cynthia is glad her brother has come home."

"Yes, I'm home now." Polly's expression took on a wistful look. "I'll see my parents soon. Have you talked to them yet?"

Uh oh. Polly's mental light bulb was loose. Mentioning her siblings might help straighten her circuits. "No, *tanteh.* Is Uncle Moishe coming? I heard he wasn't well."

"Moishe? He couldn't stay away. His kids are here, along with their children. I wonder how much he's told them. Be careful what you say to anyone, dear."

Marla opened her mouth, then closed it again. Polly would tell her what she wanted at the appropriate time. "If you'll be all right, I'm heading for my room. Which way do I go?"

Vail must think she got lost. Her stomach rumbled, and she decided to check out the restaurants after getting changed. That is, unless Champagne had arranged a family get-together for lunch. She'd study their schedules after unpacking.

"You're too young to go," Polly said, misinterpreting her words. Her eyes shone as she clutched Marla's arm. "Steer clear of Oleander Hall and you'll be all right."

Wasn't that the same section Champagne had warned her away from? "Don't worry, I'm not going in that direction. The social director told me it needs repairs and might be dangerous."

"That's not the only reason." Polly leaned forward, giving Marla a whiff of fetid breath. "Bad spirits inhabit that wing, and only they know what really happened over there."

Chapter
Two

Marla gaped at Polly. Did her aunt believe in ghost stories? "You grew up here. Who's haunting the place?"

Polly's eyes misted. "After the tragedy, our family drifted apart. No one wants to heal our dynasty more than I do. This is our last chance to mend fences and right old wrongs." Her voice shook with emotion. Glancing furtively about the lobby, she added, "Those ghost hunters may rattle a few cages. We don't want them finding anything that belongs to us. Stay alert, mind you."

"What do you mean?"

"You'll see. You're a smart girl, so I'm sure you can handle this bunch." Muttering to herself, Polly shuffled off.

Marla found herself surrounded by a motley crew of young people with eager faces. They wore jeans and T-shirts saying SEEING IS BELIEVING. An array of equipment jangled on their bodies: cameras, recorders, compasses, and other gadgets.

"We're with the West Coast Florida Ghost Chasers," said one young man with a crewcut and a toothy grin. "Are you one of the family?" He pronounced those last two words with extra emphasis, as though he were talking about the Kennedys or Donald Trump.

Considering the hotel's past history, maybe he referred to one of Florida's finest, like Henry Flagler or James Deering, Marla thought. "Which family? This is a holiday weekend. Lots of people are vacationing here." She waved her arm to encompass the expansive lobby.

"You know, Andrew Marks, the man who built the place. Aren't you one of his descendants?"

Hearing her grandfather's name from the mouth of a stranger startled her. "What if I am?"

"You can help us prove our point." At his pronouncement, the other paranormal folks nodded their heads. "Andrew's spirit walks the halls. Maybe he'll manifest himself to you."

Been there, done that. Didn't I solve Carolyn Sutton's murder to put her ghost to rest? "No, thanks. I'm here for recreation, nothing more. I don't want to be involved in anyone else's business."

The young man squinted. "But it's your family, and rumor says the treasure was never found. Those two strangers may still be here, guarding its secret."

"Treasure? What strangers?" she asked, confused.

"The two men who visited Andrew the night he died."

"I'm unaware of the resort's history. Are you implying these people are ghosts?"

The guy gave her an odd look, as though she were the one treading on unknown territory. "We're called in when people suspect a haunting. We look for evidence to substantiate their claim. In many cases, we'll disprove it."

"I don't get it."

"There have been incidents at the resort, and management hired us to determine if the entities are real. In that case, we'll ask them to leave."

"Oh, right. Tell me," Marla said, crossing her arms, "why would my grandfather's soul linger here? Does he have unfinished business relating to the property? I'd think he would hover by the cemetery where his body is buried."

"Not necessarily," a woman with mousy hair sang in a high-pitched voice. She'd been scribbling in a notepad as Vail did when he was on a murder case. "Some spirits are attached to a place, and they don't want to leave. Or, as you say, Andrew has unfinished business. Since this was the site of a traumatic event, you know, where he—"

"Miz Shore?"

Marla whirled around. "Yes?" she said to the man leering at her. He had wild hair the color of buckskin, narrow-set amber eyes, and a thin build nearly obscured by an oversized maroon staff jacket. His name tag read HARVEY LYLE.

"I'm one of the stewards, ma'am. Yer roommate called the front desk. He's wondering why ya been gone so long."

She winced. "Guess I'd better go upstairs." Glancing over her shoulder, she said to the waiting group, "Thanks for the information. I'll catch you later."

She turned to follow the man toward the elevator. She'd had enough communiqués from the spirits after her trip to Cassadaga. If Andrew's ghost inhabited this place, it had better have a reason that wouldn't involve her. Nonetheless, curiosity compelled her to learn more.

"What do you know about ghost stories associated with the hotel?" she said to the steward.

Stepping aside so she could enter the elevator, Harvey shot her a bleary look. Was it the lighting, or did his eyes look somewhat jaundiced? In the lift, he pushed the button for the fourth floor.

"Well, ma'am, I suppose yer aunt could tell ya about them spooks. Miz Polly been comin' to the hotel every year since her mama sold the place. She always stays in the same room. Looking for the loot, she is, if ya ask me." He laughed, emitting fumes of rum like a drunken sailor.

"What loot is that?"

"I'm surprised ya haven't heard about it before. Ya bein' family and all. First time I've seen the whole caboodle gathered here, though, so maybe Miz Polly plans to let you in on her secrets. Ya might ask Seto Mulch what he knows; the old crow has been here since the beginnin'. He's our groundskeeper," Harvey added with a belch that fouled the air.

Fortunately, the elevator jerked to a halt and the door slid open. Harvey led her onto the top level of Hibiscus Hall.

"Where are we? I'm lost already," she said.

"We're in the southeast wing. The main building has seven floors, but the owner's tower in the center goes to fourteen. That's where Mr. Marks used to live. After he died, the family moved down to twelve. No one goes there now 'cept the spooks."

"I've been told not to go near Oleander Hall."

He nodded vigorously, guiding her down a carpeted corridor where Marla noticed peeling wallpaper, flickering electric lights in wall sconces, and black-painted doors. Windows, spaced at wide intervals, provided a minimal view of the grounds beyond curtains that billowed without any visible breeze. Her nose wrinkled at the musty odor. For a high-class resort, she'd say the building had more than one wing needing renovation.

"Oleander is in a bad way," Harvey said, tripping over a fold in the carpet. He didn't regain his balance so readily, tottering for a moment before steadying himself. "The whole place needs fixin' but we dunno what's gonna happen. The political bigwigs are here this weekend to hash it out. One side wants to restore the hotel to its heyday; others mean to tear it down and then rebuild on the early plantation site."

"How does the staff feel about it?"

He shrugged. "Mr. Butler—he's the manager—is tryin' to get the owners to remodel instead of sellin' to real estate people who'll turn the property into a theme park. We likes things as they are, ya know?"

Stopping in front of her room number, Marla fit her key in the lock. "Thanks, Harvey. I appreciate the information."

"Yes ma'am. If ya need anything"—he winked—"anything at all, give me a holler. I'm always willin' to share a drink and a few stories."

Marla handed him a two-dollar tip before entering her room.

Inside, Vail sprang off the bed where he'd been watching a football game on television. "What took you so long?" he said, his expression edged with concern.

"I was talking to Aunt Polly, then some of those paranormal people came over. They've been hired to chase away ghosts and mentioned something about incidents. I'll tell you about it later. I want to take the tour, so we don't have much time."

"You didn't unpack." He sauntered closer, a familiar gleam in his eyes. "I was hoping we could, uh, relax a bit in our room." His arms encircled her.

She kissed him, then let her lips hover by his mouth. "That's a tempting offer, but I'm hungry." She rubbed her body against his. "Would you mind waiting?"

"Actually, I'm starving. We'll have plenty of time for this later." Releasing her, he grinned. "The spa complex has a café. If we hustle, we should be able to catch lunch on the way to the tour. It leaves from the movie house not far from there."

Marla regarded her suitcase sitting on a luggage rack. "I'll get washed and hang up my dresses. You can take charge of our schedule." Reaching into her handbag, she withdrew the papers from the social director. Vail groaned as she tossed him the stack. Before he could make any sarcastic remarks, she'd scurried into the bathroom.

At least the facilities had bright vanity lighting and modern plumbing, she thought gratefully as she scrubbed her hands. Their hotel room wasn't so bad, either. The king-size bed looked inviting, with its floral bedspread. Side tables with lamps, a generous dresser, a desk, and a sitting area seemed spacious although stodgy in design. No coffeemaker, and probably no high speed data transmission line. Oh, well. She didn't plan to spend much time in the room, even if Vail did. She'd have to drag him with her to the obligatory social events.

After quickly hanging up her more delicate outfits, lining her shoes up in rows on the closet floor, and putting her beaded evening purse in a drawer, she pronounced herself ready to go. She'd unpack the rest later.

They wound through various corridors searching for the elevator. She could have sworn Harvey had led her in a straight line, but it appeared there were more hallways than legs on a spider.

Losing all sense of direction, she came up short when they reached a roped-off section with a sign that said NO ADMITTANCE, TRESPASSERS WILL BE PROSECUTED. Beyond stretched a darkened corridor with closed doors, much like the one in the Haunted Mansion at Walt Disney World. Marla took a step forward, wondering if she'd see an apparition at the far end.

"You're not allowed in there," barked a voice from behind. Marla felt Vail's hand on her arm, steering her around.

"Who are you?" Vail asked bluntly, directing his query to the fellow who glared at them with disapproval.

"I'm George Butler, hotel manager. This is a restricted area." The man's impeccably tailored suit backed the authority in his voice. A pair of cold, dark eyes regarded them. Marla's glance swept to his receded hairline. His slicked-back hair was artificially darkened.

"This must be Oleander Hall," she said excitedly. "It's supposed to be in disrepair, but it doesn't look that bad to me." Certainly no worse than the Hibiscus wing.

The manager's shoulders stiffened. "Much of the structural damage isn't evident to the eye. Be assured it is not safe until extensive repairs are done."

"Is it true they may tear down the hotel and build a theme park in its place?"

Butler's gaze hardened. "Not if I have anything to say about it. I'm attending the city council meeting later that's being held in one of our ballrooms. It would be a disgrace to destroy such a monument to our history. This hotel, if restored to its former glory, could rake in much needed tourist dollars to help repay the construction costs."

Marla caught a reflection of light from a corroded mirror on the wall. There weren't any windows nearby. Had that glimmer come from the deserted hall? The hairs on her neck prickled. "What about ghosts? I've heard the place is haunted. You hired a bunch of ghostbusters who I met earlier."

The manager bristled. "They are paranormal investigators,

here at my request. We've had some, uh, episodes, and I felt it prudent to bring in experts."

Vail gawked at Butler. "You consider ghost-chasing groupies to be experts? What kind of problem are you having?"

"Nothing that concerns our guests."

"Oh no?" Vail's persistent tone demanded an answer.

Marla almost felt compelled to explain his role as a police detective but held her tongue. "Something bad happened here," she told him. "Aunt Polly mentioned the tower, and the young woman I met earlier hinted at a traumatic event."

Butler compressed his lips. "Then may I suggest you ask your aunt about it. She's more closely related to the history of this place than anyone else. As for the rest, Dr. Rip Spector is in charge of my consultants. If you see or hear anything extraordinary, kindly inform him."

After escorting them to the proper elevator, Butler took his leave while Marla and Vail descended to the ground floor.

Getting her bearings, she pointed toward an exit door. "Let's go out here so we don't pass through the main lobby again. Which way is the cinema?"

Vail held the door open for her. "We'll head to the spa complex first. We have to go around the tennis courts to get there. I hope they have something substantial to eat at the café. Or if you'd rather, we could hit one of the other restaurants for a sit-down lunch."

"We don't have time if we're going on the tour. We can go somewhere nice for dinner tonight. You have our social schedule. Is there anything planned besides Cynthia's cocktail party from six to eight?" Marla asked, striding along a gravel path among manicured lawns.

"Not that I could tell. I'd like to try the steakhouse. It's located in the former stables."

"Okay." Marla didn't care where they ate. She was more interested in delving into the fascinating history of the place and wondering how it impinged on current issues facing the resort.

After stuffing down turkey and cheese sandwiches at the spa café, they headed toward the movie house, located in a converted barn. Marla spotted Cynthia loitering among the tour members who'd gathered in front of the renovated building.

Exchanging air kisses with her cousin, she waited while Vail offered his greetings. *He's really being a mensch about all this,* she thought with a swell of warmth.

"Where are Bruce and the kids?" she asked.

"They're at the beach. We have so many exciting events planned, I hope we have time for everything," Cynthia said, patting her well-coiffed blond hair. Diamonds glittered on her left hand and in her pierced ears. Her husband had made his money in real estate; they had extensive property of their own in eastern Fort Lauderdale.

"I can't wait to lie on a lounge chair." Marla admitted, "but I couldn't resist the tour. It sounds like there were some strange events in the history of this place. Have you heard about—?"

"Hi, Marla. I'm glad you could join us." Champagne breezed past, drowning out Marla's words with a booming greeting to the group and a round of introductions.

"After the cocktail party tonight, some of us are meeting at the Jasmine Court restaurant for dinner if you want to join us," Cynthia offered, hovering close to Marla. "And we're having a bingo game by the west veranda at ten o'clock for night owls."

Vail grimaced. "It's been a long day, so we'll probably turn in early. Right, hon?"

"Which rooms are you in?" Cynthia said.

"Hibiscus 407," Marla answered.

Cynthia glanced at each of them in turn, moistening her lower lip. "You're staying together? It doesn't bother me, but some of the other relatives might talk. I mean, you're not married yet and . . ." Cynthia flushed deeply. "Sorry, it's none of my business."

Marla straightened her shoulders. "In this modern age, I wouldn't think anyone cares."

"You'd be surprised." Cynthia lowered her voice, leaning forward. "Everyone is asking me where Corbin has been the past few years. I-I can't tell them my brother just got out of jail." Her blue eyes implored Marla. "You won't say anything, will you?"

"Of course not." Both of their gazes swung to Vail.

He raised his arms in surrender. "Hey, I didn't hear anything. Don't look at me."

Marla felt her elbow bumped and turned to face a bevy of relatives from Massachusetts she hadn't seen in a while. "Uncle William and Aunt Harriet, how delightful." They'd arrived with the oldest of their three daughters, Joan, who was accompanied by a youthful version of herself. "Who's this beautiful young lady?" Marla said, regarding the pretty brunette, who had a slightly upturned nose and impishly curved mouth.

"Rochelle recently turned sixteen," Joan replied, beaming at her only child. "She's just gotten her driver's license."

"It's great to see you," Marla said. "Where is everyone else? Lori is here, isn't she?"

"Lori and Jeff just arrived and are getting settled. We've already seen Julia and Alan, but they didn't have far to come, did they?" Joan chuckled. Her youngest sister and brother-in-law lived on Florida's east coast.

Vail cleared his throat, and Marla stepped aside to introduce him. "This is my fiancé, Dalton Vail." She attempted to explain her family tree while he murmured a polite greeting. "Joan's father, my Uncle William, is my mother's brother."

"They'll give you a quiz before the weekend is over," Rochelle put in laughingly. She wore a typical teenager's outfit: skimpy tank top that revealed her navel ring and jeans slung low over her hips.

"So what do you do?" Joan asked Dalton as Marla gave her older cousin's head an admiring glance. Bronze highlights glinted in the sunlight on cascading waves of ash blond hair. "I thought Marla would shy away from permanent relationships after she divorced good old Stan."

"I'm in the law field," Vail stated, somewhat aloofly.

"Oh, Stan was an attorney, too."

"Not a lawyer. I'm a homicide investigator."

"Awesome!" Rochelle cried, trotting beside him as the group followed their guide. "So, like, do you carry a gun?"

"Usually."

"Have you caught many bad guys?"

"Uh huh."

"Has anyone shot at you?"

"There have been a few incidents."

"Ever been wounded in action?"

"Just a few bumps and bruises, nothing major."

"So, like, how do you keep fit?"

"I chase Marla around the block. It's tough to keep up with her fast pace."

Behind them, Joan winked at Marla. *What a hunk*, she mouthed. Marla wondered what she could do to rescue Vail from Rochelle's barrage of questions.

She needn't have bothered. After leading them through a forest of pines where dead needles cushioned the ground and a hush descended upon them, Champagne stopped to lecture.

"Tobias Rutfield established Sugar Crest Plantation in 1844 at the end of the Second Seminole War," she said in a didactic tone lacking her usual gushy timbre. "He bought thirty-five hundred acres and planted sugarcane, Sea Island cotton, and citrus. At his peak, he owned three hundred slaves. In 1924 a hurricane caused extensive damage, and it required too much money to rebuild. His son sold the property to Andrew Marks.

"When Marks took over, he decided to change the place into a winter retreat for vacationing northerners. That's when he built the main hotel. I'm going to show you the earlier structures: the sugar mill, some tabby slave cabins, Planter's House, where Rutfield resided with his family, and the conservatory."

The social director smiled. "I highly recommend the Sugar Garden Restaurant adjacent to the greenhouse for afternoon tea. It has a delightful view of the formal gardens. When you get a chance, check out our renovated structures. The movie theater is now housed in the former barn, and the steakhouse is located where horses once lived. The barbecued ribs are *astounding*."

"Yo, Marla," hissed Joan. "Have you set a date?"

"What?"

"When are you getting married? I'll have to reserve the day on my calendar."

Marla glanced at Vail's stern profile. He'd stepped apart from the women, but Rochelle still dogged his footsteps. His expression told her he was trying hard, but failing, to pretend interest in the historical monologue. "We're, uh, still coordinating our schedules."

"You're not going to tie the knot at the same synagogue where you wed Stan, are you?"

"I doubt it. Dalton isn't Jewish."

Joan's eyes widened at the same time her parents, hovering within listening distance, gave a collective gasp.

Marla turned her head toward Champagne, whose finger pointed to a small pile of shells on the ground.

"The Indians who lived here harvested shellfish for food," the blonde stated. "They piled empty oyster shells into four-foot-high mounds known as middens. Early builders used this material to make a primitive form of concrete called tabby. Ten bushels each of shells, lime, and sand were mixed with ten barrels of water to make sixteen cubic feet of wall. Planter's House is constructed of this material, with walls nearly two feet thick. You can still see the tiny holes from spreader pins that held the wooden forms where the liquid tabby dried."

She paused. "Unfortunately, Rutfield disregarded local traditions by erecting his house on hallowed ground. In so doing, he eradicated an Indian burial mound, and the land has been cursed ever since."

Chapter
Three

"You wanted to know about ghost stories," Champagne said to Marla, leading the group down a path toward jutting stone ruins. "We've had various incidents reported that have no clear explanation. The paranormal team that's here this weekend might be able to shed light on them. Personally, I think the hauntings are real."

"Do the stories relate to Rutfield or to his successor, Andrew Marks?" Marla asked, watching her footing over sandy ground sprinkled with fallen pine cones, dead branches, and the occasional stray coconut. As they approached the sugar mill, pines gave way to trees more typical of a tropical hammock: malaleucas and cabbage palms, sapadillos and seagrapes. The smell of decay weighted the air.

"You'll hear different tales regarding both men, plus some other strange things. Follow me."

A dozen construction workers, swarthy men wearing stained clothing and weary expressions, trudged past toward an open field. Although the outbuildings must have been in different stages of renovation, Marla hadn't noticed the annoying buzz of saws or whine of drills. Instead, bird songs and the distant swish of waves reached her ears. Since it was a holiday weekend, why weren't the men at home with their families?

At the ruins, Champagne paused to bounce on her feet. She waited until the laborers receded in the distance before continuing her spiel. "People have seen a lady in a long white gown roaming these ruins. Rumor says she's Miss Alyssa, only daughter to Tobias Rutfield. It appears the girl took a fancy to their Irish foreman and met him in secret assignations. The young man, who was madly in love with her, understood her father would never approve a match between them.

"One day, Rutfield told his daughter that he intended for her to marry a neighboring landowner. In defiance, she rode out to find the Irishman, but there was a miscommunication. She waited for him in the mill, where a fire erupted. When her horse returned to the main house unmounted, her father led a search party. They found the girl's remains in the storage room, where she must have been wedged in by a barrel. Those things were huge, and if one got dislodged, she could easily have been trapped. Finding her locket nearby was the definitive evidence. The Irishman mourned her deeply and left the plantation soon afterward. Supposedly, her spirit searches for him still."

"What a romantic story," Cynthia exclaimed, putting a hand to her heart.

Marla's devious mind ran in other directions. "Did they determine how the fire started? Weren't there slaves around?"

"It was a Sunday, when everyone attended religious services. Rutfield's daughter ducked out from the church right after the sermon."

"Maybe the young couple had a disagreement, and the Irishman murdered her. Alyssa's ghost is trying to let people know that's what happened," Marla suggested. "Or she set the fire herself, committing suicide because she wouldn't be forced into an unwanted marriage."

Champagne shrugged. "At least she's a benevolent entity, even if she is unhappy. The other spirits on the property aren't as tame, but we'll get to them later." She led the group forward.

"Be careful where you step, now. That rickety wooden barricade shields an old well, and you wouldn't want to fall in." Gesturing, she added, "There's one of the cisterns that captured rainwater. Rutfield used an extensive system of water collection, with pipes leading to a storage facility having a capacity of forty thousand gallons. Part of its brick building still stands north of here."

Surprised by the complexity of the ruins, Marla surveyed their surroundings. She'd expected a funnel-like single structure similar to ones she'd seen in pictures of the Caribbean Islands. Evidently, this had been a much larger facility. She gazed at a thirty-foot-high chimney that remained mostly intact. A wide gap in its base looked big enough for a person to explore. *Not me, thanks*, she thought, envisioning vermin inside.

"You can see remnants from the mill," Champagne said, pointing to rusted machinery strewn across the uneven stone foundation. "Processing the sugarcane wasn't easy. It took twelve to eighteen months to harvest, then the stalks had to be crushed. See that old sugar press?"

She led them under an archway and into the cool interior of a stone structure. Vast pits, lined with coquina shells, sank into the flooring in a long row. "The juice was collected in big vats before being sent to the boiling bench in here. These pits used to hold huge kettles, or copper pans called coppers. They were heated by fires fueled by dry cane stalks. As the juice heated, its water content boiled off, and impurities were skimmed from the top. After the juice boiled down, it was ladled into smaller coppers and finally poured into wooden pans. Sugar crystals formed as it cooled."

"What was this bell used for?" Joan asked from outside.

"The clanging bell called slaves in from the fields." Champagne paused. "A few unfortunate accidents happened, as they will in any industrial setting: slaves who lost their footing slipped and were crushed, or fell into one of the boiling pits. People have said they've heard the bell ring when no one else is about, and not a leaf stirs on the trees."

Shudders rippled through the group. "How much sugar could this place produce?" asked a man in the rear.

"The presses generated from three to five hundred gallons of juice per hour. The crystallized sugar was put into hogsheads, or barrels, holding up to sixteen hundred pounds each. Did you know a railroad once ran through here? It's all overgrown now, of course. Take a few minutes and look around, then we'll move on."

Spying Rochelle on her fiancé's tail, Marla hastened to join him. "Isn't this amazing?" Marla said, taking his arm in a proprietary gesture. They ducked under the arch to proceed outside. "Think how many slaves must have lived and died here. It was hard work, and I'll bet they operated this place around the clock except for religious holidays."

Vail flashed a grin at her, stopping by a rusted wheel that lay on the ground under the shade of a live oak. "I would think you'd be more interested in that romantic story of two lovers. Are these woods spooked at night, do you imagine?"

"Alyssa is a good ghost, remember?"

"Not if she's restless and unhappy. No one really knows how she died. Were her bones found after the fire? Was there any evidence of trauma?"

"This isn't a modern forensics case."

"I hear folks have seen moving lights out here at night," said the man who'd asked the question about sugar production. He'd come up behind them, his face florid in the sunshine. "Must be the wraiths of those dead slaves, eh?" He chuckled as though chills running up his spine provided a rush.

In broad daylight, Marla found it difficult to imagine haunted happenings, at least until they got farther from the crowd. They strolled past an assortment of relics including gear mechanisms from one of the rolling sugar presses, iron kettles, pistons, and enormous vats. She had to keep an eagle eye on her footing because the foundation rose and fell unevenly to different levels, and there were hidden corners with walled arches and unexpected drops.

"Look at that," she said to Vail. Set into a crumbling wall was an outdoor oven still fitted with some sort of metallic drum. Holding on to Vail's arm, she stepped onto a sandy plateau to get a closer view. A smoky scent drifted their way. Creeping roots and Spanish moss from overhanging trees encroached upon the ancient stones, but the wind carried more than a whiff of the past. The air whispered, and if she strained her ears, Marla could almost hear the slaves grunting while they fought heat and hunger during their labors.

A quiet crowd, absorbing the history, followed the guide about a quarter of a mile through the woods to a section holding slave quarters, where a few tabby cabins still stood. These were essentially one-room dwellings with a chimney at one end and open windows that had been covered by long-rotted shutters. Now they stood vacant, a testament to the past, jungle vines reaching through the openings like beckoning fingers.

"So, Detective," said Rochelle, sidling up to them, "do you, like, go around dusting for fingerprints and searching for clues? I mean, let's say someone gets bumped off. What's the first thing you do?"

Marla grimaced. Would Dalton be accosted by curious relatives all weekend? Intending to rescue him, she got sidetracked by Joan prattling on about her daughter's math prowess and other mundane topics. Too bad Joan's husband hadn't been able to come, Marla thought.

"Will you start a family of your own, now that you're getting married again?" Joan said to Marla in a sly tone, along with a covert glance.

"I doubt it," Marla replied with a cynical twist to her lips. "I already work sixty hours a week in my salon. Even if I had spare time, I'd rather advance my career instead of being stuck at home changing diapers."

"Oh yeah? Doing what?"

"I could become an educator, a platform artist, expand into spa services, or work for one of the major hair-care product companies. Those are only some of the possibilities. Besides, Dalton has a thirteen-year-old daughter. We've grown quite fond of each other. She's enough extra responsibility for me."

Realizing she was gritting her teeth, Marla focused on watching where she stepped on the path to Planter's House. They exited the tropical hammock and followed their leader, single file, through a fallow field toward an impressive two-story columned mansion.

"Where will you go on your honeymoon?" Joan asked just when Vail twisted around to wag his eyebrows at Marla, a look of desperation in his eyes. Whether awed by his job or attracted by his masculine appeal, Rochelle appeared smitten. The girl continued to bedevil him.

Casting him an encouraging smile, Marla answered Joan. "We haven't discussed it yet. I'm not sure Dalton can take the time off, plus I'd have to rearrange my schedule. So we'll see."

Their arrival at the manor relieved her of any further need to answer indelicate probes. They faced a southern mansion. Wide verandas extended around all four sides of the brick-and-tabby structure.

"Rutfield built the north section of the mansion first," Champagne said, pointing. "This is connected to the main structure via a breezeway. Note the twenty-five-foot-high columns that support the roof. In the early days, those were considered symbols of sophistication. Due to the risk of fire, the kitchen became a separate addition. If you want a taste of old times, you can stay in Planter's House, which has been fully remodeled into deluxe suites. We serve complimentary continental breakfast and afternoon beverage service in the lounge."

Cynthia poked Marla. "You'll have to come see our place later. We have a huge living room and a kitchenette."

"Uh, right," Marla said, returning her attention to the social director. "Are there any ghosts haunting this building?"

Champagne's glance caught hers. "Oh, surely. Major Ferringer, a Union soldier intent on destroying the place, was caught before he did any real damage and shot right on that front porch. Anytime something strange happens here, folks blame his ghost. Some guests claim to have seen him in his dark blue frock coat with epaulets. Others complain he moves their furniture, unlocks doors, or turns lights on and off. I've never had a problem with him, but it's said he favored blondes."

"Champagne," a clerk said, rushing up to them, "I'm afraid you'll have to leave the tour early. There's been another accident."

Champagne's face paled. "What now?"

"One of the workers fell off his ladder. We've called an ambulance, but Mr. Butler wants you to help with crowd control."

"Of course." Champagne offered a falsely bright smile to the group. "We're nearly finished anyway. Thanks *so* much for coming. I hope you'll have a simply *fabulous* time during the rest of the weekend."

Her frothy demeanor made Marla feel like she was at Walt Disney World. The social director exuded genuine enthusiasm when she related resort history. Why, then, did it seem forced at other times?

Marla waved a hasty good-bye to her relatives as the group broke up. Her pulse accelerating, she hurried to reach Vail, who'd forged ahead. Alarm gave wings to her feet, but Champagne surpassed them both. The petite woman had gained yards in front.

A crowd of onlookers surrounded a prone figure on the ground at the base of Oleander Hall. Beside him crouched a heavyset fellow, who rummaged in a black medical bag. His jowls nearly reached his thick neck, encircled by a stethoscope.

Vail shoved his way into the circle, kneeling by the victim's side. Splotches of red blotted the man's coveralls. Judging from the fallen ladder nearby and toppled paint cans, he appeared to be a painter, although Marla didn't think the crimson stains came from pigment.

The whine of a siren grew louder. Flashing lights heralded the arrival of rescue personnel. A path quickly cleared for the police, who charged onto the scene with paramedics in tow. Rising, Vail strode to one of the uniformed officers and spoke rapidly. The heavier man waddled over to join them while Marla hung back in horrified fascination.

It looked as though the medical team had come too late. They went through the motions of hooking up the victim to various paraphernalia, but she could see the resignation on their faces. It didn't take long before they loaded him onto a stretcher and drove away. Marla glanced at Vail, whose scowl indicated his disapproval.

Off to the side, George Butler engaged in a heated dialogue with a gray-haired gent whose weathered face revealed his advanced years. "Excuse me," Marla said, approaching the hotel manager. "Can you tell me what happened?"

"The poor man must have lost his balance. A most unfortunate accident. I got here just as our resort doctor finished examining him." He waved at the fellow hovering at Vail's side. "There wasn't anything more we could do."

Appalled at Butler's casual tone, Marla blurted, "Why was that man working on a holiday? Don't you give the staff time off? Earlier I passed some construction people crossing the fields. They were still on duty, too." What was their assignment, to look for sinkholes?

"Tomorrow is the holiday, not today. Anyway, they're with our maintenance crew. Right, Seto? Seto Mulch is our groundskeeper and maintenance chief," Butler said by means of introduction. "He keeps things in shape."

The older man nodded his acquiescence. His skin exhibited many age spots, indicating he'd spent a lot of time in the sun.

"I don't understand what the painter was doing in this section," Marla said. "I thought you told me Oleander Hall was closed until you got approval for renovations."

Mulch exchanged glances with the manager. "A section needed

coatin', ma'am. If we have the place lookin' good, at least on the outside, maybe the higher-ups will decide to remodel rather than tear it down. Be an insult to our past if they replace this fine hotel with mockups for some theme park."

"A living-history experience will draw more people than an expensive resort known only to an exclusive clientele," said a woman who broke from the crowd being corralled by the social director. "Pardon me for intruding on your conversation. I'm Donna Albright, city councilwoman. We're having a meeting here this weekend to decide the issue."

"Surely you don't want to destroy the hotel," Butler protested.

"This isn't the first accident involving workers on the property. Remodeling is becoming too risky," Albright retorted.

"That's why I have the paranormal team here this weekend. They'll settle the spooks." Butler pointed to a fortyish man with stark white hair and a build that indicated too many trips to the buffet table. "Dr. Rip Spector is leader of the ghost chasers. We're continually replacing our construction crews. They're a superstitious lot, and they claim unhappy spirits are playing pranks on them."

"I wouldn't call a fatal fall from a ladder a prank," Albright said.

Marla wanted to question Albright further, but just then two familiar faces came into view. Marla rushed ahead to exchange quick hugs with her cousins Lori and Jeff Levine.

"What's going on?" Jeff asked, his onyx eyes glinting in dark contrast to his golden brown hair.

Marla brought them up to speed. "Dalton has no jurisdiction here, so I don't know what he's telling them. It's a terrible thing to happen."

Now that she thought about Butler's explanation, it seemed illogical that they'd assign a maintenance man, even if he was part of a holiday crew, to paint a condemned wing when he should be on call for emergencies involving guests. They must have enough laborers that it didn't matter.

"I wonder if the paranormal team believes ghosts were responsible," she said to Lori. "Can't they measure for ectoplasm or some such thing to detect the presence of spirits?"

Jeff, a handsome guy with a cocky grin, leaned toward her. "You don't really believe that stuff, do you? I suppose spinning tales about weird visitations helps attract guests. People like to think they're staying in a haunted house."

"The manager is the one who hired experts to chase the spooks away, or at least coax them into leaving people alone," Marla said. Unless he'd hired them as a show for his superstitious labor force, that is. She'd have to catch Dr. Spector later to see if he'd found anything significant. One thing was certain: Polly didn't want the spirit hunters to uncover any family secrets. She'd said as much to Marla earlier.

Marla smiled at Lori, who wore her coppery toned hair in a short bob. "I'll get Dalton so I can introduce you. I don't know what's keeping him this long."

As though he'd heard, Vail glanced at her before ending his conversation. He loped over to them wearing a heavy frown.

"I tried to convince the officer to do a more thorough investigation, but he wouldn't listen to me."

"That's too bad. Dalton, this is my cousin Lori and her husband, Jeff Levine. They live in Jacksonville."

"Pleased to meet you," Jeff said, shaking hands. He glanced to his right as though startled. Marla followed the direction of his gaze to Seto Mulch, who stood staring at them. Some unspoken communication seemed to jump between the two men before Jeff nudged his wife. "Hey, Lori, let's clear out." He gave them a weak grin. "We don't want to hold up these lovebirds. They'll have things of their own to do."

Before Marla could protest, Jeff hustled off toward the main building. Lori, throwing her an apologetic look, scurried in his wake.

"What kept you?" Marla said, focusing her full attention on

her betrothed. "You're not running the police force here, you know. That man's accident was awful, but—"

His slate gray eyes bored into hers as he gripped her shoulders. "It was no accident. The deceased had marks on his forearms as though he'd tried to defend himself. He didn't fall. He was pushed."

Chapter
Four

"Pushed? How is that possible? The painter was on a ladder."
"Notice the open window on the third floor? Somebody could've leaned out, put their hands on that ladder. The victim saw this person, struggled for control, and lost his balance."

"Butler is trying to put the blame on ghosts."

"Spirits can be mischievous, but they don't kill people. Bad guys are usually responsible for doing the deed."

"You're saying this was deliberate, not an accident? Even so, it's not your precinct."

Vail gave a rueful chuckle. "You're right, but the local cops could at least take it seriously. They won't even do an investigation."

"Why not?"

"They're convinced this was merely an unfortunate occurrence, nothing more. They think the workers are careless. Someone was electrocuted less than a week ago repairing faulty wiring in the tower. The officer I spoke to doesn't think very highly of the workforce, most of whom, he says, don't speak English."

"In other words, they'd rather look the other way," Marla concluded.

"Exactly."

From reading the newspapers, Marla understood small-town

mentality, but to hear Vail practically admit it existed here was disheartening. This place had once belonged to her family, after all. She had the feeling that link hadn't ended with its sale.

"I have to talk to Aunt Polly. There are too many confusing things going on at this resort, and I'll bet she can explain a lot of them."

But when she called the elderly woman's number from the main lobby, she got no response. "I'll try again from our room," she told Vail as they stepped inside the tower elevator. She shivered. "It's awfully cold in here, isn't it?"

"I know how to warm you up," he suggested in a smooth tone.

"That's an inviting offer." She pushed the button for the fourth floor after he closed the inner grating. This particular elevator was an old-fashioned mechanism with a gate that had to close before the outer door shut. Inside, it smelled faintly of cigar smoke. While Marla experienced a growing sense of disquiet, the lift lurched upward with an assortment of creaks. Facing the control panel, she felt a sharp pinch on her butt.

"Oh my, Dalton, can't you wait until we get to our room?" She felt it again. "Stop that, will you?"

"Stop what? I'm not doing anything . . . yet."

"You pinched me."

"No, I didn't."

Turning sideways to face him, she regarded his befuddled expression. "You did it twice. Don't con me."

He spread his hands. "Are you calling me a liar? I never touched you."

A snicker of laughter reached her ears, making goose bumps rise on her skin. "Did you hear that?"

Dalton tilted his head. "Hear what? Are you all right?"

"No." Marla pounded the button for the fourth floor as though that motion would get them there sooner. The car creaked upward at an agonizingly slow pace. "I think someone is in here with us, and it's not anyone we can see. Get me out of here." Her heart racing, she scrabbled to open the inner gate as soon as they arrived at their destination.

Vail lumbered on her trail as she sped toward their room, momentarily getting lost and having to backtrack to find the right turn-off to Hibiscus Hall. She didn't offer any further explanations, not quite believing her own perception. Breathing a sigh of relief when they shut the door to Room 407 behind them, Marla allowed herself a moment to gather her reserve.

"I'm starting to believe those ghost stories," she said after her nerves settled. Advancing toward the bed, she noticed a subtle lilac fragrance. Had the maid been there recently? The bed hadn't been turned down; it was too early.

"What you need is a dose of reality," Dalton replied, gripping her shoulders and pulling her close. "Like this."

As his mouth descended on hers, Marla forgot all about spooks and other oddities. Her mind took a hiatus while she played intimate games with Vail in their private quarters.

An hour later, her tension finally abated, they made a foray to the beach. Marla chose lounge chairs facing west, figuring a full blast of sun would rejuvenate her. She lay back, limbs relaxed, until her bared stomach was assaulted by a spritz of cool water. Snapping open her eyes behind dark sunglasses, she jerked upright. Champagne Glass stood grinning with a water spray bottle in her hand.

"We don't allow our guests to get overheated," the social director said. "It's just part of our *superior* service."

"You should ask people first," Marla retorted.

Vail's muscles rippled as he shot to his feet. He wore swim trunks but looked no less imposing than when fully clothed. "We'll take a dip in the ocean if we're too hot," he said, his voice dangerously quiet.

Champagne's smile wavered but only for an instant. "Sure thing, sugar. I want you to have a *divine* time while you're here. Let me know if I can help you in any other way."

"There is one thing," he replied, giving her a level look. "These accidents that have been happening, is anyone looking into them other than your manager who hired the ghost chasers?"

She glanced around, then lowered her voice. "I can't say, but you might talk to old man Mulch. He'd like the renovations to go forward, but we're always losing workers."

"Because of the incidents?"

"The hired men believe in the curse. There's a big turnover among the labor force. You never see the same guy twice." She sucked in a breath. "I shouldn't be talking about it."

"Isn't there a meeting going on now?" Marla asked. "I met Donna Albright earlier." Leveraging herself off the beach chair, she brushed sand from her legs.

Champagne hesitated. "The council has to decide if they'll issue permits for further restoration or allow the current owners to sell the property. I think it would be abominable to build a theme park here, but no one listens to my opinion." She leaned forward, eyes glistening. "I understand one of your relatives is looking to invest."

"Oh, really?"

"He's one of the partners in the development company. Why would he destroy your family's legacy by tearing down the place? This estate has so much history. With proper funding, it could be restored to its glory—the grand hotel, plantation tracts and all." She glanced behind them and stiffened. "Well, sugar, I hope you have a *marvelous* stay. Now if you'll excuse me, I need to see to our other *delightful* guests."

Marla twisted around to see what Champagne had glanced at, causing her to adopt that falsely bright tone, and stifled a groan. George Butler was chatting with one of the cabana boys, but that wasn't what dismayed Marla. Rochelle bore down on them with three female friends, whom she promptly introduced as cousins from out west.

"This is Dalton Vail," Rochelle said proudly. "He's a police detective." She jiggled her body, offering a generous view of flesh covered in the minute bits of fabric teens considered proper swimwear. Marla bristled when Vail's intrigued glance traveled the girl's form.

"We're just leaving," she snapped, gathering her towel. "Come on," she told Vail. "We have to get ready for the cocktail party." As she marched him away, she called, "See you later."

"What's the matter?" Dalton said, reaching her side.

"You didn't have to look at her that way."

He took her arm, but she shook him off. Amusement filled his eyes. "You're jealous."

"I am not. But in case you haven't noticed, my cousin is way too young for you."

"The poor girl is entranced by the fact that I'm a detective."

"Then why don't you act like one and help me figure out what's going on around here? Have you noticed the change in Champagne's personality, like when she puts on her fake gushy act? Who is she trying to fool?"

"Obviously not you."

"She seemed nervous when she was talking to us. I'll have to catch her alone some other time."

Back in their room, Marla called Polly again, but no one answered. "Should I knock on her door?" she asked Vail, worried about her aunt.

"She'll turn up at the cocktail party. You can't expect her to stay in her room the whole time. She's probably out shmoozing."

Reassured, Marla smiled. "You're right." She laid her sleeveless black dress, lingerie, and jewelry on the bed, then opened the drawer to retrieve her beaded bag. "That's funny, I could've sworn I'd put it in here."

"What's that?"

"My evening purse. Didn't I unpack it from my suitcase and put it in this drawer?" She surveyed the smooth bedspread, dresser top, and desk. Nothing.

Vail looked at her as though she had a screw loose. "Why don't you check in there?" He pointed to her luggage on the rack.

Remembering she had to put away the rest of her things, Marla lifted the lid. Her black beaded purse sat on top of a pair of folded slacks. Feeling a sense of unease, she took the bag and added it to the collection on the bed.

Promptly at six o'clock, they entered the banquet hall that had been reserved for their family event. *You'd never know it was dark outside from the way the room glitters*, she thought, admiring the party lights strung in potted palms and the crystal chandeliers illuminating the ballroom much the same as they had in the 1920s.

Dozens of well-dressed people stood chatting in clusters, their noise level competing with orchestral background music. Circulating waitresses wearing white gloves offered hot hors d'oeuvres, while Marla spotted a table with platters of raw vegetables, cheese, crackers, and other crudités. Two opposite corners held cash bars with lines of customers.

Marla noticed gazes turning their way, along with looks of envy from her female kin. A swell of pride filled her. Who wouldn't look at the smashing man in the charcoal gray suit?

Rochelle might do more than look, given the chance. If Marla had to stick to his side like nail glue, she'd protect Vail from the teen . . . and anyone else's flirtatious advances.

Vail grabbed her hand for moral support when Anita veered in their direction.

"Marla, come meet our Colorado cousins," her mother said, pulling her toward a cluster of people. Gripping Vail's hand, Marla steeled herself for the onslaught of introductions.

"So is this the entire *megillah*?" Vail broadcast to the crowd after they'd made the rounds.

Glances of benign humor passed among her relations. "I think you mean the whole *mishpocheh*. That's family," Marla whispered into his ear. "A *megillah* is a story."

Color suffused his cheeks. "I'm trying to learn."

She smiled gently. "I know, and I appreciate it." Turning to Uncle Moishe, the eldest present, she said, "I'd like to hear the whole *megillah* about this hotel. I would have asked Aunt Polly, but she isn't here yet. Has anyone seen her this afternoon? It's unlike her to be late." Anxiety churned her stomach. Polly had initiated this reunion. She wouldn't miss their first function when it was so important to her.

Uncle Moishe, ten years older than Anita, waved his hand dismissively. "She'll show up when she's ready to make an appearance. Polly never could let this place go. Even after Mama sold it, she kept coming back. I hear she takes the same room every year, like clockwork."

"Is it true our family used to own the hotel?" Marla asked.

A hush fell over the room, and all eyes turned to Moishe. Her uncle, well into his seventies, nodded his wrinkled face. "Polly spent her early years here, so this property represents her roots. Ours, too. Papa bought the place in 1924, the same year Polly was born."

"He came from Poland, didn't he?" asked cousin Lori, Uncle William's middle daughter.

"That's right," Moishe replied. "My father's original name was Andrzej Markowski. Papa changed it to Andrew Marks when he arrived in this country. A couple of years later, he met and married Ruth. That was 1923. They moved to Florida a year later when he bought this plantation from Tobias Rutfield. First they intended to work the fields, but when visitors started streaming south in the winter, they decided to turn the property into a resort. After remodeling the original plantation house, Papa constructed the main hotel. He'd studied architecture, you know, at the University of Warsaw."

"Where did grandfather get the money to buy the place?" Marla said. "Did he bring riches from the old country?"

"Papa paid cash for the property, but I don't believe he had a stitch when he immigrated. His source of wealth remains a mystery to this day. Polly may have more answers. My sister took care of Mama until she died."

"So Andrew established the resort," Marla prompted, curious to hear the rest of the story. "Was he successful?"

"You'd better believe it." Moishe scratched his jaw. "They didn't even have to advertise. People came on the recommendation of their friends. But then came the tragedy." He surveyed the circle of eager relations, absorbing their history with the same alacrity as they downed their drinks. "Andrew died in 1943, and after that, everything changed."

Cynthia raised her hand as though they were in class. "Didn't Andrew receive two visitors right before he croaked?"

Moishe gave her a disapproving glare. "That's true. I was only thirteen at the time, but I remember them. They were very somber, dressed in black, wearing Cossack hats like you see in old Russian movies. They spoke with heavy accents. Andrew met with them in Oleander Hall. One of his favorite rooms there was a parlor overlooking the gardens."

A distant look in his eyes, he continued. "He summoned Mulch to bring his humidor, then gave orders he was not to be disturbed. According to one of the maids, Andrew looked visibly shaken when he emerged more than two hours later to go straight to his penthouse suite at the top of the tower. The maid peeked inside the parlor and was startled to find an empty room. The two men were nowhere to be seen. My father died alone of an apoplectic attack that same evening."

"He had a stroke?" Vail said. He'd remained silent throughout Moishe's tale, shifting his feet restlessly. Marla noticed how he perked up at the mention of an unattended death.

"Yep." Moishe glanced at his brother, William. "Mama got real funny toward her sister and brothers afterward, but don't ask me why. Ownership fell to her, so Ruth took charge and ran the resort until she sold it years later. We grew up here listening to superstitions about how the land was cursed because the early plantation decimated an Indian burial ground. Some said this curse killed Papa in his early forties. I've heard tales of recent problems, too. Makes you wonder why the ghosts are still restless."

"It's awfully strange that Andrew died right after those two visitors came. Didn't anyone question them?" Cynthia queried.

"They vanished, never to be seen again. If you ask me, I think my father's past came back to haunt him. We never heard much about his childhood or how he got out of Poland. Or where he got the money to buy the plantation. Maybe he stole it, and those two guys traced him to Florida to recover their loot."

"If Andrew's spirit inhabits the hotel, he's guarding his secrets well," Marla said.

Her attention diverted to Rochelle, who had sashayed to Vail's side. The young lady wore a rose sweater and short black skirt with outrageously high-heeled strappy sandals. Vail's mouth quirked into a half-smile as he nodded a greeting to Marla's second cousin. Or, wait a minute—was Rochelle a second cousin, or a first cousin once removed? She'd have to look up family relationships when she had spare time. What mattered now was reminding her fiancé why he'd come here: to meet her relatives, not be seduced by one of them.

"Did anyone meet those paranormal researchers?" she asked in a loud tone. "The manager hired them to search for spooks. I heard the top floor of the tower has remained uninhabited since Andrew's death. Maybe no one wants to stay there because it's haunted. Where did Ruth live while she managed the hotel?"

"Where did I live? Land's sake, child, I stayed with Mama," Polly said in a clear, cold voice. Hobbling into the room, the elderly lady, wearing a flowered blouse and a navy skirt, paused to survey their assembly. Her face was flushed, and her hair disheveled. Marla thought she looked as if she'd been outdoors in the wind.

Polly waggled a finger at her brother. "Shame on you, Moishe, spreading rumors about the family. It isn't ghosts I'd worry about, if I were you. Things here are worth investigating, but they have nothing to do with the spirit world."

"A painter fell off his ladder today. He'd been outside Oleander Hall," Marla said, hoping Polly might shed light on the incident.

"Whassat?" Polly's face scrunched. "Y'all want to go outside to the pool? It's too breezy."

"Didn't you want help looking for something?" Marla asked, moving closer so she could shout into Polly's ear. She'd rather avoid mentioning details with so many onlookers.

"You're looking fine, niece. Don't worry so much about what

you wear. It's what's in here that matters." Polly patted her heart. "Who is this?" she said, regarding Vail quizzically from behind her spectacles.

"Aunt Polly, I'd like you to meet Dalton Vail. We're engaged."

The older woman caught those words without a problem because her expression brightened. *"Mazel tov!* It's about time you settled down. Getting long in the tooth, you are, so you should be grateful he'll take you. Mind you, the fella had better treat you right. Come here, young man."

Marla grinned. Silver streaks glinted in Vail's black hair, but she supposed Polly considered them both babes in the woods at her age. Her mother chose that moment to enter, followed by Marla's brother, Michael, and his wife, Charlene, with their two children. More hugs, kisses, and murmured greetings.

"What do you mean, you never had a bar mitzvah?" Polly said in a rising tone.

Marla whirled around from where she'd been admiring her niece and nephew. Polly's face looked as though she had sucked a lemon and swallowed the pits. Oh no. Marla strode to her beloved's side, preparing to defend him. He stood rigid, an impassive mask freezing his features.

"Marla, you're marrying a *goy*? How could you betray us like this? *Oy gevald*, you'll ruin the family." Polly's voice dissolved into a wail, an unintelligible stream of Yiddish words.

"Aunt Polly, don't insult my fiancé. He's a fine man, and we love each other. Isn't that more important? You're always saying you want me to be happy."

"Gai avek!" Polly shrieked, backing away.

"Don't you talk to my daughter like that," Anita said, grabbing Polly's arm. "I'm thrilled for her, and you should be, too. Dalton loves her, and that's all that matters."

"What's the matter? You know very well we can't dilute the bloodline any further." Shaking herself free from Anita, Polly raked her younger sister with a scornful look.

"Interfaith marriages can work if both people respect each other's traditions," Anita insisted. "You're the one who's disrupted our reunion, just when we're supposed to be making peace."

"You're *meshugeh* if you accept an outsider into our midst, but then what else can I expect from you? You run around with that *fresser,* Roger, flaunting yourself like a tramp. My own sister! *Feh, feh, feh.* To think I considered letting you in on the secret." Polly swayed like a sapling in a strong wind. "You've made me ill. I'm going to my room." Snagging Marla with a rheumy glare, she said, "You come up later, Missy. I'll want a few words with you, and *he* better not be there."

Polly teetered from the room, leaving stunned silence in her wake. Cynthia was the first to rush forward and grasp Vail's hand. "Please forgive her outburst. Polly doesn't reflect what the rest of us feel. We're very happy to welcome you into the family. Aren't we, everyone?"

Polite murmurs of agreement followed. Mortified, Marla clung to Vail's arm as they proceeded to chat individually with each of her relatives. She was conscious of a small cluster from the Colorado contingent gossiping in a corner. Knowing she wasn't the only cousin who'd married outside her faith, Marla hadn't thought anyone would care. They'd change their minds once they got to know Dalton, she reassured herself. Meanwhile, she needed to soothe his bruised ego.

"I'm so sorry," she told him later at dinner in the steakhouse restaurant, where they'd been seated at a quiet table for two. "Polly has her own views about religion. I should have warned you."

He regarded her from across the table, looking more handsome than ever. Her heart ached that he'd undergone such humiliation.

"Don't blame yourself; you did warn me that Polly was a character. Coming here, I realized we might have some hurdles to overcome. That's another reason why I thought it best not to bring Brianna." He spoke in a subdued tone, but then his intense gray eyes softened. "Besides, I'm marrying you, not your family."

Wrong. When you wed someone, you joined their whole *mish-*

pocheh. People didn't live in isolation, although she supposed family feuds had begun for less. What about Ruth and her siblings? Why had her grandmother sectioned herself off from them after Andrew died? She'd hoped to ask Polly about the interrelationships, but now she might not get the chance. She'd go to her aunt later to smooth over their disagreement and learn what she could, Marla resolved.

"You're so wonderful," Marla said to Vail, meaning it. That he could bypass his discomfort to focus on her meant a lot.

He swirled the cabernet in his wineglass, studying her from beneath bushy brows. "And you're so hot in that dress that maybe we should skip our meal and go upstairs."

"Nonsense. You have the appetite of a horse. Two appetizers, plus a salad and entrée? I guess you didn't eat much at the cocktail party after Polly raked you over the coals."

"I lost my appetite," he agreed, "but I've regained it now . . . for other things." The hunger in his eyes told her exactly what he referred to, and her body responded.

Thank goodness he could overlook the foibles of her family. She only hoped when it came her turn to meet his side that she could behave with as much grace. From hints he'd let drop, it appeared his parents might have difficulty accepting a Jewish bride into the fold. Marla decided she'd cross that bridge when she came to it. For now, dealing with her own family problems took precedence.

Chapter Five

On their way upstairs, Marla halted by the tower elevator. "If you don't mind," she said to Vail, "I'd like to have a word with Aunt Polly about her behavior tonight. I won't tolerate her treating you so rudely."

"I expect we all have folks like her in our families. Don't worry about it, sweetcakes. As long as we face things together, we'll be fine." Lifting a strand of her hair, Vail tucked it behind her ear.

She smiled at his tender gesture. "You're so special, you know that?" Standing on tiptoe, she kissed him. "Come on, let's go to our room. I'll prove how much I enjoy being with you."

"Wait. Maybe you *should* go see Polly. The old lady knows more about this place than anyone else in your family. She might have an idea why people are dying. They may be poor laborers, but that's no reason for the local boys to look the other way. Something is fishy here."

Marla nodded. "I get the feeling that if I just understood what happened in the past, it would clarify the present. I'd like to ask Polly about Andrew."

"What about him?" The elevator arrived, and Vail opened the inner grating for her. She didn't step inside right away.

"Andrew requested his humidor when those two strangers visited him. I'm wondering what happened to his possessions after he died. Did Ruth store them on-site, divide them among her children, or sell them?"

Vail tilted his head. "Good luck getting your aunt to talk. And take your time," he said with a wry twist to his lips. "I'll catch the latest scores on TV while you're gone."

Just like a man to be more eager to watch sports than to be romantic. "Aren't you coming with me? You can get off on the fourth floor."

Closing the gate after she'd entered, he regarded her through the ironwork. "Are you kidding? This thing is haunted. Ask the ghost what he wants. Maybe he'll reveal the hotel's secrets."

Shuddering as the outer door sealed shut, Marla pushed the button for the twelfth floor. At least this time, she didn't feel a chill or smell anything strange. Nonetheless, she gripped the inner rail as the car made its rattling ascent.

The door opened onto a carpeted hallway just as Marla recalled Polly saying she kept a suite here but didn't sleep in the tower. She wondered why Polly felt the need to revisit these rooms but didn't feel comfortable enough to stay overnight. Her skin crawled as she proceeded through a series of dimly lit chambers consisting of formal parlors, a private dining area, a smoking room or library, depending on who inhabited it, and a master bedroom with separate his and her dressing rooms and baths. Most of the furniture, characteristic of the 1920s, remained in fairly decent condition, and the rooms were clean. Despite their vacancy, Marla didn't notice any cobwebs or dust. Someone must be coming in regularly to clean.

Wondering where to find Polly, Marla paused by a woman's dressing table, inhaling a fragrance of lilacs in the small space while she admired a silver hand mirror and hairbrush set. Something flashed in the glass, making her turn quickly, but no one stood behind her.

The lamps dimmed briefly, then brightened. Footsteps, faint at first, sounded overhead before passing to the right. *Polly must be upstairs*, she thought with some relief, starting for the elevator shaft. Perhaps her aunt kept these rooms so she could explore Andrew's suite on the top floor without interference.

Glad to retrace her route, Marla had just pushed the button to call the lift when she heard a murmur of voices. Whipping around, she saw nothing but the empty corridor stretching into the distance. Portraits lined the silk-covered walls. Her ancestors? She felt their energy expanding, surrounding her.

That elevator was taking too damn long. Marla turned back to push the button again when she felt a tap on her shoulder. She nearly leapt out of her skin. "Who's there?" she cried, afraid to get an answer. A quick look affirmed her isolation. Still skeptical about the existence of spirits, she nevertheless had to admit the possibility of otherworldly phenomena. They weren't something she cared to encounter, however.

When the elevator arrived, she decided not to explore the tower penthouse until she ascertained Polly's location. At the lobby desk, she got directions to the room where Polly spent her nights. Her aunt stayed in Jasmine Hall on the fourth floor, facing Oleander across an expanse of shrubbery. Sure enough, Polly was in her room when Marla showed up.

"Marla, it's about time." Polly let her in, then shut the door. "You're late." She still wore the same skirt and blouse from earlier, although Marla noted she'd exchanged her shoes for scruffy slippers. It looked as though she'd kicked off her dress shoes under the luggage rack. A trail of sand marked their path. Sand?

"I didn't realize you were expecting me at a specific time," Marla said.

"I told you there was something you have to do for me." It appeared Polly had forgotten her disapproval over Marla's choice of a mate. "I need you to help me find it."

Marla glanced at the clothes flung over the queen-size bed. Her aunt, in her confused state, had likely misplaced an article of clothing. Here she'd been hoping Polly would tell her the story of Andrew's treasure, while Polly just needed her services as a maid.

Marla's gaze swept the bottles containing an unfamiliar liquid and tablets by the nightstand. She hadn't been aware Polly took prescription medicines, but, then, she'd just recently convinced Polly to add her name to the checking account so Marla could pay her bills. These things took time, especially when her elderly aunt didn't recognize that she needed assistance. So why did she insist on Marla's presence now?

"What can I do to help you?" she asked. "Get you ready for bed? Give you a shower?" Marla's concerned glance surveyed the older woman's frail body. If she'd worked undercover as a nurse's aide for Miriam Pearl, she could certainly assist her own aunt with personal hygiene. Although if Polly needed that level of care, she had no business living alone.

"No, child, sit down." Polly sank onto the bed and indicated a space by her side. "I need you to help me find the stones."

Oh no. Was Polly losing it again? "What stones?"

"Daddy's stash. I know he didn't spend it all. He hid them from those interlopers."

Her heartbeat accelerated. Now they were getting somewhere. "Go on."

"When you read my letters, you'll understand." Polly's rheumy eyes looked at Marla in bewilderment. "I can't remember where I put them. Oh dear. I wouldn't want the wrong people to get hold of them."

"What letters do you mean?"

"The ones I wrote to Vincent. Listen to me, child. If you find the gems, you can use them to fix things in the family. It's our chance to make up for Mama's mistakes."

Marla felt hopelessly lost. "Who is Vincent?"

"Whassat? I don't smell any mint scent. What's the matter with you? Did you have too much to drink tonight?"

"Tell me more about Andrew's stones." Raising her voice, Marla carefully enunciated each word.

"Be careful when you're searching for them. Others smell the scent. But that's not the real trouble here." Polly's eyes narrowed. "They're terribly wrong in what they're doing. Greedy bloodsuckers. *Ain foiler epel farfoilt di ander.* One rotten apple spoils the bunch. Mark my words."

"Excuse me?"

"They've lost sight of what this place is about. When you find the gems, you'll buy back what's ours and spread the rest among the family. If only I could remember where I put my letters." Her hands, blue veins prominent under paper-thin skin, grasped Marla's dress. "Find them, child."

Flabbergasted, Marla stared at her aunt. She had no idea what Polly meant. Letters? Gemstones? How did these things relate to what was happening today?

"Can you explain more about Vincent perhaps? I need to understand better in order to help you."

Scrunching her face, Polly peered at her. "Don't coddle me, young lady. My time has come, so it's your responsibility now."

Before Marla could ask more questions, a knock sounded at the door. Sliding off the bed, she strode over to see who was calling at this late hour. A large woman wearing surgical scrubs met her gaze. Marla got a quick glimpse of ash blond hair in short curls, crystal blue eyes, and a wide mouth before the middle-aged woman brushed past her.

"Howdy, ma'am," she addressed Polly in a chirpy voice. "I've been sent to help you get ready for bed."

"Whassat?"

"I'm from Health Corps Staffing Services. This is a courtesy visit. I guess one of your relatives hired me as a sort of gift. You wouldn't turn away such a generous gesture, now, would you?"

"I think it's a wonderful idea," Marla gushed, noting Polly's change in expression. "You can use the help, Aunt Polly, just for the one night. Forgive me for being cautious," she told the nurse, "but may we see some identification?"

"You don't have to stay," the woman said to Marla after she'd checked her ID. "I'll take good care of the dear lady."

"I can look after myself," Polly grumbled. "Whoever hired you, give them their money back. Was it Anita?" Her eyes narrowed suspiciously. "Ask your mother if she's up to her old tricks," Polly shouted at Marla. "If this is her doing . . ."

Marla didn't wait to hear the rest. She flew out the door, shutting it behind her so Polly wouldn't have any choice except to comply. In the hallway, she realized she'd been clenching her teeth. Forcing herself to relax, she called Vail on her cell phone while approaching the elevator.

"I've just finished talking to Polly," she told him, hearing the television in the background. "I'm going to take a brief walk before I come upstairs. Do you mind? I need some fresh air."

She needed more than that, Marla thought as she pushed open an exit door on the ground floor. Outside, a cool sea breeze ruffled the hairs on her arms and brought a salty taste to her tongue. Crickets sang their nightly chorus as she proceeded over a gravel path, her ears picking up the distant swoosh of waves. Through the ages, this place had seen many tragedies. What secrets did it still hide?

Polly had mentioned Andrew's stash: stones or gems. Reverse the order, and put them together. Could his source of wealth have been valuable gemstones? She hadn't gotten the chance to ask Polly about her grandfather's origins. How had he escaped from Poland and made his way to the United States? Had he been a victim of persecution? Not necessarily, if he'd been a student at the University of Warsaw. He'd graduated as an architect. Those skills would come in handy in his new country, but instead of landing a job, he'd met Ruth, married, and moved to Florida. By then, he had the cash to purchase thirty-five hundred acres of a thriving plantation. If he'd brought jewels from the old country, that could account for his immediate wealth. It could also provide a reason for his leaving Poland if he'd stolen them. And that scenario tied in with the two strangers who spoke with heavy accents. They must have tracked the thief and come to confront him.

What had happened in the midst of their meeting to make them disappear and cause Andrew to flee the room in distress? Could the remainder of the jewels have been hidden in the humidor that Andrew had requested? Maybe he'd offered the remaining gems to the visitors to appease them, in which case there was nothing left to be found. Or had the humidor simply contained tobacco, and something more sinister had befallen Andrew's guests?

She needed more information on Oleander Hall in terms of its reconstruction. Maybe things were buried there that someone regarded as best left alone. Tearing down the place might expose old bones, for example. But how would ancient history shed light on today's events? Or was there simply no connection?

Polly had also exhorted Marla to find some letters she'd written. If her aunt couldn't remember where she put them, how was Marla to find them? Perhaps the letters were what her aunt had been searching for on the thirteenth floor.

Watching her footing around a jagged piece of coral rock, Marla compressed her lips. Like it or not, she'd have to return to the top levels of the tower to conduct her search.

She hoped the home health aide would be able to appease the older woman. Hiring her had been a gesture of kindness, but who had thought of it? Marla's mother? Uncle Moishe? No matter. Polly could use the help, even if she blustered her denial. Her condition had deteriorated even more than Marla had realized. When they got home, she'd have to see about hiring someone full-time.

Sparse ground lighting made it difficult to discern her location, but when she glanced up, she noted Oleander Hall rose directly in front of her. Her steps had carried her toward the condemned wing. Many of the windows had accumulated a coating of grime and salt deposits from the briny air. Butler had ordered the other side painted to spruce up the building for visitors, but apparently not this end, because it still bore the ravages of time and weather. Those roof tiles looked as though they were about ready to tumble to the ground.

Her gaze caught a light waving in an upper window. Squinting, she tried to define its shape. Maybe if she moved a few paces to the right . . . Her back collided with something solid, and she cried out. An answering curse made her ears ring.

"Marla, what are you doing here?" said Jeffrey Levine, cousin Lori's husband.

Marla turned to regard him, about to ask the same question, when she noticed a dark-haired beauty clinging to his arm. They sprang guiltily apart.

"I needed some fresh air," Marla explained. "And you?" She gave the woman a pointed glare.

"We were discussing the menus for Friday," Jeff said. "This is Brittany Butterworth. She's the resort pastry chef."

"My friends call me Brownie," the lady said in a syrupy tone.

"Oh, really?" *I didn't know you had a sweet tooth, Jeff. Was it desserts you were discussing, or a different kind of honey?* The woman certainly exuded feminine appeal, with wide, dark almond-shaped eyes framed by a waterfall of ebony hair that hung to her waist. She wore a sarong that wouldn't suit well in the kitchen but would work just fine in the bedroom. As her nickname implied, the chef presented a sweet confection that men must feel tempted to sample. Marla's nose detected a familiar lilac fragrance.

"Brownie's been telling me about the meals planned for our family events," Jeff said.

"Is that so?" Would Jeff *fudge* his response if she accused him of cheating on his wife? Then again, he'd get his just *desserts* if she tipped Lori herself. Or maybe she should e-mail Jeff a *cookie* to a family therapist. Marla smiled to herself as her cousin's spouse led them toward the well-lit pool area.

"On Friday we're having a beach picnic with shelling. It should be a blast," he said. "Then that night is the outdoor luau.

Sorry, no roast pig on the menu; it's not kosher. We'll have chicken instead. You gonna do the rumrunner's jog? Sounds like a hoot."

"Where is Lori?" Marla asked bluntly.

"Poor girl has a headache. I came out for a stroll and ran into Brittany, er, Brownie."

I'll bet you did more than run into her. "Don't tell me you just met," she scoffed.

"Lori and I have been to the resort before. It's one of our favorite getaways. We've always complimented Brownie on her dessert cart selections."

Yeah, right. "How often do you come here? I understand Aunt Polly returns every year."

"Oh, our visits don't usually coincide with hers. We'll both be disappointed if this place is torn down, though."

"If that theme-park idea gets passed, it'll ruin things for everyone," Brownie said in a smooth voice with a gritty undercurrent, like molasses tinged with coffee grounds. "Do you realize they don't plan to build another hotel? At first I thought it would be a great opportunity to step up and take charge as master chef. But now, I think the changeover could turn into a disaster. Who'll come to see a recreation of some old buildings with costumed cast members?"

"The town council met earlier to debate the issue," Marla said. "Did you happen to hear the results?"

"The developers are putting up a strong argument. They say a living-history museum will bring more jobs to the area as well as tourist dollars," Jeff replied. "That's baloney. They get plenty of tourists here already. I don't see any advantage to destroying Andrew's legacy."

Marla peered at him closely, but she couldn't discern his thoughts from his placid expression. How much did he know about their family secrets? "So I gather you and Brownie are opposed to the theme-park idea. You'd rather see the money put into remodeling. What about the ghost stories?"

"The spirits would be a lot happier if we fixed their home," Brownie said, her dark eyes gleaming in the moonlight.

As they parted company, Marla considered her options. Should she report this encounter to Lori? If it was truly a chance meeting, as Jeff claimed, she'd only stir up trouble.

A cough sounded behind her. Glancing over her shoulder, Marla noticed a figure on one of the lounge chairs by the pool. "Michael, are you alone out here?" she asked her brother.

His face, a male reflection of her own, gave her a weak grin. "I had some thinking to do. I thought I'd sit and listen to the waves. Maybe the right decisions would come to me."

She didn't like the sound of that. "What's wrong?"

He waited while she sat on the adjacent chair. "A lot of things. The stock market . . . You know how things took a dive. People tend to blame their financial advisers."

Marla felt her blood chill. It had been only a few months since she'd consulted a psychic in Cassadaga, a spiritualist camp in Central Florida. The Reverend Hazel Sherman's words had been clear: *Your brother is experiencing tremendous emotional difficulties that he's created for himself. It's producing a snowball effect. . . . He's having to make some major changes in his lifestyle. . . . A lot of it has to do with his finances. He's gone off the edge.*

Hazel had said a lot of other things, too, about Michael's relationship with their father and Marla's need to reconcile with him over past differences. She hadn't paid any heed to the fortune-teller's meanderings. Why should she, when Michael and his wife seemed to lead the perfect upscale life in Boca Raton?

"What do you mean?" she said when she found her voice again. "Everyone lost money when the market plunged. You couldn't predict what was going to happen."

Michael stared at a trail of ants on the pool deck. "I made some bad choices. Not only for myself, but for my clients. They called me on it, wanted the money back that they'd lost, started lawsuits." Swiping his hands over his face, he regarded her wearily. "I didn't tell Charlene the extent of it, but I got us into a pretty big hole."

Marla swallowed. If the psychic's forecast about Michael had turned into reality, then what about the warning to her?

You're going to take a trip, and it involves family issues. Something bad is coming up around this trip.

There may be a death before the end of the year.

Chapter
Six

"Why didn't you tell me you were having problems?" Marla asked her older brother. "I could have helped. Does Ma know?"

Michael shook his head. "Don't say a word to her. I haven't told her anything."

"So what are you doing to meet your debts?"

"I got a loan."

He shuffled his feet while Marla swatted at a hovering wasp. Sniffing fragrant jasmine from a nearby hedge, she skirted away from the insect vector. Encouraging Michael to talk was just as sensitive an issue as dealing with hornets. If you weren't careful, you'd get stung.

"It isn't good to keep problems to yourself," she said. "Stress builds up until it makes you sick."

"No kidding. I'm probably responsible for running the store out of antacids these days." Michael smiled ruefully, his toffee-colored eyes so much like her own that Marla's heart ached.

"Why do I get the feeling you're making light of something serious? You should trust the people who love you."

Michael pushed himself off the lounge chair, straightening his tall frame. "If I can correct my own mistakes, no one else needs to suffer along the way. You should understand. You didn't tell the folks when Tammy's parents threatened to sue."

"Daddy had just recovered from his first heart attack when Tammy drowned. My grief caused our parents enough pain."

"You hired a lawyer on your own, didn't you?"

"I had to do something when the toddler's parents blamed me. I'd only gone to answer a phone call they told me to expect. I wasn't a bad baby-sitter."

Yeah, and look at what you had to do to earn money for the attorney. She'd posed for some rather explicit photographs. Her face flushed at the disgraceful memory.

She rose and stretched. "You have nothing to hide. Everyone experienced losses in the lousy economy."

Wearing sandals, Michael still topped her five-feet-six-inch height by several inches. "If Charlene finds out how much I've lost, she won't see me in the same light anymore. It's my job to provide for her." His eyes reflected the glare from the balloon-shaped globes lighting the pool area.

"You're the one who drives a BMW and has the latest plasma TV on your family room wall. Charlene doesn't care about those things."

"She works too hard. I've been hoping she could retire soon. This will put a crimp in our plans."

"Whose plans, hers or yours? I thought she was aiming to make principal of her school."

He jabbed a hand through his mocha brown hair. "Just because you enjoy working so much doesn't mean Charlene does. She'd like to stay home with the kids."

"Oh yeah?" Marla planted a hand on her hip. "I never got the impression that Charlene means to quit her job, especially when Jacob is in kindergarten and Rebecca is almost old enough for preschool. You want her to stop working because it'll make you feel more manly. It's merely another status symbol for you to be the sole breadwinner."

Like Stan, my dear ex-husband. The jerk couldn't understand why I wanted to go to cosmetology school. No way I'd ever burden myself with another controlling male. Marla didn't like to see her brother in that role, either.

"I don't know how we got down this road," Michael said in a morose tone.

"Speaking of roads, remember when you told Daddy about your car accident and he loaned you the money to fix your car?"

"I should have dealt with my own problems instead of burdening him. Pop had his fatal attack not long afterward."

Old resentments surged from an inner well she hadn't known still existed. In her heart, she'd blamed him for their father's death. If Michael had stayed home during the rainstorm like Mom had insisted, he might not have skidded on the wet road and hit that other car. His disregard for safety could have led to worse, but enough stress came from the incident anyway.

Hadn't the psychic said her brother had to move past his emotional difficulties? Reverend Sherman's insights revealed that Michael had meant to apologize to their father, but he hadn't been able to do so before the man died. Her dad had made his peace; now it was her brother's turn. She had to offer forgiveness, too, if she meant to help him.

Besides, Marla had taken out a loan recently, and she hadn't told Michael about it. True, Miriam Pearl had offered the funds after Marla had solved the murder of the old lady's granddaughter. Marla needed it to buy some rental property from her ex-spouse. But from the rent received plus her income from work she'd been able to make the payments to Miriam each month.

"At least tell Charlene about your situation," she said. "It's better to forewarn her instead of surprising her if you run into a snag. She's smarter than you think. I'll bet she's already guessed what you've avoided telling her."

"Don't worry, I'll be fine. I have a plan to set things straight. But I do appreciate your listening." Tapping her under the chin, he grinned. "I'm always here for you, too, sis."

In another instant, he'd turned on his heel and left.

Marla stood alone with the buzzing insects and steady rhythm of the waves. Troubled by their encounter, she watched her brother's retreating figure until the dark night swallowed him.

She'd stepped forward a few paces, intending to return to her hotel room, when a moving shadow on the rear veranda caught her eye. Changing direction, she climbed the stone stairway to the Grand Terrace.

Dr. Rip Spector faced Oleander Hall, holding some sort of device in his hand. Marla cleared her throat, startling him because he jerked upright.

"Sorry, I didn't hear you approach." Lamplight gave her a glimpse of his stark white hair, curious hazel eyes, and surprisingly young face. She'd put him in his mid-forties.

"I'm Marla Shore. My family is here for a reunion this weekend. Mr. Butler told me he hired you to chase away the ghosts," she said, cracking a grin.

"Indeed. I'm attempting to get a base reading on the EMF fluctuations." He spoke stiffly, as though used to people's skepticism.

"Pardon me?" Her glance fell to the instrument he held.

"Electromagnetic field. Spirits produce a disruption of energy in the area, but so do many of our common household appliances. This EMF field meter measures readings, but I have to locate normal sources before I can detect unusual spikes."

"I see." She noted the open canvas bag on the ground displaying an array of other equipment. "Have you found anything interesting yet?"

"Oh yes." His voice filled with enthusiasm. "This place abounds with spiritual energy. So much has happened here in the past, it's no wonder."

"Are you allowed into Oleander Hall?" she asked.

"Of course, although Mr. Butler has requested we clear the times with him before we work there."

"I thought I felt a presence in the tower elevator."

The ghost hunter laughed, which eased the lines on his face and gave him a more carefree appearance. Marla wondered what he did for his day job. "That's probably old Andrew, who wants to scare people away from his penthouse."

"Why is that?"

Dr. Spector shrugged. He had a bulky frame, made wider by too many good meals. "Could be he's just territorial. I don't think that's the case with the anomalies in Oleander. I've caught a ball of light in the parlor with my camera and EVP—electronic voice phenomena—on audio. I'm no psychic, but those spirits seem restless."

"Can you find out what they want?"

"That's not my job. We're here to capture evidence of spirit activity and convince the entities to leave. If you're respectful, and you tell them to go, they'll realize they don't belong there anymore."

"What about the man who fell off his ladder today?" she said, careful to keep her voice neutral. "According to the manager, some of the workmen believe a ghost may have caused the disaster."

"Poltergeists can be dangerous, not because they want to cause harm, but because they possess a great deal of energy." He gave her a level stare. "I don't believe that unfortunate business was related to our otherworldly friends."

"The police say it was an accident."

"So I would presume." He tilted his head. "If you're really interested in learning more about what we do, come up to my room. I can show you photos of orbs and other phenomena."

"No, thanks, I don't have time right now. Besides, I'd rather check out Oleander Hall. Can you call me when you're going inside the old wing? I promise I won't interfere with your research." Unless she mistook that gleam in his eye, he'd look for an excuse to run into her again.

Her thoughts swerved in a new direction the next morning. After a leisurely breakfast and a brisk walk around the resort, she and Vail split up. He headed to a volleyball game on the beach, while she joined a bowling tournament in the sports and spa complex. Needing time alone with her family, she figured this

HOOD COUNTY LIBRARY

would be a good opportunity to bring up Polly's mention of the family riches.

"Aunt Polly told me about some gemstones our grandfather owned," she said to her assorted cousins. "I'll bet this is where he got the money to buy the plantation. She believes the remainder of his loot is still here. Polly has been searching for it but unsuccessfully so far, and she's asked for my help."

Lori, who'd come with her husband, widened her eyes. "No kidding. What kind of gems? Diamonds?"

"Where did grandfather get them?" inserted Cynthia, looking her usual svelte self in belted linen slacks and a silk blouse.

"Good question," Marla replied. "Maybe he stole them, and those visitors in Cossack hats were detectives who tracked him down. Supposedly Andrew was upset after he left them in his parlor. Why else would they have come to see him?"

"They could have been foreign investors," Cynthia offered. "What if they'd put up the money for the hotel and wanted payback? If Andrew didn't have the funds, that would be enough cause to give him a stroke."

"Didn't you say Ruth stopped talking to her sister and brothers after Andrew died?" Lori asked Marla. "If the remaining stones were missing, maybe she suspected her siblings stole them. She could have blamed them for their father's fatal attack." Lori stopped speaking to applaud Jeff, who'd just scored a strike.

Marla gestured. "Aunt Polly said she wanted to right old wrongs this weekend. Since our great-aunt and great-uncles are no longer living, that would refer to our Colorado cousins."

"I don't think they know any more than we do about the past history of Sugar Crest," said Joan, one of Marla's teammates. Her daughter Rochelle was noticeably absent. Marla wondered if the teen had gone to the beach with her new friends, where she'd likely run into Vail. It made her impatient to leave.

"Polly recommended this place for our reunion, didn't she?" Marla addressed her query to Cynthia.

The blonde nodded. "I can't tell you how surprised I felt when Aunt Polly said our family used to own the resort. My

OOD COUNTY LIBRARY

mother was the next eldest after Polly, but she'd never said a word to me. Lori, you and Jeff have been here before. Did Uncle William say anything to you?"

"We're just as much in the dark as you are, aren't we, sweetheart?" Jeff said, smiling at his wife as he walked up to them. "You know, I'm getting a hankering for a mug of hot coffee."

Lori scrambled to her feet from the bench where she'd waited for her turn. "I'll get right on it, dear."

"Try not to spill it this time, okay? Oh, and get me a couple of chocolate doughnuts while you're at it."

Lori seemed to shrink into herself. "I may not have enough change."

Frowning, Jeff pulled out his wallet. "I thought I just gave you a ten yesterday. I told you not to squander it. Here's twenty. That had better last longer."

Watching their exchange, Marla bit her tongue to keep herself from defending her cousin. Not one to allow a man to push her around, she felt her hackles rise, especially when she remembered her encounter with Jeffrey and the cute chef last night. *It's not your place to interfere,* she reminded herself, digging her nails into her palms. Nonetheless, she resolved to catch Lori alone later and offer a few words of advice.

Her turn came, and she rolled the ball down the lane, where it ended in the side gutter. Oh, well. Bowling wasn't her thing; it was the conversation that interested her more.

"What do you think, Marla?" Jeff asked. "Is there something valuable hidden here that belongs to our family?"

My *family, pal.* "If anyone looks for the stuff, it should be me. Polly didn't tell any of you about the gems. She wanted me to help her find the stones."

"Hey, they don't belong to her," Cynthia protested. "We're all Andrew's heirs. If there's going to be a treasure hunt, I want in."

That's what you get for introducing Cynthia to adventure. After facing down a couple of murderous crooks in a funeral home with Marla, her cousin was too eager to participate in another investigation. "We don't even know what to look for or where to begin,"

Marla said, hoping to discourage false hopes. *Oh no? What about Andrew's penthouse tower suite, that everyone claimed was haunted but was situated above the floor where Polly had grown up?*

"Maybe it's hidden in the old sugar mill," said one of the other cousins. "You know, guarded by that lady ghost." She gave a delicious shiver.

Marla had given up trying to learn everyone's name. They needed name tags. Restless to get outside into the fresh air and look for Vail, she shifted on the hard bench while another ball clunked onto the alley and thundered toward the pins.

Her temples throbbed by the time the game finished and she'd turned in her shoes. She sauntered outdoors, wincing at the bright sunlight. Their big family dinner wasn't until three o'clock, so she still had some morning hours free. Her steps took her toward the beach, where apparently the volleyball game was long over. Sun-warmed sand sifted through her toes as she walked without her sandals, checking the occupants of the lounge chairs. Giving cousins Alan and Julia a passing greeting, she moved on to the pool, where she found Cynthia's brother. He sat in animated conversation with some of her younger relatives, dealing cards at a table. After muttering her greetings, she turned and headed for the main hotel.

She should've known Vail would escape at the earliest opportunity to watch the latest sports games on television. He lay stretched out on their bed, his lazy eyes welcoming her as she threw down her purse and regarded him with a smile.

"Back so soon? I thought you wanted to explore the nature preserve next door," she said in an airy tone.

"We'll do that together another day." He patted the bedspread. "I've another type of exercise in mind. Just put that Do Not Disturb sign on the door, and I'll show you what I mean." His sexy grin left no doubts.

Casting aside her intent to change into a swimsuit, Marla stripped off her clothes while Vail watched with blatant desire. It was a heady sensation to know she could turn him on so readily. Her nerves tingled with sensitivity, making her ache for his touch. Like an adolescent just discovering the power of her body, she paraded naked in front of him while his gaze followed her movements.

Sharing a room with Dalton came with certain disadvantages, Marla noted later that afternoon when she'd showered and changed into a Wedgwood blue dress. After a couple of hours at the pool, she could have used a nap, but he'd been ready to resume their private games. While she'd trade his form of distraction for sleep any day, dark circles under her eyes required an application of coverup. Finishing with a coat of apricot lip gloss, she called her mother's room to see if Anita needed any help. It was nearly time for their family dinner.

"I'm fine, but you might check on Aunt Polly. She doesn't answer the phone when I ring her room. I haven't seen her all morning. I know she's avoiding me."

"Ma, they don't have Caller ID here. She has no way of knowing it's you on the other end of the line."

"I'll bet she can tell."

"I doubt that's true. Anyway, we'll see her at dinner." Marla hesitated, clutching the receiver from the phone on the nightstand. Vail had just spritzed himself with cologne, and she could smell his favorite spice scent. "Aunt Polly told me about some gemstones that Andrew might have hidden. Were you aware of any valuables belonging to the family?"

Her mother snorted. "Polly makes up what she wants to believe, although if she's searching for jewels, that would explain her trips here every year. She insists on staying in the same room for some reason, or so the staff have told me. I wouldn't put any credence in her claims. I think Papa borrowed his money, and there wasn't anything left."

"What about those two visitors Andrew had the night he died? They could have been creditors calling in their loan. Did Ruth ever say who they were?"

"My mother was very distraught that night."

"Why did she get mad at her sister and brothers?"

"How should I know? I was too young to notice."

"Polly also mentioned some letters that she wrote to a man named Vincent." Marla heard a brief hitch in her mother's breath.

"If you want to humor her, go ahead," Anita said sharply. "I need to finish getting ready."

Dalton approached her after she hung up. "I gather your mom doesn't agree with Polly's talk about precious gems. Maybe you shouldn't waste your time, either."

"You just want me all to yourself."

His response nearly demolished her plan to reach the ballroom early. When she emerged from his passionate kiss, she wobbled on shaky knees to the bathroom to reapply her lipstick. *Everyone will know what we've been up to most of the day,* she thought, examining her heightened complexion in the mirror.

But when they joined the congregation in the hall outside the banquet room, Marla's state of composure wasn't utmost in her relatives' minds.

"Where's your diamond ring?" cousin Julia queried when Vail was out of earshot, getting her a drink from the lobby bar. Marla needed to fortify herself for the coming ordeal, and so, she suspected, did her fiancé. Her apprehension was justified by Julia's snotty remark.

She glanced at the circle of curious faces surrounding them. "We haven't had time to go jewelry shopping. We've been too busy. This is the first break we've had."

"Are you going to quit work when you get married?" said Brenda, from the Colorado contingent.

"I like my job, and I've worked hard to build my salon. Why would I want to give it up?"

"I don't suppose you'll get married in that same temple where you and Stanley had the ceremony. Are you still a member?"

"No, I'm not, and since Dalton isn't Jewish, we'll probably look for a hotel or something."

"Now you're on Polly's blacklist," sneered Cynthia's brother, Corbin. His hair stood in spikes as stiff as his smile.

"She needs my help. We're on speaking terms again."

"Aunt Polly won't speak to me since I married Christine," said an older cousin, Jon. He was Uncle Floyd's son, a younger brother of Polly's who'd died from cancer. "It's her loss, not mine."

"You'd better believe it," Corbin said. "She's alienated half the family with her attitude. That's why I can't understand how come she brought us all together for this weekend."

"Has anyone seen her?" Marla said, craning her neck to search the crowd. Instead of her aunt, she spied Vail juggling two wine-glasses while heading in her direction. After expressing her appreciation to him, she took a long sip of chilled chardonnay, then relayed her concern. "Polly isn't here yet. What do you suppose is keeping her?"

"Who knows?" Vail shrugged. "Maybe she met your ghost in the tower elevator."

"That's not funny."

When the ballroom doors opened and a hostess ushered them inside to take their seats, Marla's apprehension grew. Polly's chair yawned conspicuously vacant at the head table. Resisting an urge to gnaw her fingernails, she waited impatiently while the serving staff poured their water and presented a mushroom pie en croute for an appetizer. Her gaze fixed on the doorway, she finally gave up and tossed her napkin on the table.

"I'm going upstairs," she told the assemblage. "Something must have happened to Polly. It's way past the time when she should've been here."

Chapter
Seven

"I'll come with you," Lori offered, half rising from her chair.

"Sit down." Jeffrey gave her shoulder a squeeze. "No one asked you to interfere. If Marla takes anyone, it should be her boyfriend. He's a cop."

Marla's mother twisted her hands. "Do you think something has happened to Polly? She wouldn't miss Thanksgiving dinner, not when it was her idea that brought us here."

"Could be Polly just wants to focus attention on herself," Moishe speculated, digging into his appetizer. "She's been acting mighty strange this weekend."

"You're right," Marla replied, "and I don't like it." She waved at Vail, directing him back to his seat. "Don't let the waiter remove my food. I'll see what's holding her up. I don't need help."

As she passed through the lobby, she realized Vail's hasty push to his feet was probably motivated by his panic at the thought of being left alone with her relatives. Too late now. She headed toward the central tower before remembering Polly's sleeping arrangements. Turning toward Jasmine Hall, she crossed into the outer wing through a set of double glass doors before hitting the elevator call button. Ghosts didn't reside in this section, at least she hoped not.

"Howdy, Miz Shore," said Harvey Lyle with a wink as he passed by holding a room service tray. "Happy Thanksgiving."

"Same to you. How come you're not off for the holiday?"

"Somebody's got to be here, ma'am. I volunteered since I ain't got no folks around these parts."

The elevator door slid open. "My aunt didn't show for our family dinner. Have you seen her today?"

Harvey grew a puzzled look. "Miz Polly called and asked for a tray earlier. Said she wasn't feelin' well. Her voice sounded kinda raspy, so I figured she musta come down with something. Be a shame, with her settin' up this reunion and all."

"What time did you deliver the tray?"

"Just before noon. I set it outside and knocked like she told me to do."

"Did you pick it up yet? Is she still in her room? No one answered when I rang there."

"Been too busy. The boss has me hopping."

"Can you stop by her room after you drop that off?" She nodded at his tray. Since he was already in the Jasmine wing, it would make her feel better to have backup, especially if Polly was too ill to answer the telephone.

"Sure enough. Sorry I didn't get to it sooner. Ya won't tell Mr. Butler I been slackin' off, will ya?"

"Of course not. You're doing the job of several people today. I'll see you shortly."

Her nose wrinkled at the musty scent that met her as she entered the carpeted hallway of the fourth floor. An eerie silence prickled the hairs on her arms as she strode forward. Most guests had dispersed to the different restaurants or activities; few would be still in their rooms on this beautiful afternoon.

Her senses unusually alert, Marla approached Polly's door with caution. It was slightly ajar, making her wonder if a maid had left it open. But there weren't any cleaning carts outside, and likely the housekeepers had the day free. What about the nurse's aide from the night before? Had she returned this morning to help Polly get ready for the banquet?

Marla poked at the door with her finger to pry it open wider. Wincing at the creaking hinges, she called Polly's name. No answer. Venturing across the threshold, she sucked in a breath when she saw the limp feet at the foot of the bed. She advanced, heart pounding, while her gaze trailed from the feet up a pair of bony legs to a flimsy lime nightgown. When she saw her aunt's face, eyes fixed at the ceiling, she knew.

Her knees threatening to buckle, Marla steadied herself with a hand on the wall. Polly's state of repose appeared peaceful. Almost too peaceful, she thought, noticing how neatly Polly's thin gray hair was parted to the side. How long had she been like this, since the health care aide left? Otherwise, you'd think her hair would be mussed from sleep. *It doesn't matter. Get help, and don't touch anything.*

Unable to resist, Marla scanned the area for clues. Harvey's meal tray sat on the desk, uneaten food congealed like the blood in Polly's veins. Someone must have brought it inside after Harvey left it by the door.

Hearing a faint rustling sound, she whirled just in time to see a shadow dart from her vision.

Sweat broke on her brow. The open door to the bathroom beckoned. Clicking on the light, she peered inside. A faint lilac scent lingered in the air. Pill bottles, cosmetics, and other personal items littered the counter.

Backing away, she collided with a man's torso. Two scrawny arms folded around her.

"Shucks, Miz Shore, if ya want to play around, can't ya wait till I'm off duty?" the steward said. His breath smelled like rum. He must have taken a quick swig on the way upstairs, making her wonder where he hid his booze.

"Get off me, Harvey. My aunt is on the bed, not moving. I don't think she's breathing, either. We need to call someone."

Turning, she saw his face lose its color. "Oh my gawd. I'll get the boss." He took a few steps then faltered, gaping at Polly's frail form. "Oh my gawd," he repeated.

"Is there a hotel phone near the elevator? It's best if we don't disturb things in her room, just in case."

"Too late for that." Harvey pointed a shaking finger. "Looks like someone's been poking through those drawers."

"You're right." Marla had taken the room in at a glance before, but now she saw Polly's corsetlike undergarments spilled onto the floor. "A nurse's aide showed up last evening to help my aunt get ready for bed. I don't suppose you met her?"

"No, ma'am. I'd better get help. Do ya mind stayin' here by yerself?"

Marla pulled her cell phone from her purse. "I'll wait in front of her door." She followed him into the hallway. After he disappeared around the corner, Marla phoned Vail.

"I need you here. Something terrible has happened. Don't say a word to anyone, okay?"

"What's wrong?" he said in a hushed tone.

"It's Aunt Polly. She . . . she's gone. I think she might have died in her sleep." Her eyes filled with moisture. "Please come right away. You can give my family some excuse."

Her relatives would find out soon enough. She could imagine her mother's blood pressure rocketing. Why this of all weekends? *My time has come, so it's your responsibility now.* Polly's words from their earlier conversation tripped into her mind. Had her aunt felt a premonition?

"I'm on my way." Vail clicked off, leaving her standing in the corridor accompanied by an uneasy silence.

Wondering if the shadow she'd sensed inside Polly's room had meant anything or been a figment of her imagination, she muttered a quick prayer for her aunt's soul. Perhaps she'd sensed Polly's spirit as it departed to its rest. Or maybe someone had actually been in the room. Glancing up and down the hallway, she wrapped her arms around herself while waiting for company.

Vail arrived on the heels of the manager.

"I called the paramedics, and our resort doctor, too, after Lyle notified me," Butler explained. He looked like an undertaker in his black pinstripe suit and slicked-back dark hair. He took a quick glance at the deceased before waving a hand dismissively in the air. "Poor thing, her heart must have given out."

Vail's long stride brought him to the bedside. He bent forward, peering at Polly's face with a frown on his own. "I think you'd better summon the police while you're at it."

Marla gave him a shrewd look. "The door was unlocked when I got here, and it appears someone's been rifling through my aunt's drawers."

Straightening, Vail compressed his lips. "I see."

"Is there a problem?" boomed a loud voice from the hallway. A portly fellow toddled inside to join them.

"This is Dr. Angus," Butler said to Marla. "I'm sorry to say he's been called upon to do his duty all too often. We get lots of retirees, you understand. Some of the old folks rent rooms for the entire winter. It isn't unusual to find them . . . well, you can guess. I hope I didn't drag you from your holiday dinner."

"No bother." Dr. Angus huffed a few wheezy breaths. "Where's the patient?"

"In here." Butler reached the nightstand and picked up the telephone before Vail could stop him. "I'll call the cops, although it'll be a waste of their time."

"Look at her eyes," Vail said to the doctor.

"Petechial hemorrhages can mean many things," Dr. Angus commented after a brief examination of the body. "They often occur in natural diseases." He indicated the prescription bottle on the bedside table. "It's nearly empty. The lady must have been ill."

Startled, Marla stepped farther inside the chamber. "How is that possible? When I was here last night, the bottle was full. I didn't even know Polly took medicine before then."

"You saw her last evening?" Dr. Angus replied. His jowls quivered as he bobbed his head. "Did she appear sickly?"

"Aunt Polly hasn't looked well lately," Marla admitted, "and she'd lost weight. I've been helping with her affairs at home, but she hadn't said one word about having a serious illness."

"Your aunt had something wrong if she had to take a morphine sulfate solution. This prescription label has a phone number. I can call the pharmacist to get more information, and perhaps the name of her personal physician. If she overdosed by mistake, that would have caused respiratory depression. The elderly are especially vulnerable to changes in dosage."

Marla bit her lower lip. "You could ask the nurse's aide who was here last night. She was a gift from someone in the family and came to help Aunt Polly get ready for bed. I'd like to know what time the woman left, and what state Polly was in."

It occurred to her that the aide might have been the one who tossed through the drawer contents, looking for money. Or could someone else have been here, searching for clues to Andrew's supposed treasure? What about those letters Polly had exhorted her to find?

"Will the police dust for fingerprints?" she asked Vail in a low tone. "When I first came in here, I thought I saw someone. It might have been my imagination. You know, like a moving shadow from the corner of my eye. Or else I'm just spooked by all these ghost stories."

Grasping her elbow, he steered her from the room. "I'll speak to the officers. You should join your family. I can stay to make sure things get done properly."

She warmed to the concern in his eyes. "I'm not hungry, and I don't want to ruin the dinner for everyone else. Not yet." Hugging a hand to her stomach, she blinked moisture from her eyes. "Poor Polly. She has no children. I suppose my mother will want to make arrangements."

"She'll have to wait until the coroner releases the body. There isn't much else anyone can do right now. You'll have time enough after we get home."

Marla drew in a tremulous breath. "I need a drink. This is too weird. That psychic's prediction came true."

Vail gave her a brief hug and released her. "Just think: now Andrew's ghost has company."

"Gee, thanks, that makes me feel a lot better."

"Go downstairs. Find out which one of your relatives ordered the nurse's aide. And have something to eat before you keel over. I asked the server to keep your plate warm."

"What would I do without you?" She stroked his cheek, already bristly after his recent shave.

His eyes glinted like polished metal. "I need you more," he whispered, his lips brushing her forehead.

Marla turned away, wanting only to escape with her lover and forget what had happened. Unfortunately, duty propelled her to the ballroom, where her family was enjoying coffee and pumpkin pie.

Anita jumped from her seat upon spotting Marla. "Where is Polly? Why isn't Dalton here with you?"

Marla halted, shifting her feet while she mustered her courage. She studied a spot on the wall when she spoke. "I have some bad news. Aunt Polly . . . She passed away in her sleep."

Anita clutched a hand to her heart. "What?"

Moishe and William rose in unison. "You're saying our sister is gone?" Uncle William said, his voice hoarse.

Marla nodded, swallowing a lump in her throat.

"I don't believe it," Anita cried. "We just spoke to her. She might have had memory lapses, but Polly didn't say anything about ill health other than normal complaints."

"Maybe she felt this coming on, and that's why she planned the reunion."

"You could be right," Cynthia inserted. "She seemed adamant about coming to Sugar Crest."

"She wanted to die here," Marla suggested, "to guard the family treasure with the other spirits. Which one of you hired the nurse's aide to tend her last night?"

Polly's siblings exchanged puzzled glances. "Be clear, *bubula,*" Anita said. "What are you talking about?"

"I was with Polly last night when a health care worker arrived. She said someone had sent her as a gift for the evening." When no one admitted their generosity, Marla gave them all a scrutinizing glare. "If none of you paid for this woman, who did?"

"Call the service that sent her, and they'll tell you," offered Rochelle in a small voice. She sat at the far end flanked by her young cousins.

"Do you suspect this aide had something to do with Polly's death?" Anita snapped.

Shrugging, Marla pulled out her chair. "Who knows?" She sank down, grabbing her wineglass and draining the contents.

A waitress in a black dress and white apron approached. "Ma'am, would you like your dinner now? I've been holding it for you."

"Yes, thank you." It would be a while before their next meal, especially if their activities were cancelled.

Her relatives plied her with questions to which she responded in monosyllables in between bites of turkey dinner. She wasn't terribly hungry but forced herself to eat. Another glass of wine left her light-headed but calmer.

Dr. Angus was probably right in assuming that Polly had died of natural causes. If her aunt had to take morphine, she must have been hiding a serious problem. Perhaps she'd merely hastened her own death by taking too much narcotic analgesic. But, then, who'd hired the aide, why were Polly's undergarments strewn on the floor, and what had aroused Vail's suspicions?

Marla remembered her own evening purse had been displaced. She *had* unpacked it and put it in the nightstand. Somehow the beaded bag had moved on its own back to her suitcase. Person or poltergeist? Were there truly ghosts here, or human beings who aimed to perpetuate the legends?

Watching her relatives chatting animatedly about the latest family fiasco, she wondered if one of them was lying about hiring the aide. It should be easy enough to discover if the woman had come from a service. Maybe she'd left a receipt in Polly's room. *I'll have to get in there later, after things quiet down.* Among other items, Marla needed to obtain Polly's checkbook. Since her name was on the account, she'd have to pay any final bills. More importantly, she wanted to locate the letters her aunt had mentioned. Perhaps they gave a clue to Polly's illness, but that made sense only if they were recent. No doubt about it, she needed access to Polly's personal belongings.

"If the police don't pursue an investigation, I suppose someone will have to pack Polly's things," she addressed the assembly. "I'd like to help."

Anita's expression showed relief. "You're her closest niece. That makes sense. If you can handle those details, I'll plan the memorial service. Moishe, what about you?"

The older gent cleared his throat. "We're flying home to Denver on Sunday. We've already paid our regards to Polly by being here for this reunion."

"I see," Anita said coldly. "William?"

"I can't stay for the funeral. We have a flight to catch, too, and I have appointments next week. We'll attend in spirit. You'll have enough nieces and nephews to make a *minyan* if you allow women to participate in the prayer circle."

"I'm Reform these days," Anita told them. She glanced at Marla, her scornful look telling her daughter what she thought about her siblings.

"Hey, Marla," called Joan. "Does this mean we're calling off the treasure hunt?"

A barrage of inquiries followed, and Marla felt compelled to explain the situation to those who hadn't heard about it earlier. "Polly told me about a stash of gemstones that Andrew kept as his source of wealth. She seemed to believe some are still hidden on the resort grounds. I'm guessing Aunt Polly returned here every year in order to search for them."

"Oh, cool," squealed one of the younger cousins. "Do you think that's what those two strangers were after, the ones who met with Andrew the night he died?"

"Could be." She shoved her half-eaten plate of food aside. "You can look for the precious stones. I have better things to do." Feeling a crushing need for privacy, she murmured farewells before exiting outdoors into the waning afternoon sun.

Once alone, she inhaled a deep breath of warm ocean air. Being surrounded by relatives all weekend was beginning to take its toll, along with the tragedy of Polly's death. She needed time by herself to filter through all that had happened.

As she padded along the gravel path, she realized her steps

were taking her in the direction of the old sugar mill. Had it been her imagination, or had she heard a bell tolling in the middle of the night? She'd bolted upright in bed, but her foggy brain had processed the sound as a dream. Curious to revisit the site, she considered that haunted ruins would be a good place to hide an item of value. If she dug around, maybe she'd unearth Andrew's wealth—or Polly's letters, which could prove to be more valuable. Either way, it wouldn't hurt to look.

As she approached the crumbled stone structures, her ears picked up an eerie whistling, as though the trees issued a warning. Dead leaves crunched underfoot while she skirted jagged chunks of coral embedded in the dirt. A rodent scampered up a nearby cabbage palm, and another small creature of some type slithered around a clump of crotons.

Drifting on the breeze came a faint clanging. Marla twisted her neck to see if someone was ringing the bell outside the boiling bench, but the bell was not the source of the sound. Rather, it ebbed and flowed from the interior of the single standing structure, which housed vast pits.

"Is anyone there?" Marla called, listening intently. Open windows gaped like mouths waiting to devour anyone who ventured inside. The stone building, dark and cool, beckoned to her.

As she crossed the threshold, she thought she heard a girl's voice humming a plaintive song. Her breath quickened. Maybe she shouldn't have come here alone. But even as her pulse beat a rapid rhythm, she scoffed at the notion that the place harbored ghosts. She'd prove no one was here: neither a real person nor an ethereal body.

Marla took a few steps toward one of the depressions in the floor. Lined with rock made from crushed marine shells, it was first in a row that stretched to a far archway. Smells of stale sweat mingled with sickly sweet molasses, and she pictured slaves laboring in the heat from the fires while sugarcane juice boiled and frothed in huge copper kettles. Their voices seemed to surround her, accompanied by the crack of a whip, then a scream . . .

She screamed herself as a force shoved her from behind. For a moment, she was airborne, flailing her arms and legs. Then she was falling, falling, her shoulder hitting against a hard surface with a painful jolt before her head banged into a solid protrusion.

White lightning flashed before her eyes. Then blackness absorbed her.

Chapter
Eight

Marla heard a moan escape her lips before her mind allowed consciousness to seep in. Throbbing pain in her left shoulder brought her fully awake. Blinking, she studied her surroundings without comprehension. She lay at an angle on her side in some sort of bowl made from knobby concrete. No, not concrete . . . coquina. She'd fallen into one of the pits inside the sugar mill.

With realization came fear. She had definitely felt a push from behind, meaning whoever had propelled her might still be around. She dare not cry for help. Testing first her arms, then her legs, she was gratified to find her limbs intact. She'd have to deal with a sore shoulder for a few days, that's all. She knew that bumping her head hadn't produced a concussion because she didn't feel dizzy. She must've been merely stunned.

Pushing herself to a sitting position, she wondered if the intent had been to cause bodily damage or just to scare her. Ghosts didn't shove people. Someone at the resort intended harm, whether physical or emotional. Had this same person thrust the painter's ladder from the wall of the condemned wing?

Her neck prickled when she heard the bell tolling outside. Listening acutely, she caught no other sound except the rustling of dried leaves and the harsh cry of a seagull. Was it the wind swaying the bell, or someone's hand?

An urgent need to escape the sugar mill forced her to her feet. Stretching her arms above her head, she decided the rim was too high for her to reach. Nor were there any footholds on the rough interior, once white but now ash gray. She scraped her fingertips along the hard surface, hoping to find indentations that she could use for leverage. The dents she found were too shallow for use. The pits had withstood the test of time fairly well, even retaining the honeyed scent of boiling sugar.

Jumping didn't help. It jostled her sore shoulder, making her bite back a cry of pain. Should she call for help? No; the wrong person might answer. Realizing her vulnerability, she anxiously peered upward but with relief sensed she was alone.

Surely someone else would come along the path on this warm afternoon. In the meantime, she surveyed the sorry mess of her torn hosiery. Hey, could she lasso her pantyhose on that same protrusion her head had slammed into? That would give her the means to climb partway up. But then what?

Worry about it later. Slipping off her pumps, she removed her stockings. Too bad about the dress, but it was destined for the cleaners anyway. She hiked up her skirt before swirling the pantyhose over her head. After several tosses, she finally hitched one legging on the jagged prominence. Gritting her teeth at the ensuing ripping sound, she pulled gently until it held. Thank goodness for support spandex.

Hopefully her assailant had left the vicinity. Taking the chance, she threw her shoes over the edge so they'd be available later. Now for her acrobatic act. Gripping the makeshift rope, she inched her sweaty soles a couple of notches up the side of the pit while her shoulder screamed in protest. Her white-knuckled grasp of the hosiery grew slick, making her fingers slide. With an ominous tearing noise, her pantyhose gave up the struggle, and she landed with a thump on her butt.

Muttering an expletive, she stilled when her ears picked up scrunching footsteps growing louder. Someone whistled in accompaniment, and the tune sounded strangely like the theme song of the Pirates of the Caribbean ride at Disney World. *Yo ho, yo ho—*

"Help," Marla yelled. "I fell into the pit."

The boyish face of Dr. Rip Spector appeared at the rim. His stark white hair spiked in contrast to his deep hazel eyes. Merriment mingled with curiosity in his expression. "Miss Shore, what are you doing down there? Exploring on this fine day? I'd have thought you'd be eating your Thanksgiving dinner by now."

"Can you get me out of here?" She wasn't in the mood for a social discussion.

"Dear me, you are in a fix, aren't you? Should be more careful in a place like this, with ruins and all." He shifted his bow tie, worn with a blue dress shirt.

"A ghost pushed me in. Is there a rope handy?"

He clucked his tongue. "Don't make fun of the spirits. That may very well be why you're in this predicament. Wait here. I'll get something better." Returning a few minutes later, he brandished a vine fresh from the nearby woods.

"That doesn't look strong enough," Marla said. Not that she had much choice. She didn't relish being left alone while he summoned help from the hotel.

To her surprise, the leafy vine held her weight. She hauled herself upward by crossing one palm over the other while the ghost chaser grunted at the other end. Afraid she'd lose her grasp, she held on tight. By the time she collapsed outside the pit, she could barely breathe.

"You look as though you've been through the wringer," Dr. Spector commiserated, his labored breathing indicating the exertion had claimed his energy as well. Then again, he might have been the one who'd initiated her adventure. Odd that he was the only member of his group in the vicinity. Where were all the rest? Eating turkey and mashed potatoes?

"I'm lucky you happened by the old ruins," she said, rubbing her aching shoulder as she slipped into her shoes.

He pointed to a pile of equipment lying at the open archway. "I came to get some readings. There's a lot of electromagnetic energy in this particular area, but it fluctuates with the time of day. I want to compare the results to my measurements from yesterday."

"Don't ghosts come out only at night?"

"I've captured anomalies during the day as well as at night. Spirits can be active any time." He squinted as they moved into the sunlight. "We do more readings at night because there are fewer distractions, and it's quieter. It's also better for video to have a dark background."

"Why do things show up on camera that you can't see with the naked eye?" she asked, curiosity overwhelming her need to rest.

"Presumably these entities emit near infrared radiation, what we term NIR. You can capture this with a video camera but not with your eyes. It's also possible that if you saw an entity in front of you, your brain might not recognize it, and so it's dismissed. Once the camera registers the anomaly, your mind can process it properly."

Oh yeah, like I'm not going to see something that's directly in front of me. "Are you saying you can take a picture of an actual ghost?"

His eyes crinkled. "Not exactly. The most common type of anomalies that we catch on film are orbs. We might also see vortices or energy rods, and you know, unusual sources of light. Rarely do we capture an apparition." He tilted his head. "The old lady, your aunt. Is she all right?"

Marla's skin crawled. "Aunt Polly passed away some time in the early morning. Apparently, she'd been ill and may have taken too much of her medication. Why do you ask?"

His startled surprise seemed genuine. "I saw a figure move across her window last night. Remember we chatted on the terrace? After you left, I set up my equipment in Oleander Hall. While the video cameras were running, I went outside to do a quick inspection of the exterior wall. That's when I caught movement on the periphery of my vision."

"Could you tell if the form was a male or female?" This could be important, if he'd spotted someone inside Polly's room. Then again, how had he known which window belonged to her?

Spector scratched his head. "Sorry to say, but I was more focused on the corner suite in the haunted wing. We've definitely gotten some EVPs in there, and I was looking for any potential sources from outside."

"EVPs . . . what's that?"

"Electronic voice phenomena . . . voices captured on audio tape or digital recorders that are not heard by human ears. We try to duplicate them from other sounds in the vicinity to eliminate natural causes." He paused. "I did point my camera toward your aunt's window, but the figure had vanished in the interim."

"Do you take digital photos?" If so, she'd like to see them for herself.

"Most of the time. I also use thirty-five millimeter because it takes better resolution photos, plus you get a negative which proves the photo wasn't altered. I'll often cover both angles by using a digital until I see something, then I'll whip out my thirty-five. But that's when I'm not carrying the video camcorders. We've got infrared, fiber-optic, and digital video equipment that we can hook up to our computers and let run all night."

"I see. And have these films revealed anything yet?"

"We're still analyzing the data."

"With the photos, how do you know you're photographing an orb rather than a speck of dust on the lens?"

"Orbs have a spherical shape. I've caught them where we have EMF fluctuations. We've got videos where anomalies have gone through walls, hit ceiling fans, veered around people. If you have free time while you're here, I can show you."

Marla shifted her feet. "I'm more concerned about what you spotted in my aunt's window. Did you see anything else?"

"I saw lights flickering on the beach, but by the time I'd moved my gear past the dunes, nothing showed."

"Too bad." Marla still thought it meaningful that he'd glimpsed an oddity in the vicinity of Polly's room. Her skin itched, compelling her to move on. "Well, if you'll excuse me, I have to get cleaned up," she told Spector while he stuffed his equipment into his backpack. "Thanks again for your help."

The ghost chaser hustled to join her on the path to the hotel.

"I'd like to learn more about your family history," he said in a rush as though reluctant to let her go. "Tragedies, love affairs, squabbles." He slanted her a curious glance. "I don't suppose you know anything about that final meeting between Andrew and his two guests?"

"Only that he died shortly thereafter."

"With its rich historical background, this place already is a magnet for tourists. You'd think the city council would want to preserve it. Any idea how the vote went yesterday?"

"I'm not sure they've reached an accord. I haven't seen any of the council members today, so I assume they went home for the holiday." Marla winced as she tripped over a tree root and jostled her sore shoulder.

"Can you imagine tearing down this magnificent hotel? It's a showplace for the era in which it was constructed. What a shame to lose so much history," Spector told her.

"The council members don't care. To them the bottom line is all that counts. Which would make the city more money: renovating older structures, or tearing them down and bringing in wealthy investors for a new attraction?"

"The entities that dwell here are attached to the resort and the remaining outbuildings." Spector wrinkled his brow. "They must be disturbed by the construction. Maybe that's why the workers are encountering so many accidents. It's the only way the spirits can communicate their displeasure."

You got that right. But aren't you here to help move them on to their final rest? Or won't that happen until they complete their unfinished business?

They strolled past a crew of gardeners pulling weeds from a bed of red and pink impatiens. The men, swarthy individuals wearing soiled overalls, stared at her with blank expressions. Didn't they get time off for a holiday meal?

"There's also the impact to the environment to consider," Spector added in a thoughtful tone. "A major construction project would disrupt the local ecology. I've seen hundred-year-old live oaks on the property, not to mention the tropical hammock, mangroves, and shoreline. If you ask me, money is changing hands, and that's where this notion of a theme park comes from."

"Mr. Butler would rather see the resort fixed up. His bosses must be the ones soliciting the real estate people."

"Didn't your family own this place in the past? Too bad you can't buy back the property."

"Look at all the work that needs to be done. Whichever way the wind blows, it'll cost a fortune."

"It's incredible how long it takes them to do repairs," Spector agreed. "With so many workers, they should be more efficient. Perhaps they're delaying things on purpose."

"You could have a point."

Glancing at his watch, he squawked. "Oh no, I'm late for our restaurant reservation. Take care, my dear."

He hurried away before Marla could question him further about his investigation and other things he might have noticed.

No matter. He'd reminded her that she should talk to Seto Mulch. Icing her shoulder would have to wait. Why had Mulch assigned a gardening crew on a holiday? What did he know about the maintenance work on the hotel? Was he privy to the family secrets?

After sparing time in her room to wash and change into a clean pair of black slacks and an apricot top, Marla scribbled a message to Vail on the telephone pad before heading outside. Hearing elated shouts and applause coming from the tennis courts, she aimed across the grass toward the caretaker's cottage that bordered the woods to the west. She'd studied a map and figured his place burrowed through the hammock toward the grand entrance rather than the beach. Wearing canvas walking shoes helped her avoid the pinecones strewn along the sandy ground. Shifting her purse, she rolled her sore shoulder with a grimace of pain.

"Miss Shore, what are you doing here?" trilled a female voice. Marla whirled. Brownie the chef emerged from behind a stand of bamboo and hurried toward her.

"I thought I'd have a chat with Mr. Mulch," Marla said, wondering at the falsely cheerful grin on the woman's face. "He's the only one left from the early days, so I'm hoping he can clarify some things for me about the resort history. And you? With so many groups here this weekend, I'd think you'd be busy in the kitchen." *Or maybe you don't want to ruin your nail polish so you delegate your duties instead.*

Chin thrust in the air, Brownie gave her a disdainful glance. "Everything is well organized. I just brought Seto his dinner. The old guy likes to eat by himself." She winked, her long lashes shading eyes the color of melted chocolate. "Good luck getting him to talk. He'll spout off against those real estate developers, but you won't get him to give anything else away. Don't think I haven't tried."

"Just what are you interested in finding out?" Marla said sharply.

A veil slipped over the pastry chef's expression. "With all these ghost stories, Seto must have seen something. He's been taking care of this place forever. I think his goal is to join the spooks when his time comes." Her sultry laughter trailed off as she strode away, leaving Marla staring after her.

How peculiar. Did Brownie know about Andrew's legacy, including his gems? Was that why she coddled the groundskeeper, to learn what he knew about the lost wealth?

Compressing her lips, Marla emerged from the trees in front of a Bahamian-style cottage painted coral with white shutters. It had a modest porch holding ceiling fans, a couple of patio chairs, and a worn welcome mat. The jalousie windows were open to let in a fresh breeze.

As she climbed the steps, she heard the old man's voice talking loudly. Either he had another visitor, or he was on the phone. While she stood frozen, debating whether she should ring the bell or leave, she couldn't help overhearing his words.

"Sending your spy won't get anything out of me, sonny. You haven't found what you're looking for before, and you won't find it now. A pretty face don't sway me, even if she is a good cook. I been here so long that I'm a fixture. I seen plenty, but what's past is best lain to rest."

He cleared phlegm from his throat. "Of course I agree with Butler. Old bones are better left buried. A bit of plaster, some fresh paint, modern plumbing, and we're back in business. You tell me whose side you're on."

He paused to listen, then his voice rose. "I'm not a fool. I know who you are. It's stamped on your features as bright as day. The apple don't fall far from the tree, sonny. If you're here to cause trouble, be warned that I'll stop you. Ain't no doubt about it, yes sirree."

After Mulch slammed down the receiver, Marla counted to five slowly before punching the doorbell. Tramping footsteps heralded his approach, then the door swung wide to reveal the old man chewing on a celery stick. In the fading sunlight, she noticed the creases in his face had deepened so that he appeared fatigued.

"Sorry to bother you on a holiday," Marla began, "but I wanted to have a word with you. Do you have a few minutes?"

"I suppose I can listen while my meal is heatin' in the oven." Signaling for her to enter, he stood aside for her to pass. Inside, Marla faced a cozy living room with comfortable furnishings, old-fashioned lamps, and a scent of pine and woodsmoke. Her glance lit on the fireplace, its interior blackened from use.

An image popped into her mind of Polly's room at the hotel. A fireplace adorned one wall. Was that where she'd seen the moving shadow? Marla hadn't thought twice about it at the time. The recess appeared decorative rather than functional, but that wasn't unusual in Florida. Fake logs deluded transplanted northerners into believing they still lived in a cold climate. Her room didn't have a fireplace, nor did Anita's.

"Something wrong?" the old guy asked her, swallowing a last bite on his stalk.

Sure, let's start with that conversation you just had on the telephone. Was Brownie the spy you were referring to? Who were you addressing as sonny? What did you mean, old bones were best left buried?

"Oh no, I was just admiring your place," she said aloud. "How long have you lived here?"

He gave a hearty chuckle. "Ever since I can remember. My daddy worked for Rutfield before Andrew Marks took over. Andrew brought in fresh money and fixed things up. I was so excited when he hired me. Hard to believe I started as a busboy in the main dining room, ain't it? I was fifteen then, back in 1927. Those were the good ole days."

Marla did a quick calculation, putting him at ninety-two years old. "Andrew was my grandfather. They say he had some mysterious visitors the night he died."

"Everyone wants to hear that tale." Glaring at her with sharp eyes, he seemed in no hurry to elaborate. His handsome features, although sporting the ravages of time, indicated he must have charmed the ladies in his day. White brows rose above a well-defined nose and firm lips. His skin, tanned from years in the sun, held scars that were likely from removed skin cancers, a common occurrence in the sunny South.

"Aunt Polly requested my help," Marla said. "I understand she's been returning to the resort every year since her mother, Ruth, sold the property."

The groundskeeper's expression softened. "Oh, if Polly sent you . . . Why don't you take a seat. What's your name again?"

"Marla Shore." She didn't know if he remembered the manager introducing them.

"Poor gal. My Polly hasn't had an easy time of it."

His Polly? "I imagine you felt close to the family, growing up here as you did."

"After my daddy passed on, it was up to me to keep the place in shape." He grinned proudly, showing yellowed teeth.

"Andrew must have relied on you a great deal. My aunt has been searching for something she feels rightfully belongs to us. I'm wondering if you know what she means?"

A look of pain entered his eyes. "Polly will never find her heart's desire, because Vincent took it from her."

Chapter
Nine

"Who's Vincent?" Marla demanded. "Aunt Polly told me about him, but I still don't know who he is. She wrote some letters that she said Vincent may have taken."

"Impossible. She wrote them after he'd gone. I'm surprised Polly even mentioned his name after the grief he caused. I'd steer clear of the subject if I were you." Anger laced his tone, arousing Marla's curiosity even more.

"What's in those letters?"

"Stuff."

His guarded look prompted her next comment. "It's gallant of you to protect her privacy, but she wanted my help," Marla reminded him. "Is it just the letters she wants me to find, or something more?"

Mulch didn't seem to hear her, or else he'd gotten lost in daydreams of the past. "Polly was cute as a button when I first laid eyes on her," he said with a sad wag of his head. "You know how they say familiarity breeds contempt? I was like the big brother she never had. She trailed after me once I finished waitin' on tables and went to pitch in at the fields. We both loved the land, and Polly liked to get down and dirty with the flowers and such. She was like a fresh bloom herself, all curled up and ready to open to womanhood. But she never saw me as nothin' more than a hired hand."

Why, you old sot. You fell in love with Polly. "And Vincent?"

"His name ain't worthy of discussion."

"Why would he be interested in Polly's letters? What was his relation to her?"

Compressing his lips, Mulch shook his head.

"I heard Andrew paid cash to purchase the plantation," she said, changing tactics. A dry throat made her voice raspy. After the heavy afternoon meal, she needed a drink of water.

"You heard right."

"If he immigrated to this country a couple of years before, he couldn't have brought much money with him. I understand he'd been a student at University of Warsaw. How could he have acquired such wealth in so short a time?"

"Where he got the dough wasn't my concern."

"Maybe not, but did it interest those strangers who turned up one night in 1943?"

Mulch clasped his gnarled hands. "Those two fellows arrived outta the blue and asked to see the boss. They wore funny hats and spoke with accents. Andrew got upset when I told him two men had come to see him, and they looked like foreigners."

"Why was that?"

"Appears he was expecting 'em. *I always knew they'd find me,* that's what he muttered under his breath. He said he'd speak to them privately in the parlor. They were in there for a while before Andrew sent for his tobacco."

"Oh yes, the humidor."

"Next thing we know, the boss heads to his suite, where he takes sick. Three days later, he's six feet under."

Marla leaned forward. "And the two men?"

Staring into space, Mulch didn't answer at first. "Gone."

"Gone where? Did anyone see them leave?"

"No ma'am."

"Maybe they're still here, and their ghosts are haunting the hotel."

He looked at her through lowered brows. "Are you believing that hogwash Butler spreads around?"

"I've felt Andrew's spirit in the tower elevator."

"Oh yeah? Mebbe so. Or mebbe ghosts are part of this theme-park mystique."

"The theme park hasn't been built yet."

"No?" They stared at each other while Marla got the feeling she was missing the point.

"How about the accident yesterday? Some say a spook pushed the painter off his ladder."

"Ain't no spooks doin' bad deeds around here. Ruthie would turn over in her grave if she knew what went on."

"What's that?" Marla asked, leaning forward.

"It's best you don't know. Tell Polly to stop her snooping, too. She may be searchin' for her letters or the gold at the end of the rainbow, but all she'll find is trouble."

Gold? Did he mean that literally or figuratively?

"My aunt took ill last night. When she didn't show up for Thanksgiving dinner this afternoon, I went to her room to check on her. I'm sorry to be the bearer of bad news, but it appears she'd died in her sleep." Sleep induced by an overdose of morphine, perhaps.

The analogy jumped out at her: Polly, taking sick in her room and dying alone. *Just like Andrew.*

A chill wind passed over her, causing goose bumps to rise on her arms. Was history repeating itself for a reason?

"Polly . . . dead!" Mulch leapt to his feet, the stricken look on his face confirming his feelings toward her aunt.

"I'm sorry. I realize you were fond of her."

"It's more than that. I've held my tongue out of respect. Now I can have my say."

"What do you mean?" Marla rose to face him.

"Never you mind." Ushering her toward the door, he said, "Make sure you bury your aunt proper. She was a fine lady."

At the threshold, Marla halted. "I'm surprised the chef didn't tell you about Polly when she brought your dinner. Then again,

I'm also wondering why Brownie delivered your meal. Don't her duties usually confine her to the kitchen?" *Unless she's spying for someone. What did she think Mulch knew?*

"You'd best ask the woman herself."

If his glowering look was meant to send her away, Marla ignored it. "My aunt requested a tray brought to her room, and Harvey Lyle served it. Why didn't he bring yours?"

"Mebbe he just delivers to guests. I'm on staff."

"Oh, I see." The notion struck her that Polly may have been dead already when someone called to order her tray. "Did you order a nurse's aide to care for Polly last night?"

Mulch pushed the door open. "Polly ain't never needed no help. She may have been a bit drafty in the attic lately, but she managed okay."

"Last night, a nurse's aide showed up at her room and said someone had sent her as a gift. None of my relatives claimed responsibility."

His eyes narrowed. "Describe this woman."

"She had a fairly large build and blond hair . . ." Hair that could have been a wig, she realized belatedly.

Mulch's bony hand gripped her arm. "Polly had no right to get you involved. Leave this to me, young lady. Go now."

Dismissed, Marla sought Vail at the resort. She found him reclining in their room watching football on television. Not again! A frown of annoyance creased her forehead while she tossed her purse on the dresser and slipped off her shoes.

"Where have you been?" she asked him. "I left you a note. You could have called me on your cell phone."

Vail's eyebrows lifted. "I thought it was obvious that I was hanging around the investigation. I convinced the medical examiner to do an autopsy. I hope that doesn't offend you."

She bit her lower lip. "Don't tell my mother. She might be upset. I'd just as soon see Polly buried peacefully, but then I'd be left with too many questions. So you did the right thing, Dalton. I'm glad someone listened to your advice this time. Will they share the report with you?"

He nodded. "I reminded them what a scion of the community Andrew had been when he was alive. Then Ruth kept the resort going afterward. This place provided most of the jobs for the townsfolk in earlier days. It's payback time."

Swinging his legs off the bed, he leveraged himself to his feet. "What happens now?"

"Ma will need my help packing Polly's things. I should find her. I would expect she'll cancel the rest of the weekend to sit shivah at home."

"I dunno, your family's planned this reunion for months. Polly would want you to stay together."

"That's true." She closed the distance between them and gave him a quick kiss. He smelled like shampoo and spice aftershave. His hair, soft and fluffy, begged for her touch. A pirate sifting gold coins wouldn't get as much of a thrill as she did fingering his silken strands.

Vail's eyes burned with passion as he drew her closer. "Mm, you're turning me on, sweetcakes." Nuzzling her neck, he murmured into her ear. "Wanna learn some new routines from your personal trainer? I could show you a few hot moves."

Her body tingled in all the right places. Maybe it was because she sought a relief from stress, but his offer struck the right chord. In no time, she'd shucked her clothes. Their lovemaking came fast and furious, no doubt providing a release valve for both of them.

"I love you, you know," Vail said in his seductively low voice when they lazed naked in each other's arms. "You make my life worthwhile."

"I love you, too." She stretched to kiss him on the mouth. "You've given me a different perspective on things. I never thought I'd *want* to take care of a man, let alone his child." Stan had soured her on marriage, and Tammy's death made her fear losing a child she loved. Now she felt ready to accept those risks. "You and Brie have changed my world to a better place."

"We still haven't set a date."

"There's no rush. I'm enjoying the slow progression."

He stroked the swell of her breast. "I want you to be mine. Why put it off?"

"We haven't decided where we're going to live." *Not in your house. I can't compete with memories of your dead wife.*

"I've been thinking about that, and I figured—"

The phone rang. Marla jerked away, reaching for the receiver at the same time he did. What had he been about to say?

"Marla, where did you run off to earlier?" Anita's voice snapped at her. "Michael called the funeral home and left a message on their machine. We want to arrange a memorial service for Polly."

"You'll have to wait until her body is released," Marla said, always the pragmatist.

"I know, but we can get the ball rolling."

"Too bad she never got a Pre-Need plan."

"Polly never thought about doing anything for the sake of others. We'll get a plot in the same cemetery where your father is buried."

Hearing the strain in her mother's voice, Marla said, "I'm sorry this occurred during what should have been a happy occasion. Are you canceling the rest of the weekend?"

"No. I've given it some thought and talked it over with Cynthia. Polly had a reason for us to be here. You'll figure it out."

I'm not doing too well so far. "Thanks for the vote of confidence."

"I know you'd rather stay behind closed doors with your beau, but you can't shirk your duties entirely. I need you to help me go through Polly's things. Mr. Butler claims she has stuff in the tower."

Marla's eyebrows lifted. That meant a return visit to the twelfth floor. "Where do you want to start?" She smiled at Vail as he traced a zigzag down her spine with his finger.

"In Jasmine Hall. That'll be easier, and you may pick up on a clue the police overlooked. I'm not so sure Polly would have taken an overdose on purpose without concluding her business here this weekend."

"Why was she taking a painkiller? Did you know she was ill?"

"Did Polly ever confide in me?" Anita countered. "That's why I sent you to look after her. Anyone could see she was getting more frail, not to mention more forgetful. I hope the autopsy will tell us what plagued her."

Marla's jaw dropped. "You're aware of that?"

"I'm not stupid. Your boyfriend spent an awfully long time in her room. He must've been convincing the cops that Polly's death might be more than it seems. At times it's useful to have a detective in the family."

Marla's heart soared. She'd never felt more cared for or more secure than she did right now with Vail beside her. "You're right," she said softly.

Her mother's tone sharpened. "I learned something interesting. When I asked Mr. Butler why Polly kept a suite in the tower when she didn't sleep there, he said it was her right. He murmured something about the terms of sale when Ruth transferred the property. It sounded like she retained partial ownership."

"No kidding?"

"We should get a copy of the legal documents to see if we're entitled to anything. Maybe this is why no one can rent rooms on the top two floors."

"Wow," Marla said. "Do you know what this means? If our family controls those levels, they can't tear down the hotel without our permission." Marla ruminated on the possibilities. "That makes this whole theme-park discussion a moot point. The resort would have to be renovated."

"What if Ruth made Polly her sole beneficiary?"

Marla lurched upright, mindful that Vail was ogling her nude body. "That's an interesting idea. If Polly alone controlled the penthouse suites, she could have presented an obstacle to the sale. The hotel conglomerate couldn't negotiate with the developers without her consent. Now that she's gone, they can proceed with the deal. But how can we see if this is true?"

"It's a holiday weekend, so I presume offices in town will be closed."

"Cynthia's husband is in the real estate business. I can ask Bruce to use his connections to get information."

"I saw him hobnobbing with some of those city council people. Maybe he's looking to buy property in the area."

Who had told Marla that one of her relatives was considering investing in the theme park? An unpleasant suspicion germinated in her mind.

"There's no rush in cleaning out the tower suites," she said. "I've already taken a quick look at the twelfth floor. It smells like mold and has a lot of old furniture. I'd rather start in Polly's room as you suggested."

"I'll meet you there," her mother agreed.

Marla would rather search through Polly's things on her own. "I know you've been wanting to spend time with Charlene and the kids. Why don't you give her a call? There isn't anything else scheduled until the movie tonight, so you have a few hours free. I can deal with Polly's stuff. If I discover anything important, I'll let you know."

"It wouldn't be right."

"You need to relax, Ma. Don't feel guilty."

"Oh my, there is one thing I forgot."

Marla felt a twinge of alarm. "What's that?"

"Polly must have a will. Did you ever get into her safety deposit box at the bank?"

"She let me in once. All I saw were stock certificates, the deed to her condo, and some bond funds." Vail tickled her side, and she suppressed a giggle. "If no one can find a will, I suppose you and your brothers would inherit. She has substantial cash in her bank accounts."

"She could have hidden a will in her condo."

"We'll see when we get home. If you can deal with the funeral parlor, I'll handle things at this end. Go on and have a good time with Charlene. I'll catch you later."

After hanging up, she turned to Dalton, swatting away his roving hand. "Stop that, or we'll never leave this room."

He gave a leering grin. "That's okay with me."

She saw the desire in his eyes and tamped down her own. "Ma raised some interesting questions. Let me shower and get dressed and then I'll tell you."

"So your mother doesn't know if Polly had a will drawn or not," Vail reiterated after she'd repeated their conversation. They wound through the corridors on their way to Jasmine Hall. Marla had called ahead to the front desk to make sure Polly's door was unlocked.

"Aunt Polly may have retained part ownership of the resort. I can't believe Ma never heard about it before, though." Marla's nostrils wrinkled at the musty odor rising from the carpet. "That makes it more likely that Ruth favored Polly as her main beneficiary, in which case people had a motive to do away with my aunt in order to proceed with their theme-park plans."

"The construction accidents play into that scenario. Proponents for the property sale would point to the dangerous state of disrepair of current structures," Vail said.

"Not if unhappy ghosts are causing the mishaps. Mr. Butler seems to believe that if he rids the resort of its unearthly inhabitants, the incidents will stop. Unless he hired the ghost chasers to appease the superstitious workers."

"The haunting could be a smokescreen."

"For what?" Marla asked, keeping pace with his long stride.

"I'm not sure. Do you think Butler really believes in ghosts?" Vail's lip curled in a cynical smile.

"Don't you? I'll admit I'm skeptical, but after riding in the tower elevator, I can understand why he'd need help. The twelfth floor gives me the creeps."

"I wonder how long it's been since anyone ventured into the penthouse. If that was Andrew's domain, you'd think someone would have explored it by now."

"We'll have to look for his humidor there. You know, my grandfather sent for his tobacco when he was visited by those two strangers. Maybe his loot was hidden inside, and he used it to pay them off." Relating her family history, she added, "Seto Mulch said he couldn't talk when Polly was alive, but now there's nothing holding him back. Evidently, he was in love with her. I heard him on the telephone talking to someone. Seto said he wouldn't allow this person to cause trouble, and that he knew Brownie, the chef, had been sent to spy on him."

They reached Polly's door, and Marla preceded Vail inside. Her gut clenched as she surveyed the empty room. Someone had disposed of the linens and aired the bed, but an unpleasant odor lingered in the air. She noticed the medicine bottle was missing, although everything else seemed pretty much intact.

"Where do I start?" she asked helplessly, surveying a silver comb and brush set on the dresser top, a tissue box on the night table, and a denture cup. A powdery film coated most surfaces. Vail must have gotten the cops to dust for fingerprints. She noticed someone had picked up the clothing from the floor.

"No one has accounted for that nurse's aide who came last night. Did you learn anything about her?"

Vail grimaced. "Nope. I'm hoping the techs will pick up something we can trace."

"We?"

"I intend to stay fully informed about this case."

Marla hadn't realized she'd tensed, but her muscles eased at his words. Rolling her injured shoulder, she was relieved to find its residual soreness gone. She looked into her fiancé's smoky eyes. "Thanks, Dalton. It means a lot to me to share things with you, the good as well as the bad."

"I know." He gave her a quick embrace, patting her on the back, then set her aside so they could begin work. Reaching the closet, he opened the creaky door and yanked out a worn suitcase, the old kind without wheels. "Why don't you pack her clothes in here. Your family can decide if they want to give her stuff to a thrift shop."

"I'd better check her pockets. Polly was so paranoid, she probably hid cash around."

Unfortunately, the only items in the pockets she discovered were used tissues, rusty bobby pins, and in one, a plastic rain hat. While Vail tossed bathroom implements into a handy laundry bag, Marla tackled her aunt's purse. Nothing was more personal than combing through another woman's handbag, and Marla felt uncomfortable violating Polly's privacy. Inside her wallet were a few small bills, a social security card, Medicare information, and business cards from doctor's offices. Polly hadn't even owned a driver's license. Worse were the folded plastic bags that Marla suspected were for taking home leftovers from early-bird specials. She mauled through several more pathetic items, growing increasingly depressed. Finally, she threw the purse—minus the wallet—onto the pile of folded clothing in the suitcase.

Stretching, Marla strolled across the carpet toward the window, but along the way, her gaze caught upon the fireplace that she had wondered about earlier. A grating in front guarded the recess, but there appeared to be no evidence of charred wood or even an exhaust vent.

"Dalton, look at this," she said, stooping to unfasten the grate. Removing the obstacle, she crouched on her knees to peer inside. The concave opening was deep, with a bricklike lining and a dust-free floor. It reminded her of a gaping oven, and with that image came the memory of the story of Hansel and Gretel, who shoved the witch into the oven to be rid of her.

Hearing an odd whistling sound, Marla tilted her head to listen. It sounded like wind rushing through a gorge. Could there be an opening behind here somewhere? Her pulse accelerated as she traced the edges with her fingers. The rough surface scraped her skin, but she felt no unusual protuberances.

"What is it?" Vail said, his bulk hovering at her shoulder.

"I don't know. Isn't it illogical to have a fireplace with no chimney? I mean, the rooms could have been modernized for electric fires, but even then the hearth wouldn't be this clean. There should be some residue or other indication of use."

"Hmm, I see what you're saying." His strong fingers probed the edges along the outer arch.

A latch clicked, and suddenly Marla was staring into a dark, dank tunnel. "Omigod, it's a secret passage!"

"I've always wanted to find one of those."

His excited tone made her glare back at him. "I'm not Nancy Drew, and you're not one of the Hardy boys. People are dying here, need I remind you?"

"Right. Get moving." Grinning like a puppy, he let a lock of peppery hair fall onto his face.

Shaking her head, Marla shuffled forward. On her hands and knees, she ended up twisted like a pretzel when she attempted to squeeze through the narrow opening. For someone as slight as Polly, however, it would pose no problems. If the old lady had been through here recently, she must've been more spry than Marla had realized. And that made her death all the more suspect.

Marla dragged her legs through the narrow stretch until the space widened. A cobweb snagged her arm, eliciting a muttered cry while she brushed off the sticky substance, imagining spiders crawling through her hair.

"I don't suppose you have a flashlight?" she said to Vail, thinking of her own purse that she'd locked in her suitcase in their room. An earthy scent tickled her nostrils, making her sneeze. Surrounded by four solid walls, she crept ahead in the yawning blackness, listening acutely for scurrying creatures. All she heard was the strange whistling, ebbing and flowing like the ocean waves outside.

"Actually, I have this emergency light," he said, flicking something on that produced a fairly strong bluish glow.

"Hey, I just came to a landing of some sort."

Following her pronouncement came a slamming noise accompanied by a couple of resounding clicks. It originated from behind them.

Vail cursed.

Marla glanced back in alarm. "What was that?"

"I hate to say this, but I think we've just been locked in."

Chapter
Ten

"What do you mean?" Marla said, rubbing her shoulder. "How could the panel shut on its own? There wasn't any breeze in the room."

Then again, how could her purse have jumped from the night-stand drawer to her suitcase? Could this be a ghostly presence at work, or someone much more real? Of the two possibilities, she preferred the first one. It didn't bode well that a person with mischievous intent kept such close watch on them.

"No luck," Vail said, after he'd scuttled back to test the entry. His grim face confirmed their plight. "Keep moving forward. We'll look for another exit."

Folding her body onto the landing, Marla inhaled a deep breath of musty air. "I think we can stand here. Give me your light." She took the keychain device and shone it around the walls. Sure enough, there was enough space to stretch. Moreover, a spiral staircase faced them.

Tucking her legs underneath, she pushed herself upright. Her head cleared the ceiling by a couple of inches. Vail stooped when he stood.

"Which way should we go?" she asked.

"We started out on the fourth floor. If we go down, we'll probably come to either an exit outdoors, or a panel that opens into one of the major corridors at ground level. Unless you want to go up and see where it leads."

"I'd like to know who uses these passages." A scrabbling noise made her clutch his arm. "The cobwebs aren't too bad, nor is there much dust. That panel opened rather easily, too. I'd say someone's been through here fairly recently."

His light flickered, and she gripped his bicep tighter. The whistling noise abruptly stopped. Muttering voices sounded as though they came from the other side of the wall.

"What's that? Do you hear them?"

Vail glanced at her as though she'd sprouted wings in her ears. "Hear what?"

"People talking. Do you think we're next to someone's bedroom?"

"Who knows? We should draw a diagram of the tunnels to overlay a blueprint of the hotel. Right now, let's climb the stairs," he suggested. A smile tilted his lips. "That is, if you're game."

Despite their situation, he looked incredibly sexy with his eyes glimmering in the bluish light and his silver-streaked hair tumbling onto his forehead.

"Why not?" Marla said, shrugging. "This has been a great day so far, having Thanksgiving dinner with my relatives, dealing with Polly's death, falling into the pit, getting cryptic stories from the groundskeeper, and now being shut inside this maze. Let's hope we can find a way out."

"Whoa, what pit? Did I miss something?"

Forging ahead, she grasped an iron railing as she forced one foot above the other on the narrow stairwell. "I forgot to mention that I took a walk out by the sugar mill. In the section with the boiling vats, I sort of fell into one. Dr. Spector came by and helped me."

He gave a strangled grunt. "You went off alone, just happened to topple into one of those enormous cavities that are too obvious to overlook, and the chief ghost chaser just happened to be sauntering past in order to lend a hand? Give me a break."

"Dr. Spector acted very kindly. I don't think he pushed me inside the pit."

"Oh, so now you were pushed? This gets even better."

"Go ahead, be angry with me. That's why I didn't want to tell you." Sweat beaded her upper lip and brow. Without air flow, she felt overly warm. Or was it her sense of guilt for withholding information from her fiancé that suffused her with heat?

"I just want you to be safe," his voice grated from below.

"I know, but I'm not prepared to sit in our room for the entire weekend. We have too many questions that need answers."

"You're impossible."

"That's why you like me. I'm not afraid to do what has to be done."

"No, that's not true. I *love* you because you give my life meaning. I don't want anything bad to happen to you."

"I worry about you too, so let's drop the subject. I'll be more careful hereafter."

"I've heard that before, sweetcakes."

Ignoring him, she paused for breath. "Gads, do these stairs go on forever? We must have climbed several stories."

"I think we're in the tower."

Marla placed her foot on the next step. A stone crumbled, and she pitched forward. Grabbing the rail, she caught herself while Vail snagged her from behind. She hauled herself back with his assistance.

"Stop running like you're catching the subway," he said in a curt tone. "This looks like it levels out up there. It should be easier going soon."

"I hope so." Her legs trembling, she pressed her hand to the wall. Slime coated its surface, most likely mold growing in the dank darkness. Grimacing with distaste, she skipped the broken step but nearly lost her balance again when she heard eerie laughter pealing in the distance.

Get me out of here, her instincts cried. Yet curiosity compelled her onward. If they were indeed in the tower, which floor would they end up at? Was this why Polly made a show of staying in Jasmine Hall, because she had ready access to Andrew's suite or the level below?

They reached an intersection, where the choice presented itself of either continuing the climb or facing a blank wall.

"This doesn't make sense," Vail said, bending his knees to keep his head from banging the ceiling. "Why is this landing here?" His fingers cataloged the wall. "I don't feel any locking mechanism."

Marla stood next to him, wondering if they should keep following the staircase until its end. But what if they faced the same puzzle above? Borrowing his light, she splayed it on the edges of the rectangle. Mildew made it hard to distinguish any cracks. Shifting the angle of the light, she looked for changes in reflectiveness. One particularly knobby spot caught her eye. Pressing it with the palm of her hand, she was gratified to hear a clicking noise. A rush of air followed as the hidden panel slid open.

"You did it," Vail exulted, charging into a corridor that stretched into the dismal blackness. Not a single window illuminated the carpeted hallway. As soon as she stepped across the threshold, the panel closed behind them with a soft hiss.

"This has to be the twelfth floor," she said, sniffing a musty odor, "although I don't remember it being this dark. The stairs must continue up to Andrew's suite."

"You won't get me back in those tunnels." Vail pointed toward the elevator shaft a few paces ahead. "We can reach the fourteenth floor the normal way, or find a fire exit. How much did you see the last time you were here?"

"I just explored the first few rooms. Hold on, something isn't right. Look at the elevator." She walked over. "There's no call button."

"Huh?" Reaching her side, Vail peered at the closed doors to the elevator shaft. He used his key light, which Marla had returned to him, to see clearly. "That's odd."

"Maybe we're *not* on the twelfth floor."

"Then what's this? Number thirteen?"

"Could be a hidden level. We can't go too far without better lighting, though."

"You're right. We'd better look for a real stairwell."

Marla's neck prickled at a rhythmic clomping sound. Vail's startled glance told her he heard it, too. Her apprehensive gaze turned toward the hallway. Coming toward them were footprints sinking into the carpet, but they saw no one. A chill wind swept them like an enveloping cloud. Marla could almost smell the effluvia.

She *could* smell it. Cigar smoke mingled with the strong scent of rum. A piano started playing, and she heard a sound like glasses clinking.

"Yikes!" Pivoting, she nearly flew toward the hidden panel. Her hand pounded the rim, searching for the release. "Dalton, is that you?" she shrieked when someone pinched her bottom.

"What? I'm not doing anything."

An icy finger tickled her neck. She inhaled sharply. The air felt weighted, as though it had assumed a leaden quality.

Vail found the proper knobby protrusion, and the panel opened. "We'll return with lanterns," he promised.

"Oh joy. I can't wait." She could tell from his pallid complexion that he'd encountered some anomalies, too. Had the ghost hunters checked out the tower at all, or were their explorations confined to Oleander Hall?

"I wonder what purpose this level served," Marla said once they were inside the passage again. She put a hand to her chest, feeling her heart's rapid thumping.

"I'll ask Butler. He may be aware this floor exists."

"Seto Mulch knows this place's secrets, although he's not eager to divulge them. He might talk more readily when I tell him what we've found." Facing the spiral staircase, she moaned. Her legs already ached from the climb. "Now where?"

"Upstairs? At least we know the tower elevator reaches the penthouse."

"We must have missed an exit onto the twelfth floor. That is, if Polly made use of this route. I don't think she was physically fit enough for this much exertion." And if Polly wasn't the one brushing away the cobwebs, who was?

"Unfortunately, it's too late to ask your aunt." Vail led the way upward. "Be careful; this last step is a bit wobbly."

Now that they knew what to look for, finding the portal mechanism wasn't as difficult. Waning sunlight filtered into the corridor as they entered the fourteenth floor. Tall windows were framed by gossamer white drapes, now a faded gray. The rarified air, uncontaminated for years by human habitation, had an earthen scent as though mice were the hall's sole remaining residents.

Passing the elevator, Marla opened the first door on the right. It squeaked on its hinges, making her grit her teeth. Hoping the spooks were busy on the lower level, she advanced briefly into a lady's bedroom. From what she could see of the furnishings that weren't covered with sheets, it was decorated in Louis XVI style with faded red damask wallpaper and upholstery. To the left of the fireplace hung an engraving by a French artist. An antique clock and tarnished silver candlesticks decorated the mantelpiece.

The next few rooms revealed lacquered boxes and other knickknacks, as though the rooms had been sealed and left untouched. A comfortable sitting room, two spacious master suites, and five more guest bedrooms branched off the hall. Marla hesitated inside the masculine paneled suite that must have belonged to Andrew.

"This is incredible," she said to Vail, who stooped to examine a brass lion-footed brazier beside yet another fireplace. "The artworks in here alone must be worth a fortune. Andrew had to be very wealthy to acquire pieces like this." She pointed to a pair of miniature bronzes horses.

"No kidding. I'm surprised no one's made off with this stuff." Straightening his spine, he regarded her with an oblique expression. "There must be a reason why this level has been preserved."

"Andrew's gemstones could be stashed in this room. Do you see a humidor?"

"Nope. It could be anywhere, unless it doesn't exist. How much of the stories we've heard is legend, and how much is real?"

"Bless my bones, I wish I'd known about this floor when Polly was still alive. I'll have to ask Ma and her brothers what they remember. They must've been up here when they were little. They may have even lived on this floor." A return visit to the caretaker was in order. He must have overseen repairs.

Sparing a moment, she listened to the silence. "Isn't it odd the spirits don't haunt this place? Does that mean they're trying to tell us something about the twelfth or thirteenth floors?"

Vail held up his hands. "I'm not the one to second-guess any ghosts. We have enough things to check out without their interference." He ticked them off on his fingers. "One, does someone in your family retain part ownership of the resort and, if so, exactly which parts? Two, find the source of Andrew's wealth. Three, figure out the purpose of the hidden level. Four, follow the secret passage to its ground entrance."

"That one is easy, but you've forgotten a more important item. Polly urged me to find her letters. I have no idea what letters she wrote to someone named Vincent, but they meant a lot to her. I'll bet they hold the answers we're seeking."

"Well, we didn't find them in her luggage, so they must be elsewhere. Why don't you recruit your mother's help in searching through the twelfth floor? It might bring back useful memories."

"Memories she'd prefer not to surface, you mean? Good idea, but not today. It's been too traumatic for her."

"Then let's go join your family. Talk to your relatives. Maybe something will slip out that will give us some insight."

Striding into the hallway, Marla pushed the button for the elevator. Various groans and creaks accompanied its ascent. "You don't have to get involved," she told Vail, feeling guilty for spoiling his weekend. "This is my family, and I can deal with it."

The look he gave her spoke volumes. "Your family is mine, now," he said quietly.

Her throat clogged with emotion. "Thanks, Dalton. I owe you for this. We'll go away another time, just the two of us."

"Oh no, you're not getting away with things so easily. Next time is your turn."

"Huh?" She pulled open the inner grating when the elevator door slid open.

"Pam's parents said they want to come for Christmas. They haven't seen Brianna since her mother's funeral. I couldn't very well refuse them the right to see their granddaughter." He grinned sheepishly while following her inside the lift. "It'll be our first holiday season together. You won't mind entertaining for them, will you?"

Thunderstruck by his words, Marla could only swallow and shake her head. She'd hoped to avoid dealing with the December holidays, at least until they had a chance to discuss their respective traditions and what they would do to celebrate. Apparently, Dalton had decided for her. And of all things, to invite his dead wife's parents to join them!

She compressed her lips, unwilling to say something she might regret later. This didn't bode well for their relationship if he made plans without consulting her first.

Later, she confided in Anita, "I'm not even comfortable with the idea of putting up a Christmas tree," as they strolled in the balmy evening toward the old barn that had been converted into a movie house. Her family had reserved the entire venue, and even the adults looked forward to watching the latest Harry Potter sequel again. Vail strode ahead, chatting with cousin Cynthia's husband, Bruce.

"I'll admit he should have considered your feelings on the subject," her mother said, walking with a slump that told Marla she hadn't quite recovered from the shock of Polly's death. "What does he expect you to do, provide Christmas dinner?"

"Hanukkah falls on the same week. I thought I would do the menorah lighting at his house. We could still exchange gifts."

"You'll have to work out the details. Let him know your expectations may be different than his. The man probably just needs more education about Judaism."

"I suppose so. It'll be even more difficult with Pam's parents being there. I *really* don't like that idea."

"Brianna has the right to see her grandparents. You can't erase them from her life, *bubula.*"

"I know." Marla tripped on a rock jutting from the sandy path. Recovering her balance, she contemplated how her path through life had likewise suddenly become more rocky.

Her younger cousin Rochelle was hanging about the theater's entrance with her pals. When she spotted Vail, the teen led her entourage in his direction. Her slim hips swayed in a pair of jeans so tight that Marla wondered how she sat down.

"Hello, Detective. We were hoping you could tell us what's going down." An eager smile lit her youthful face.

"I'm sorry, I'm not following you." Vail's shoulders hunched, his sign of tension.

"I noticed you spent an awful lot of time in Polly's room today. Didn't she die in her sleep?"

Vail gave Marla a startled glance. Since when was the girl keeping watch on their movements? True, it must have appeared peculiar that they'd gone into Polly's room and vanished for hours. In the time it took to explore the passages and then retrace their steps, the fireplace panel had opened without a hitch. They had emerged back into her aunt's bedroom so easily that Marla doubted they'd ever been locked out. Or maybe the locking mechanism had been jammed. Accidentally? Or on purpose, by a human hand, or by a ghost who wanted them to find the thirteenth floor?

"It's a blessing when an old person dies peacefully," Vail told Rochelle, hedging around the truth. "Right, Uncle Moishe? Marla hoped you could tell us what it was like to live here."

Oh, so now he was putting words in her mouth. Marla bit back a retort and gave her uncle what she trusted looked like a demure smile. "You were born after the hotel was built, right?"

Moishe nodded. Beside him stood his wife, Selma, her hooked nose and garish clothing reminding Marla of a brightly colored parakeet. "I was born in 1930, so I never got to live in Planter's House. Polly spent a few years there before Papa moved the family into the hotel. We had rooms on the top floor. Those were the grand old days, when we had the run of the place and the help treated us like royalty."

"Are you reminiscing again?" Moishe's eldest daughter, Rachel, bounded into view with her sisters. "I leave you alone for just a few minutes and already you're telling tales."

"These kids wanted to know what it was like to live at the resort. Shall I tell you how Mama made gefilte fish in the bathtub?"

"No, that's okay," Marla said hastily. "Did you, uh, notice how the tower elevator goes from the twelfth to the fourteenth floor?"

"Papa said that was because guests might be superstitious. Ain't that right, William?" He nodded at his younger brother, accompanied by three chattering daughters and their families.

William, with a harried expression, replied, "This place always had its share of ghosts and ghoulies. Papa didn't need no people refusing to stay on a thirteenth floor. Folks are too stupid to realize it's the same no matter what number you call it."

"Yet was there actually a real level sandwiched between the two top ones?" Marla persisted.

"*Bistu meshugeh?* You're letting your imagination run away with you, girl."

"I wonder," Anita said, a pensive look on her face. "Polly once told me about . . . Nah, it's nothing."

"What?" Before she could press her mother for answers, they arrived at the converted barn.

They shuffled into the theater amid a mad rush for seats. The gaggle of teenagers sat up front while adults vied for seating away from their hooting laughter. Rochelle held herself aloof from the pack and managed instead to obtain a place on Vail's left side.

"So, Lieutenant, do you get to the movies often? I've always wondered what police officers did in their spare time. Do you, like, patrol shopping malls?"

Vail rolled his eyes. "Actually, my daughter and I—Brianna is almost *your* age—we go to parks. We like to look at the foliage and play a game identifying the trees."

"That sucks. Marla, is that all you guys do for fun?"

Marla pursed her lips. "I've never gone for walks with them," she said tautly. Brianna had told her not so long ago of the things she and Vail had done when his wife was alive. Now Marla felt even more closed out of his life. He'd never asked *her* to take a stroll in the park. Maybe she needed to take the initiative and schedule some excursions herself.

Just then the lights in the movie theater flickered and went out. Silence descended with an expectant hush. Someone coughed. Marla shifted in her seat to watch the screen, but it remained blank. When the film still didn't come on, she realized something might be wrong.

Chapter
Eleven

"Don't be frightened," Champagne Glass's effervescent voice rang out as Marla's eyes adjusted to the dark. "It's only a short circuit. We'll have it fixed momentarily."

The social events coordinator flounced up the aisle, dimly illuminated by emergency lighting. She wore her golden hair in a frothy swirl atop her head. In khakis and a tucked-in cotton blouse, all she needed was a whistle on a lanyard to complete her impression as a camp leader. Her manner oozed confidence as she reassured the theater occupants.

Marla felt the years receding. Her muscles eased, as she succumbed to feeling like a teen tour groupie.

"This should give you a taste for what we'll experience tomorrow night," Champagne said, pausing by Marla's seat. "I hope you're all planning to come to our *marvelous* campfire. We'll be toasting marshmallows and telling ghost stories."

"Are you inviting Dr. Spector?" Marla asked in a dry tone.

Champagne gave her a sweet smile. "I'm afraid he's here on business, sugar. Nighttime is when his people do their best work. He'll be too busy to engage in tall tales."

"Dalton and I met a few spooks today up in the tower. Spector might be interested in hearing about them."

"I don't think so. His research is confined to Oleander Hall and the sugar mill ruins." Lifting her chin, Champagne turned her attention to the assembly. "Let me remind you what we have on track for Friday, folks. In the morning, you'll have your choice of a tennis tournament or a Nature Center tour. Join us for a *divine* picnic lunch on the beach with shelling. We get some pretty big specimens here, you know. Then relax until dinner when we'll have our *fabulous* poolside luau. Later on, our campfire starts at ten o'clock for you night owls."

Her poise faltered when the movie screen flickered on. "Here we go. Enjoy the film." She left as quickly as she had arrived, no doubt rushing to another group to remind them about the next day's activities.

Marla pushed aside her concerns to focus on the movie. Vail's hand clasped hers, and she found it soothing to lose herself in the story of wizards, magic spells, and flying broomsticks.

When Friday morning rolled around, Harry Potter's adventures drifted through Marla's mind as she lazed in bed. Instead of traipsing along on some group tour, she'd rather investigate the strange events at the resort, just as Potter did at Hogwarts. Nonetheless, hoping that she could learn more about Vail's various interests, she suggested to him that they join the excursion to the Nature Center.

Lying beside her and wearing nothing more than his boxers, he grinned as he traced her mouth with his finger. "I'm more tempted to stay here with you, *sugar*," he said, imitating Champagne Glass on the last word.

Marla grimaced. "That woman is a total fake."

"I agree, but I think she puts on the schmaltz for the guests' benefit." His hand sloped downward, melting away her ambitions for the day.

"I don't trust her. When I mentioned we'd seen ghosts in the tower, she cut me off. She knows something."

Vail's manner changed abruptly. "Let's get dressed and catch a quick breakfast. There are a lot of people we need to see today. You wanted to pay another visit to Seto Mulch, and I'll ask the manager about the thirteenth floor."

"We have plenty of time. I know you'd like to walk through the woods. You can start educating me about some of those trees." She hoped her coaxing tone didn't betray her anxiety over his response.

"Later. It's a good opportunity for us to question the staff while your relatives aren't underfoot."

Bouncing to her feet, Marla tugged her silk nightgown into place. "I'm sorry if they irritate you."

"That's not what I meant." Standing, he grasped her shoulders and pulled her close. "It's hard for me to ignore my instinct to chase bad guys. Maybe I should just stick to the devoted-fiancé role." As he rubbed his body against hers, his motion gave a different meaning to the word *hard*.

"I just don't want you to be uncomfortable around my family." *Like I'll feel around yours.*

"Don't worry, I'm fine. Although if Rochelle asks me another question, I might arrest her for harassment."

They headed for the All-American Bar and Grill inside the main building. While the hostess greeted them, Marla spotted Champagne sipping orange juice at a table with a large woman who wore a red kerchief around her head. Was she imagining things, or did the woman bear an uncanny resemblance to the nurse's aide who'd cared for Aunt Polly? Her nose and complexion were different but those things could be altered with prosthetics and makeup.

"Good morning," Marla called, bustling over before the hostess seated them. "We enjoyed the movie last night," she told Champagne, whose face looked uncharacteristically drawn.

"I'm so glad." Her voice came out hoarse, unlike her usual gushy tone, and she swiped a hand at her cheek. Had she been crying? When Marla stood her ground, Champagne waved a flaccid hand toward her companion. "Marla Shore, allow me to introduce Wanda Beake. And this is Marla's, uh . . ."

"Fiancé," Vail supplied, joining them.

"We're very fortunate to have Wanda here," Champagne said with a weak smile. "She'll be conducting the nature tour at nine o'clock. Wanda is just back from her latest bird-watching trip to Ecuador, so her insights are *amazing.*" Champagne squared her shoulders as though to register her enthusiasm.

"It's a pleasure to meet you," said the bird-watcher in a singsong voice that sounded nothing like the nursing aide's raspy tone. A pair of expensive binoculars hung around her neck. "I got in late last night. Those long flights are such a drag. I'm so grateful the hotel sent Mr. Lyle to pick me up. I'd never find this place driving in the dark. Would you believe it's my favorite resort, and I've traveled all around the world? You guys been here before?"

"This is our first time." Marla gave her an oblique glance. "I'm surprised you'd take another vacation so soon after coming back from South America. I'd be exhausted."

Wanda's laughter trilled. "Who's in a rush to get home? After hiking through the wilds of the jungle, I need a little pampering. My bills and junk mail can wait. Besides, this is the perfect time of year to catch the migratory birds in Florida. We'll be spotting some colorful ones today. I hope you're planning to attend."

"They'd probably rather run off to the beach, wouldn't you?" Champagne said with a barely perceptible shake of her head.

"Now, dearies, you'll have plenty of time for that later. I'll look for you at nine." Wanda gave Champagne a pointed stare.

The social director's lower lip quivered. "She's an *excellent* guide and very well versed in our ecology. It'll be a *super* tour. You simply can't miss it."

"We'll be there," Marla cut in, shooting Vail a warning look when he opened his mouth.

"I'd prefer not to join any of the planned activities," he growled as soon as the hostess seated them.

Marla held her reply until the waiter had taken their orders. "That woman reminds me of the aide who showed up at Polly's room. Did you notice her complexion? It's fairly pale, like she hasn't been out in the sun. Anyone traipsing through a rain forest is gonna get tanned."

"Not if she wears a hat, or it rains a lot."

"Champagne looked visibly upset. I'd never seen her so rattled before. I got the impression she didn't want us to take the tour. That makes me even more curious."

He sat back and regarded her lazily. "Do I have to go with you?"

She choked and grabbed for her water glass. "Of course, you do. You're the one who likes nature stuff."

"Oh, and you don't?"

Her hand gripped the goblet tighter. "You and Brianna go to parks all the time. You've never asked me along. Is that an exclusive event, or am I invited? Pam used to go with you."

His eyebrows lifted. "I don't believe it. You're jealous."

"Don't be absurd."

His mouth expanded into a soft smile. "You're welcome to come with us anywhere, hon. I figured you were too busy to spend time at Secret Woods."

"I'm never too busy where you're concerned." *Liar.* Did she really want to get hooked into family excursions? Next they'd be taking road trips, which wouldn't be much fun if they had to share a room with his teenage daughter. She lowered her lashes so he couldn't read her expression. Sorting through her feelings took too much energy.

Inevitably, Vail chose to accompany her on the tour anyway. Her mood lifted when she spied Cynthia and Bruce at the entrance to the nature trail. They had their kids along, Annie and Kelp. Her parents being ocean conservationists, Annie's full name was Anemone. The young adults jostled each other past the gate. Wanda Beake waited on the other side.

"Welcome to our guided tour," Wanda called. About two dozen other people, including some of Marla's distant clan members, ranged before her. "This morning, you'll have the opportunity to view four of our ecological communities: a hammock, savannah, dunes, and the shoreline. Each has its own vegetation and wildlife. Please remain on the boardwalk until we reach the beach. Leave nothing behind, and take nothing with you."

As the bird-watcher led them into the hardwood forest, Marla caught up to Cynthia. Her cousin wore an attractive crimson and black printed blouse with black slacks, appropriate for the cooler morning air. She and her husband owned an estate that fronted a mangrove preserve in eastern Fort Lauderdale. Marla figured they would want to explore the park.

"Did your mother ever talk about this resort?" Marla said to Cynthia. "I'm amazed no one in the family seemed to know about it before."

"I'd heard nothing until Aunt Polly called regarding the re-union." Cynthia's blue eyes skimmed Marla's ebony ensemble, a short-sleeved knit top that zipped up the front with matching sweat pants. "Mom told me stories about how Ruth celebrated the Sabbath. Grandmother plucked the feathers off chickens destined for the oven and made challah from scratch. I wish I'd known her. She died five years before I was born."

Marla bypassed a dried coconut in their path. The trail consisted of packed earth made spongy underfoot by a layer of dead pine needles and leaves. Pink bromeliads bloomed in a cluster just inside the entrance. As they followed a wooden arrow pointing the way, she brushed past a sea grape tree with broad, round leaves. It stood next to a weeping bottlebrush, its branches hanging gracefully like a willow. The cool air was redolent of humus.

"My mother didn't talk much about her early years," Marla said, "except that her dad passed away when she was three."

"That must have been traumatic. Ruth had to raise their eight children on her own afterward."

"She had the energy to manage the hotel at the same time. It's too bad I don't remember our grandmother."

"As the eldest, Polly would have helped her a great deal." Cynthia gave Marla a sly glance. "Did our dear aunt spill any of her secrets? I know she talked to you. Like, did Andrew's treasure really exist?"

"Oh, so we're back to his hoard of jewels? I think we have a better chance of finding a pirate lode than any stash of Grandfather's." Marla hesitated. "I wonder what happened to cause the rift between Ruth and her siblings after his death. Polly wanted me to find some letters that she said would explain everything."

"Look, there's an osprey," Wanda's excited voice cried.

Marla spotted the gray-backed bird with its white chest and purplish-brown head. It had a rounded beak and long, narrow wings. She thought its imperious eyes gave it a majestic appearance. Higher in a live oak branch draped with Spanish moss, she noticed a bald eagle while Wanda passed around her binoculars.

A sea breeze brought a flutter of dead leaves from overhead. Gumbo limbo and shady shower trees vied for space with strangler figs. They passed a thorny paurotis palm and ducked through an archway of vines. Many of the plants bore labels, for which Marla was grateful. It would help her learn to identify the foliage. She recognized the hand-shaped fronds and toothy stems of a saw palmetto and some ubiquitous cabbage palms.

"Birds love the sweet fruit of this hackberry tree," Wanda stopped to lecture. "Its seed is covered with a datelike pulp. And here's a Florida elm. Our moist, tropical hammocks have not been affected by the Dutch elm disease that killed American elms to the north."

Marla didn't look at the stately tree trunk. Her attention diverted to several holes in the ground that she hoped didn't harbor snakes. A sweet, spicy scent tickled her nostrils while her canvas shoes scraped over sand. The silence was broken only by rustling branches, bird calls, and distant ocean waves.

Off the trail on a grassy swath, a stream of workmen trudged silently south. They wore uniforms emblazoned with the Nature Center logo, but Marla thought they looked remarkably similar to the construction crews.

"What are they doing here?" she asked Wanda, catching up to their tour leader.

"The park staff is working to eliminate those Australian pines and Brazilian peppers," Wanda said, pointing them out. "These trees aren't natural to the area, and they're a threat to the native plant species and wildlife habitat."

"Is this property administered separately from the resort?"

Cynthia's husband replied. "The park belongs to the same parcel as the hotel. It's the real treasure, wouldn't you say?" Bruce stooped to avoid an overhanging areca branch as they continued along the guided path.

Did Bruce mean a treasure in the ecological sense, or something truly valuable like underground oil? Nah, Andrew had acquired his wealth before he moved to Florida, not afterward.

"Have you been searching for Andrew's gemstones?" Marla asked her cousins while Vail chatted with her other relatives.

"Who can resist a treasure hunt?" Cynthia said. "We've been looking in Planter's House, because that's where Andrew and Ruth lived when they first came to the plantation. Lori and Joan divided up the main floor of the hotel. Julia is too busy getting her nails done today to bother. Your brother and Charlene said they'd search the old ruins."

"Do you really expect to find anything?"

"Personally, I think Andrew's secret is tied to his death." Cynthia scratched her arm. "Rumor says the condemned wing is haunted by those two men who visited him the day he died. I think we should concentrate on locations that are supposed to be spooked."

"I'll bet you're right. Dalton and I will take the top tower floors." Andrew's stash might not exist, but Marla still hoped to find Polly's letters and maybe a copy of her aunt's will. Drifting toward Bruce, she meant to ask him about his real estate interests when her cell phone rang. With a twinge of guilt, she remembered her intention to call Nicole to make sure everything was all right at the salon, and to phone Tally to wish her friend a Happy Thanksgiving. She should check on Spooks in the kennel, too.

Barry Gold's cheerful voice greeted her. "Hey, Marla. Just wanted to check in and see how you're doing."

Marla gulped and glanced over her shoulder at Vail. She didn't want him to catch her talking to the optometrist, who happened to be the highly eligible son of Anita's boyfriend. "I'm great, thanks. How are things with you and your dad?" Barry had gone north to help settle the estate of his great aunt.

"We should be back by next Wednesday. Any chance we can attend services together on Friday night?"

Marla's heart lurched as Vail turned in her direction. "I don't think Dalton would like it if we went out together, even for religious reasons."

"I'll call you when I'm back," he persisted. "We'll talk about it then. I picked up two more films for my John Wayne collection. You still have to come over and watch one with me."

"Have a safe flight," she said before hanging up.

"Who was that?" Vail said when he reached her side.

"One of my friends. Did you learn anything new? I noticed you were working the crowd."

"Not a whole lot, unfortunately. You?"

"Cynthia and my cousins divided up their search field. They're looking for Andrew's loot. I said we'd take the top floors in the tower."

"Sounds like a plan. I want to get back there today."

"Me too. We should have some time after lunch."

Wanda brought the group to a halt after they climbed to an elevated walkway overlooking a grassy marsh. Something slithered past in the water.

"We have an interesting vista from this savannah," their guide's voice boomed. "This grass is called hairy gramma. It's a short midwestern prairie species, rarely grown in Florida. Look carefully and you might spot some alligators."

So? It's not as though I haven't seen them before. Marla glanced at her younger cousins' scared faces and smirked. *Be grateful it isn't summer. You'd be eaten alive by the mosquitoes.*

Swarms of bugs flew close to the water, making her scurry ahead to the mangrove swamp, where tannin colored the shallow depths. Wanda halted the group to point out an anhinga sunning on a branch. Skirting an egret in her path, Marla approached Cynthia's husband.

"Hey, Bruce, you said this park is part of the same parcel as the hotel. What do think about the plans to turn the whole thing into a theme park?" she asked him with a playful note.

His face reddened, and he glanced away. "My opinion doesn't matter. It isn't my decision."

"What if our family still had a stake in the resort's ownership? Would you recommend selling the property, knowing the hotel would be torn down?"

"If the living-history museum gets the green light, the outlying structures could be restored to their original appearance. The sugar mill, slave cabins." He couldn't conceal the zeal in his eyes. "Think in terms of Sturbridge Village, or the historical recreation in Portsmouth, New Hampshire."

"What about the barn and the stable? They've already been converted into a theater and restaurant." Marla tilted her head. "And don't forget the conservatory, with its delightful tearoom overlooking the garden. Would you destroy those also? I thought you favored preservation. The old hotel, if properly restored, would showcase Florida in its 1920s heyday."

"You must have been talking to George Butler. He's adamant about reconstruction. He has his repair crews working overtime just to put the place in a better light. It won't sway the city council. Donna and the others have already voted in favor of the property sale."

She grabbed his arm. "How do you know this?"

"I, er, ran into her." Scowling, he pulled back.

"Just what is your interest in this place, Bruce? Have you been attending those council meetings?"

"What if I have? They're not closed-door sessions. Anyone can attend."

"Are you aware there might be stipulations about the terms of sale dating from when Ruth signed over the property? Have you examined the legal documents?"

"We haven't gotten that far—" He cut himself off, casting her an angry glare.

"So you *are* one of the potential investors."

"If I am, that's my business."

She planted a hand on her hip, aware the others in the group were crossing into the dune community while she hung back along with Bruce. A harsh bird cry filled the air, followed by an ominous snorting noise. Glancing down, she shifted her feet away from the edge of the boardwalk that ran from the mangrove swamp to the shore. No need to tempt the gators.

"It may be my family's business, too." She met his gaze squarely. "This is one case where I support the resort staff. I think the hotel would be magnificent if it were restored, ghosts and all."

"You haven't seen the condition of Oleander Hall. It's deplorable. There have been too many accidents that show just how rundown the place is."

"You've been inside the condemned wing?"

"Yep. It's full of rotted beams, peeling paint, mold. There's even garbage strewn across threadbare carpets that are a tripping hazard in themselves. Empty food wrappers, soda cans, you name it. The rats probably outnumber the dust mites in that hellhole."

Soda cans? Who'd left those, the work crews? To her knowledge, they weren't allowed inside Oleander Hall until restorations were approved. External repairs were merely cosmetic in nature. She'd have to speak to Dr. Spector to see if his crew had been snacking on the job.

So much for asking Bruce about Ruth's legacy to their family. Either he wasn't aware of any obstacles that might deter a sale, or he wasn't letting on that he knew of any.

Dismissing her, her cousin's husband trudged off. Marla hurried to catch up to the group. She paused on the walkway that bridged shifting sand dunes. Sea oats, railroad vines, and dune sunflowers inhabited this fragile ecosystem. Marla spotted a great blue heron along with a roseate spoonbill, excitedly pointed out by Wanda Beake. Terns trotted along the beach while pelicans graced the skies.

If only her thoughts were as clear as the blue sky overhead.

Musing over her conversation with Bruce, she considered the implications of his involvement. If he had an interest in the proposed theme park, how far would he go to achieve his aims?

"When do the police expect the autopsy report to be ready?" she asked Vail as they stood on a bluff overlooking the beach. She spoke in a low voice so no one could hear them. Her neck itched, and she ran a finger around the inside of her collar. She'd rather be lying out in a swimsuit than wearing a pants outfit in the rising heat.

"It could take a few days. What did Bruce say? I saw you talking to him."

"I know this sounds terrible, but I'm wondering if he had a reason to want Aunt Polly out of the way." She repeated the gist of their conversation.

"No fair. He told you more than he told me," Vail said with a teasing gleam in his eyes.

She gave him an affectionate punch. "That's because I'm less intimidating than you, even when you're not officially on the job. Do you think Cynthia knows about his interest in developing the resort?"

"She made the arrangements for this weekend." Vail regarded Marla with a thoughtful expression. "It's possible Bruce mentioned the city council meeting, but Polly is the one who selected this place."

"I think Cynthia would have said something before now if she knew. She's likely to oppose him."

"And if Polly turns out to have met an unsavory end?" Vail asked.

Shrugging, Marla tilted her head. "We still don't know what Butler meant about my aunt having rights to the top floors. If legal terms were really in her favor, and Bruce knows about it, he'd have a motive to get rid of her."

Chapter
Twelve

"Have you seen my floss?" Vail said later that morning, when they were back in their room. He shuffled through his toiletries in the lavatory. "I thought I put it next to the toothpaste."

"You can use mine." After a refreshing shower, she'd donned a rust-colored short-sleeved sweater and a pair of khakis. Standing in front of the dresser mirror, she brushed her hair.

Just after she put the brush down, the hotel room door burst open. Startled, she glanced up but saw no one in the doorway.

"Who's there?" Vail called.

"I don't see anyone." Striding over, she peaked out. The corridor was empty. Strains of theme music from *The Twilight Zone* sifted through her mind. "I could have sworn I'd locked it when we came in," she said, shutting the door.

"Must be your spooks again," Vail said in a jovial tone.

"That's not funny." Had she left the door ajar, or did a breeze kick it open? "Look, what's our plan?" she asked, disregarding the ethereal possibilities.

He emerged from the bathroom with a towel around his neck. "I'll talk to Butler. You can corner the groundskeeper. We'll ask them both about the thirteenth floor, and if they know anything about the legal terms of sale. Butler may have a set of blueprints for the hotel. We'll meet back here afterward to explore Andrew's suite."

"We should see where the rest of the passages lead. Did you get your flashlight from the car?"

"Right there." He pointed to the dresser.

"I want to find Harvey Lyle," Marla said. "According to Wanda, the steward picked her up at the airport last night. I'd like to confirm her time of arrival. And I still haven't finished asking Ma questions."

"Wouldn't Anita tell you if she knew something important?"

"She may need her memory refreshed. If I bring her to the twelfth floor, where she grew up, it might ring some bells. I have a feeling my family history is involved in whatever's going on around here. For all we know, we might be sitting on a mountain of wealth, either through Andrew's legacy or Ruth's disposition of the property. Will you be able to check the town records today if city offices are open?"

"For you, I'd do anything." He gave her a slow, sexy grin. "It's a long time until lunch. Wanna kill a few hours?"

"Don't get ideas," she retorted, even while her body responded against her will. "If we get sidetracked, it'll be dinnertime before we accomplish anything."

"Is that so bad?" He sauntered closer, his eyes gleaming.

She held up a hand. "Whoa, boy. Save it for later."

After he left, Marla phoned her mother's room. When no one responded, she decided to track down Anita later.

Heading outside, she aimed toward the groundskeeper's cottage. A troop of laborers clomped by, carrying paint buckets, brushes, and other equipment. They all had a similar look, with their olive green overalls and swarthy complexions. She halted to watch them, wondering where they came from. *No labor shortage here, even on holidays.* When one man carrying a clipboard scowled at her, Marla hastened on her way.

A seagull lent its plaintive cry to the wind as she avoided a gnarled root in her path, then nearly tripped on a trailing vine, causing a lizard to scamper under a nearby rock. A black crow flitted into her path as though daring her to trespass. Watching it take off with a flutter of wings, she skirted past a grayish-white trunk with lichen growing in green splotches on its surface. Sun-warmed frangipani spiced the air, filling her nose with fragrance. She passed a cluster of cycads whose fine-combed fronds stretched outward like multiple arms raised in supplication.

Marla's nape prickled as she approached the front door to Seto's house and saw that the drapes were pulled tight. When she'd visited Mulch before, sunlight had streamed in through the windows.

Knocking on the door brought forth no response, so she circled around to the back, which faced the woods. Seto's house couldn't be too far from the grand entrance to the resort. The drone of traffic reached her ears along with a gurgling sound. Following its source, she discovered a garden hose attached to a faucet on the side of the house. Water trickled from the hose's mouth. So the precious liquid wouldn't go to waste, Marla twisted the spigot. It turned easily, making her wonder why someone had not thoroughly shut off the valve.

She followed the stream of water to the rear kitchen door. Putting her hand on the knob, Marla shouted a greeting. As the silence grew longer, she gazed down at the water flowing over a concrete slab and under the transom. Mulch must have had the painters here. The water had a faint pink tinge.

Would the old man paint his house pink?

Pushing the unlocked door open, she peered warily into the darkened kitchen while a strong odor of bleach slammed into her nostrils. Shadows danced on the walls. She fought an urge to retreat, but, calling Mulch's name, she forced herself to search the house. The groundskeeper wasn't there, and she noted a strange discoloration on his linoleum floor.

Tearing out the back door, she raced toward the main hotel lobby and its bright, spacious interior. She located Champagne Glass in the social director's office. The blonde gave her a confectionery smile so sweet it could displace chocolate on the dessert menu. "Hey, Marla, how come you're not out enjoying this *lovely* day?"

Marla spared a glance at the woman's desk piled with papers. "I'm worried about Seto Mulch. He's not in his house. His outdoor hose was leaking water into his kitchen, and it had a reddish tint."

"Really? That's odd." Various emotions flickered across Champagne's expression before her brow smoothed. "Why, sugar, that could just be rust from the hard water."

"Don't you think Seto would have turned off the faucet more securely? Anyway, the trail led into his kitchen. The water shouldn't be pink in there. And his back door was unlocked."

"Oh dear." Champagne chewed her lip. "He might be prepping for the luau tonight," she suggested. Marla noticed she'd lost her cheery demeanor. "You could find him supervising the gardeners by the pool. What were you doing at his house, Marla?"

"I wanted to ask him some questions about my family history. Do your people carry beepers?"

"I'm afraid not; we use cell phones, but Seto refused to get one. He's still back in the dark ages in respect to technology." Champagne's mouth curved in a wry smile.

"What about a work schedule? He must account for his whereabouts to someone."

"You can ask George Butler. The manager keeps tabs on his key people. But Seto often wanders off on his own, especially to the sugar mill. I've seen him there lots of times when I lead tour groups. I think he's aiming to keep Alyssa's ghost company." Nervous laughter bubbled from her throat.

"Do you really believe in spirits?" Marla said. "People are dying here, but not to join their ancestors. First that man on the ladder, then my aunt, now Seto is missing. I've noticed that the resort employs an unusual number of laborers, and construction work continues without any end in sight. What's going on?"

Champagne cast an anxious glance at the open doorway. "I don't know what you mean."

"May I shut the door?" At Champagne's nod, Marla secured their privacy. "Aren't you the least bit concerned about these things? I've noticed how you assume your cheerful act in front of guests. Is your performance aimed at your audience or your employers?"

"I-I'm sorry. I can't . . . Look, Marla, I know you want to help. But that could be dangerous around here."

"I'm more worried about Seto Mulch right now."

"He has to be somewhere on the property. You'll see."

"I'll check it out, but I'd appreciate it if you could ask around as well."

"Of course." Champagne cast her eyes down.

"What is it?" Marla sensed she wanted to add something.

"If you could get inside Mr. Butler's office . . ."

"Yes?"

"You may find many of your answers there."

Is he involved in something that disturbs you? Marla wanted to ask. Embezzlement would give the manager a reason for wanting to preserve the hotel. Any sale might prompt an examination of his accounting books. "Go on," she said instead.

"It's the theme park. He's already—"

A knock rattled the door before it banged open. Wanda Beake swooped inside like a bird of prey. "Champagne, dearie, I'm so sorry to interrupt, but I need to review this schedule with you." She waved a sheet of paper. "Oh, Marla. You ran off so quickly this morning that I didn't get a chance to ask if you enjoyed our little tour." Her mouth widened in a grin, but Marla thought her eyes looked unfriendly.

"It was *wonderful,*" she said, imitating Champagne's exuberance. "I was just talking to Champagne about the lack of a salon on premises. My cousin had to go into town earlier to get her nails done. It would be highly convenient for guests if you had a beautician on staff."

Champagne picked up the cue. "You're right, and we have the facilities at the spa, but we can't find qualified people willing to do part-time work."

"I have a salon in Palm Haven," Marla explained. "Maybe I'll mention it to your manager later. You could always work out an on-call arrangement with a local establishment." Taking her leave, she breezed out the door, hoping the naturalist regarded her as nothing more than a fluff-head. A search for Butler led to a dead end. Instead, she ran into Harvey tagging someone's luggage at the bellboy's station.

"Have you seen Seto Mulch?" she asked him, the urgency of that errand returning.

The steward leered at her. "I ain't run into him yet today, ma'am," he replied, "but I'll take a look-see with ya as soon as I store these bags."

"That's okay." She shifted her handbag. "By the way, what time did you pick up Wanda Beake from the airport last night?"

Harvey scratched his bristly jaw. "It was pretty late. Didn't get there until after dark. Ya'd think they'd schedule flight arrivals during the day to these small aero-ports."

"Were many people getting off the airplane?"

"I waited outside at baggage pickup, but there weren't no crowd at all."

Maybe that was because the bird-watcher had come in earlier and hidden out for the day.

"Harvey, why is there no thirteenth floor?" she asked, changing the subject abruptly. "You know, the tower elevator goes from twelve to fourteen. Anyone who can count will realize the top floor is number thirteen. Or is there an actual level in between the two?"

"Impossible. Ya can't get off nowhere else. Did hear some wild rumors, though."

Pulling a key ring from his pocket, he unlocked the storage room and stashed the suitcases inside. Returning, he winked at Marla as he pocketed his keys. *Those would be useful to borrow sometime,* she thought. Would they gain her entrance into Oleander Hall?

"What kind of rumors?" she said, anxious to pursue her search for Mulch, but also wanting to hear what Lyle had to say. Harvey signaled for her to follow him into the telephone alcove, where he pulled a flask from his jacket. "Want some? It's good stuff."

She wrinkled her nose at the strong whiff of rum when he uncorked the container. Taking a deep swig, he smacked his lips before replacing the flask. "Maybe booze ain't what yer after." His loopy smile revealed a broken tooth. "Gals like you go for guys like me, even if ya pretend yer too hoity-toity." He swaggered toward her, making a lewd gesture. "We could do it quick-like, or go somewhere more private."

Marla forced herself to remain still. "Tell me what you heard about the thirteenth floor first."

He leaned so close, she could see the jaundiced tint to his eyes. "This hotel was built during Prohibition. Folks used to come here to get their fix, if ya know what I mean. A secret floor would be just the place. No access, though, so I don't see how it can be true. Keep in mind, this is just hearsay."

"I would imagine the blueprints display the layout."

"The boss has a set in his office. Keeps them locked up."

Marla assessed the lecherous gleam in Lyle's eye and what she would have to do to gain entry into the manager's office. There had to be another way. Right now, it was more imperative to locate the groundskeeper. Seto Mulch had worked for Andrew and then Ruth. Prohibition? She hadn't even considered the era, but the more she thought about it, the more the secret passage made sense.

"My boyfriend will get angry if he finds me here," she warned, ducking Lyle's outstretched arm.

The steward snickered. "Be waitin' for ya next time, honey buns."

"Not if I can help it," Marla muttered on her way outdoors. The door swung at her, and she nearly collided with Donna Albright.

The councilwoman's flushed face regarded her warily. "I'm so sorry," the older woman said. "I forget these doors aren't automatic and which way they open. I wasn't paying attention."

"That's all right." Marla stepped across the threshold, but Albright's next words stopped her from going any farther.

"By any chance, have you run into Mr. Mulch? The old guy was supposed to meet me, but he didn't show."

"What do you mean?"

"He left a message on my machine that he had something to say regarding the hotel property, and I should meet him by the volleyball court at eleven o'clock. He stood me up."

Marla glanced at her watch. It was almost lunch hour. Time to exchange news with Vail. "Champagne told me he's fixing the pool area for tonight's luau. It's possible he got delayed."

Albright's lips pursed. "I don't appreciate my time being wasted."

"How did the vote go on Wednesday?"

"We still have some issues to clear up. There's a lot of opposition from the hotel staff, and they make some valid points."

"I thought the council voted in favor of the acquisition."

"Who told you that?" Albright's spine stiffened.

"My cousin's husband, Bruce, a real estate developer," Marla said. "He admitted he'd like a stake in developing the theme park. Have you done a title search to see if the current owners have the right to sell the property?"

"We haven't progressed that far. Is there some reason why you'd anticipate a problem?"

Marla shrugged. "I'm wondering who holds the documents, that's all. This place used to belong to my grandparents."

"So I'm aware." She glanced behind Marla, and an expression of distaste wrinkled her face. "Oh Lord, here comes that ghost-busting gang. I'll see you later."

Marla rushed outside before the paranormal team could intercept her. Locating Vail took some time, but she managed to track him down after he finally answered his cell phone. She caught up to him inside the gym, where he was demonstrating how to lift free weights to Rochelle and her young cousins.

"What are you doing here?" she said, raising an eyebrow. He wore tan shorts and a dark green polo shirt, an outfit that displayed his sinewy limbs to good advantage. "I thought you planned to speak to the manager and then head into town to the property appraiser's office. It's nearly time for the beach picnic."

"The city center is closed for the weekend, and I just missed Butler. He was busing a bunch of those workmen back home, or so I presume. I saw him leave with a group in a van."

"I can't find Seto Mulch, and there's something suspicious in his kitchen. I need you to take a look, if you can tear yourself away from your admirers." She nodded at Rochelle, who stood in a corner giggling with her bikini-clad pals. Vail's glance kept drifting in their direction.

"It's not what you think," Vail said from the corner of his mouth. "She reminds me of Brianna. No way I'd ever let my daughter out of the house looking like that."

As though you'll have a choice. And if she reminds you of your daughter, why are you showing off your muscles? "Have you accomplished anything?" she asked in a tight voice, folding her arms across her chest.

His appreciative smile at her evaporated her anger. "I saved myself a trip into town," he said. "Apparently, a fire destroyed all the official records dating before 1970. That's what one of those city council members told me."

"Oh no," Marla moaned. But then her initial dismay gave way to hope. "Wait, it's possible Butler keeps copies of the sale agreement and deed in the hotel files. Champagne told me some of the answers to our questions might be found in his office. Harvey said his boss keeps a set of blueprints there, too."

"You've been busy."

"What are you looking for?" Rochelle's voice squeaked from behind, giving Marla a start. Her friends likewise crowded around the detective.

"Things that could help us solve some of the mysteries about this place," Vail said indulgently.

"Want us to help?" the girl offered. "We're going to lay out this afternoon, but we have tonight—there's not much to do here in the evenings."

"You can go to the campfire," Marla suggested.

"That's for little kids. We don't need to hear ghost stories when the real thing is right around the corner. My mother says you're going to explore the penthouse suite. Can we come?"

"Definitely not." Marla snapped.

Vail leaned toward the cluster of teens. "I'll give you an assignment," he said in a hushed tone. "It's really important, okay? Watch for Mr. Butler. Let us know when he gets back to the resort."

"He could've gone home for the weekend after he took those men into town," Marla said on their way to the groundskeeper's cottage. "I doubt Butler lives on the property. There isn't any need, with Mulch serving as caretaker."

"So maybe he keeps his secrets hidden elsewhere."

"We can worry about him later. I'm more concerned about Seto. I suppose the old coot could still be around the resort. I did a quick search before meeting you, but I didn't see him anywhere. Do you think he went with Butler?"

"No, Butler was alone in the front seat," Vail said.

Marla glanced at him. "By the way, you handled Rochelle very well. She seems to fancy herself as an apprentice sleuth."

"I'm just hoping she stays out of harm's way."

As soon as they arrived at the Bahamian-style house, Vail assumed his professional demeanor. A quick look inside brought a scowl to his face. He rejoined Marla by the exterior faucet and pointed to the rust-colored stains where the water had dried.

"Someone tried to erase the evidence, but there's been blood spilled," he said. "I'd like to talk to the crew by the pool area before we report Mulch as missing."

Their hunt turned up gardeners planting pentas by the rear terrace. Speaking barely decipherable English, they didn't provide much information. One of them spoke angrily in Spanish to the others, and then they all fell silent, concentrating on their work.

"Marla, where have you been?" Anita summoned her daughter from the pool deck, where she sunned on a lounge chair, wearing a one-piece swimsuit and oversized sunglasses. "Come here and talk to your cousins from out west." Her gesture included Vail. "Dalton, you and Yosef can talk shop. He's a prosecuting attorney."

"I can't think of anything I'd rather do less," Dalton muttered in an undertone. Giving a resigned sigh, he marched over and shook the man's hand after Anita made introductions.

"This is some great *shandeh*, isn't it?" Vail said in a loudly cheerful voice.

"Shindig," Marla corrected, nudging him. "*Shandeh* means shame. Shindig isn't even a Yiddish word."

"Christ, what do I know?"

Marla's relatives dissolved into laughter.

"*Oy, az dos hartz iz ful, gai'en di oigen iber,*" Anita said, wiping tears from her cheeks. *When the heart is full, the eyes overflow.* Her mother's glance told Marla that she appreciated Vail's efforts to fit in.

Her fiancé looked as though he'd swallowed his tongue. "I'd love to stay and chat, but I have a prior engagement. Please excuse me," he said in a choked tone. "I'll catch you at lunch." He loped off before Marla could protest.

"Ma, you embarrassed him," she chided her mother.

"I'm just trying to introduce him to the family. Some of your cousins have married *goyim*. It's not as though intermarriage is so foreign to us."

"I still say you should have stayed with Stanley," Julia remarked. "He was the perfect husband: a rich Jewish attorney." As usual, her cousin's lipstick could have used more precise lining. It made her mouth look too wide.

"Stan was a jerk," Marla shot back, feeling the sun heating her shoulders. The temperature must have warmed into the seventies. "By the way, Barry called this morning to wish me a happy Thanksgiving."

Anita wagged a finger at her. "Now there's a good catch.

Single, never been married, an optometrist. I'll admit, he may not be as sexy as Dalton, but he'd be a steady fellow. Lust wears off after twenty years or so."

Marla was tired of her family debating her love life. "Have any of you seen Seto Mulch? He's the old guy who hobbles around the resort, supervising everyone else."

"You don't mean the manager?" said a fresh-faced blonde Marla didn't recognize.

"No, Butler has gone into town. I need to find Mr. Mulch."

"What's so urgent?" Anita asked, applying coconut-scented sunscreen to her legs, still shapely for a woman in her sixties.

"I wanted to question him about the original hotel construction. You know how the tower elevator goes from twelve to fourteen? I'm wondering what happened to the thirteenth floor."

"People are superstitious, *bubula*. Lots of companies do the same thing in their office buildings."

"Have you taken the elevator? It takes longer to go between twelve and fourteen than between any of the other floors."

"That's the creepiest ride I've ever been on," whined Julia. "Alan wanted to tour the penthouse to see what it was like in Andrew's day, but we'd only gone up a few floors in that rattling death trap when the weirdest thing happened. The lights went out, and I felt something brush against my cheek."

She leaned forward, giving a revealing view of her cleavage in a designer swimsuit. "I think it's haunted by Andrew's ghost."

"You want to see ghosts?" bellowed a voice behind Marla. She spun around to face Dr. Spector's amused hazel eyes. His stark white hair went along with someone who encountered spooks for a living. "I'm going to take readings in Oleander Hall," he announced. "Care to join me?"

Chapter
Thirteen

Marla smelled the stale odor as soon as she entered Oleander Hall behind Dr. Spector. His stocky frame, laden with equipment dangling from his backpack, provided a bulwark against the wave of negative energy that seemed to emanate from the condemned wing. Marla thought she felt a presence charging the air as she followed him down the silent corridor toward the parlor where Andrew had met the two visitors. Her canvas shoes trod along the faded carpet while she imagined faint whisperings and creaking doors.

"What's that?" she asked in a hushed tone, hearing the soft thud of footsteps overhead.

"We're not alone in here," Spector said.

His insouciant voice offered little reassurance, and as Marla passed a rattling doorknob, she hastened her steps. "Are your people on the floor above us?"

"Nope. Mr. Butler said this is where we should concentrate our efforts. We've caught an orb in the parlor as well as EVPs, so something is definitely here." Halting in front of a pair of double oak doors, he pushed one open. "Come see for yourself."

The rich scent of cigar smoke drifted into her nostrils. A quick scan of the spacious room revealed sheet-covered furniture, dusty draperies, and portraits of men in Confederate uniforms on the walls. Their eyes seemed to follow her as she stepped inside the parlor, illuminated by sunlight streaming through the drapes. Windows made up two of the walls, the room occupying a corner space at the far end of the wing. She noticed a seating arrangement in front of a fireplace, and a lacquered cart that must have held cordials beside one of the armchairs. Not during Prohibition, she reminded herself.

"Someone should write the history of this hotel," Dr. Spector said, displaying a digital thermometer. "I heard that Andrew Marks sat in a thronelike chair in the lobby and examined each guest who registered. If he didn't like their looks, he would demand their departure. This room is where he entertained his private visitors."

Marla glanced at a flotilla of dust motes suspended in the air. "I would have liked to meet him." A sudden chill raised goose bumps on her arms.

"I'm reading a temperature drop," the ghost hunter said, panning the room with his handheld device.

"What does that mean?"

"An entity may be present. Inhuman spirits will siphon energy from any living source in a room."

"So it could be those two strangers who met with Andrew just before he died. Why would their ghosts linger at the resort?" she said without admitting her skepticism. "Did you ever learn what happened that night?"

"They met Andrew, but no one saw them leave. Something is keeping them from moving on. I've told them they didn't belong here, but they're being stubborn." He cocked his head. "Why don't *you* tell them? They might listen to a member of Andrew's family. Just be respectful, and don't be frightened. Negative spirits feed off your emotions."

Marla detected a movement from the corner of her eye. When she turned to focus on it, nothing was there. Swinging her gaze past the mantelpiece, she stopped to stare at a pewter candlestick. Had she seen it slide sideways, or were her eyes deceiving her?

"Hello," she said hesitantly. "Is there a reason you're still around? We want to fix up this place, but repairs can't be done while you're bothering people. You need to go to your final rest." As though in response, strains of piano music reached her ears. "Where is that coming from?" she whispered, her lips dry.

"Perhaps the music studio near the ballroom. I believe they held concerts there in the early days." The portly fellow reached for his digital thermometer.

"What's directly above us?" The music swelled, then faded until silence surrounded them.

"The upper floors have guest suites."

"So how is it that we can hear someone playing the piano all the way over here?"

Dr. Spector shrugged. "I'm not permitted to explore as fully as I'd like. Sometimes I think Mr. Butler . . ."

"Yes?"

"I'm not sure he takes us seriously."

"How so?"

"Well, these types of effects . . . they can be reproduced. Entities are not always so . . . obvious."

Hmm. The only way they could hear sounds from the other end of the hotel would be if there was a conduit of some sort—unless it was piped in to scare away unwanted curiosity-seekers. Even that would require wiring, most likely behind the walls. Was that why Butler didn't want to see this wing torn down, because of what it might reveal? Why would he want to keep people away when he'd ostensibly hired Spector's team to get rid of ghosts so restoration could proceed?

"Have you been through this entire ground-floor level?" she asked Spector, who now busied himself taking instrument readings.

"We've done some scans, but not much else is going on except in here," he replied curtly, focusing his attention on his work. "I think something occurred in this room, besides Andrew's encounter with his visitors. That would have been upsetting enough, from what I've heard, and the residue from his emotions may be playing a part in what's keeping the anomalies close by, but I'm guessing there's more to the story than we've been told."

"Andrew died that night."

"Yes, but he died in his penthouse suite."

"I've felt a presence in the tower elevator."

"Precisely. He's guarding his domain. Or else he's just so fond of the place that he doesn't wish to leave."

Assuming ghosts existed, and Marla was willing to accept the likelihood in view of her recent experiences, what would be keeping the two foreigners from seeking their rest? Were they, like Alyssa's ghost, seeking to relate what had happened to them?

"I'm going to take a look down the hall."

Wandering into the corridor, she padded along while her heart thumped rapidly. She pried open a couple of unlocked doors and peeked inside rooms eerily decorated with covered furnishings. Their shapes rose like apparitions in the dim natural light. So far she hadn't seen anything that would indicate termites or other hazards, but, then, she didn't qualify as a building inspector, either.

Her foot scraped against something slimy. Crying out in alarm, she leapt backward. *Get a grip, girl. It's only a bug.*

Gathering her wits, she took a closer look. That blob wasn't an insect. It looked more like a mangled chicken wing. Something had been gnawing at it, true, but how did it get there? Was Spector's crew this careless about their meals? A metallic glint drew her gaze to a candy wrapper in a corner.

Angry at these signs of flagrant disrespect to the place, she marched back to the open parlor, where Spector was concentrating his efforts. As she entered, her glance flickered to the mantelpiece—and her eyes bulged. Unless she was hallucinating, now both candlesticks had moved. Stepping nearer, she squinted at the layer of dust that remained undisturbed. Instead of gracing the ends of the fireplace shelf where she had seen them originally, the candle holders now stood at the center.

"Did you move these things?" she demanded.

Dr. Spector, passing his measuring device slowly over the small round table set between two armchairs, peered at her. "Excuse me? I haven't touched anything over there."

Crouching, she pushed aside the screen protecting the fireplace interior. Not even a speck of soot darkened its yawning cavity. Could this be similar to the fireplace in Polly's room? Her pulse quickening, she slid her fingers around the stone archway rimming the hearth without applying any pressure. If this was an entrance to the secret passage, she didn't want Spector to learn about it.

This could be the means by which Andrew's visitors had left, she realized, if indeed they had vanished after their meeting. Or if something more ominous had occurred to them, they could have been disposed of through this hidden exit. Seto Mulch would have known about it. He'd lived during those times and served Andrew loyally.

Had the young busboy, by then promoted to steward, been so loyal that he'd eliminate a threat to his employer by any means possible? Had he kept the secret all these years because he admired Polly and didn't want her to discover what a vile deed he'd committed? If Andrew had known, that could account for his stroke. He might've even helped Mulch get rid of the men. But Marla had no proof of her theories. Andrew could have just paid them off and shown them out through the discreet exit.

Besides, what difference would it make to current events? Mulch must have been privy to something more relevant. Remember that phone call? He'd known the identity of the other speaker and had said he wouldn't allow that individual to cause trouble. Brownie was spying for this person. Marla had assumed the groundskeeper spoke to Butler, but hadn't she caught Brownie with Jeff Levine, her cousin's husband? What if Mulch had been speaking to Jeffrey? Then again, why assume a man was on the other end of the line?

Obviously someone who knew the resort layout was using the passages. Butler was the most likely suspect. Marla had seen someone in Polly's room after her aunt's death. What if that person had escaped into the fireplace outlet? With a shiver she remembered how her evening bag had been moved. Maybe there was another entrance into her room that she and Vail hadn't yet discovered.

When Spector left briefly to pick up another piece of equipment from his hotel room, Marla set about examining the fireplace arch more thoroughly. Not a single stone could be moved, nor did any of the indentations produce the unlatching sound she'd heard in Polly's room. Defeat left her breathless. Either she had been mistaken, or this entrance was somehow jammed or deactivated. She remembered the downward branch at the intersection she and Vail had taken. It possibly led to Oleander Hall. The only way to find out for sure would be to follow it through its entirety. Short of getting the blueprints from Butler's office, she saw no alternative.

Making a quick stop in her bedroom to freshen up and grab Vail's flashlight, she headed for the tower elevator. She could always enter the passages from the twelfth floor. Gritting her teeth, she slid open the grating to the ancient lift and stepped inside.

The elevator rattled through its slow ascent while Marla mentally ticked off the seconds. She jumped back when a chill breath blew across her neck. In the next instant, she felt a tap on her shoulder.

"Stop it, Andrew," she ordered brusquely. "I'm not in the mood for being teased."

A low chuckle sounded, while something scraped her arm. Marla screeched, leaping into the wall. That elicited a knocking noise. It came from outside, as though someone wanted to get in from the shaft. *You idiot. You're supposed to wait for Dalton and go together after lunch. He's probably waiting for you by the cabana stand and will worry when you're late.* Tremors raced up her spine. The knocking seemed to correspond with her heartbeat, a paced rhythm that grew insistently louder until the entire elevator shook. Sweat beaded her brow. *If only this damn thing would move faster.*

The noise abated suddenly as she topped the tenth floor. This isn't the Tower of Terror, she reminded herself. Despite the groans and rattles, we're not going to plunge into the depths. Pressing a hand to the wall, she felt its vibration between her fingers. Shallow, gasping breaths made her light-headed.

When at last the door opened, her knees were so wobbly that she staggered across the threshold. A long corridor stretched before her. Resisting the urge to turn and run, she experienced a moment of panic when the elevator descended, leaving her alone. She had enough presence of mind to switch on the flashlight.

Should she search for Andrew's gemstones or Polly's letters? Did either really exist? She wasn't sure what to look for, only that she'd felt a compelling urge to come here by herself.

The soft thud of a door shutting gave her pause. Real or imaginary? She'd gotten to the point where she couldn't believe her own ears. When a figure emerged out of the gloom, her heart lurched. She shone her flashlight ahead, lighting up the flushed face of Jeffrey Levine.

"Marla, I should have known I'd find you here." He spread his hands in a welcoming gesture, but she'd heard the annoyance in his tone.

"Are you looking for Andrew's treasure?" she retorted. "Cynthia told me we'd divided up the resort. This is my territory."

"I wanted to get the lay of the land. This level is just like it was in Andrew's day. Why do you suppose it's been so well-preserved?"

"Good question. People would pay a lot of money to stay up here, especially with the rooms restored to their original condition. It could be there are structural faults that aren't immediately visible. You know, roof leaks and such." *Or it could be that the hotel doesn't own the top levels, and whoever does halted progress for their own reasons.*

"If that's true, you shouldn't be here alone," he said. "Strange things happen to folks at this resort."

"You don't seem to be scared off by ghost stories."

"Who said anything about ghosts? That guy who fell off the

ladder, Polly dying this weekend, and that weird group of ghost hunters are too much for coincidence. You'd think someone is trying to chase people away."

Not to mention the missing groundskeeper. "Why would that be?" she asked. As Jeff neared, she realized how his muscles bulged under his black shirt. She hadn't been aware of his strength before, but now it made her take a step backward.

His onyx eyes gleamed in the reflected light from her torch. "You tell me. Have you made any discoveries?"

She met his gaze levelly. "Nothing significant."

He grinned with an expression she'd almost call relief. "Maybe you'll find something decent that Aunt Polly can wear for burial. You wouldn't want to put her away in those *shmattes* she favored."

"Being so religious, she'll probably get buried in a shroud. That'll be my mother's decision."

"You won't find much here."

"You've been to her rooms?"

He waved a hand. "I've breezed through all of them. The history fascinates me. You'll let me know if you learn anything relevant, won't you?"

His malevolent gleam made her answer carefully. "Sure, Jeffrey. I'll let you know what I find, but I doubt Andrew's loot really exists. I think Polly made up the whole *megillah* just to rile everyone."

"Or to draw us together, that being her aim this weekend."

Hadn't Polly said she wanted to make amends? Marla had never found out what she meant. Had she been referring to Ruth's falling-out with her sister and brothers? But their Colorado relatives seemed oblivious to any schism. Marla would have to probe deeper into their family history to learn what had prompted Polly's remark.

"Dalton is waiting for me, so I can't waste time," she told her cousin-by-marriage. "Excuse me, Jeff."

"Polly's door is the third on the left, past her parents' suites. Want me to keep you company?"

She narrowed her gaze. The man seemed in no hurry to leave.

"No thanks, I'm sure Lori is expecting you." *Not that you care about your wife.* Jabbing the elevator button to summon the lift, she waited until he'd begun his descent before rushing down the hallway.

Now, where might Polly have hidden her letters? Why did they matter to Vincent, whoever he was?

She surmised it had been Ruth's decision to move everyone to the twelfth floor after Andrew died. Perhaps Ruth suspected the gems were somewhere in the penthouse, and she didn't want the children disrupting things while she searched for them. It was even likely she had found his stash and used it to support herself and the family. But wouldn't she have shared that find with Polly, her eldest?

Having identified Polly's room without any trouble, Marla stepped inside—then stopped in shock. Drawers were spilled open. Clothing was piled on the closet floor. On the dresser, tracks showed through coatings of dust. Had Jeff searched through her aunt's belongings here as well as in her room downstairs? He couldn't have been looking for the treasure. They all knew Polly didn't have it. The only thing he could've been looking for were her letters . . . or possibly the old lady's will. But why would he care? A nagging memory surfaced, and Marla recalled smelling lilacs in her aunt's room. Of course. Brownie favored lilac scent.

So was Brownie spying for Jeff, and not Mr. Butler? Were Jeff and Brownie working together for some reason that Mulch considered trouble? As her theories expanded, Marla felt her blood chill. Was Jeff responsible for the old man's vanishing act?

I know who you are. Mulch's words repeated themselves in her mind. She'd have to ask Anita what she knew of his background.

Marla regarded the task before her with slumped shoulders. She didn't have time now for a thorough search. Glancing at her watch, she noted the dial read twelve-thirty. As though she and Vail had a mental link, her cell phone rang and his voice greeted her.

"I'll be there shortly," she said. "Save me a chair."

"Where are you?"

He'd be angry if she told him. "I'm, uh, on my way." She hung up before he could worm the truth from her.

Polly must have stored her recyclables here, Marla figured, discovering a collection of metal lids from coffee cans, washed plastic containers from ready-made puddings, foam trays from the supermarket, and scraps of aluminum foil. Empty jars took up an entire shelf in the closet, where clothing no longer in style hung inside out on dusty hangers. Marla rifled through the garments, checking pockets but finding nothing except shredded tissues. She came across a pile of monogrammed handkerchiefs, reminiscent of a lifestyle full of tea parties, formal courtships, and calling cards.

Her back aching, she got a whiff of mothballs from a woolen blanket and stifled a sneeze. A dress bag hung in a shadowed recess next to a crocheted shawl, but she'd search them later.

Straightening her shoulders, she retreated into the room to yank open the drapes. There, now she could see better. After flicking off the flashlight, she rifled through each drawer in the mirrored dressing table and then in the oak dresser. Under a pile of full-length folded slips was an ivory silk negligee. She lifted it with reverence, amazed Polly had ever possessed such a delicate item. Spaghetti straps led to a plunging neckline edged in lace. The gown must have belonged to her aunt when she was younger, and taller, before osteoporosis had shrunk her size. *It looks like something a woman would wear on her wedding night.* Could her spinster aunt have taken a lover? This would have been so out of character for Polly that Marla stood as though hypnotized at the thought, fingering the silk fabric.

Aware that she was overdue to meet Vail, she replaced the nightgown in its drawer. Then she spotted an empty cereal box stuffed with papers on the night table. Maybe the letters were in there! Her excitement waned, though, as she sifted through grocery coupons, empty junk mail envelopes, and outdated financial statements.

Maybe Jeffrey had taken the letters, if her aunt had hidden them here. Marla didn't want to acknowledge the likelihood that she'd been duped, and that Polly had sent her on a wild goose chase with her senile ramblings.

Wait a minute. If Polly wanted to leave someone a clue, what might she have done?

Instinct propelled Marla back to the closet, where she stared at the flowered print blouses, straight skirts, and shift dresses. Her gaze meandered downward. Nestled on a floorboard was an old blanket.

Wrinkling her nose at the musty smell, she dragged it out and spread it on Polly's faded bedspread. Nothing fell from its folds except clouds of dust that made her sneeze repeatedly.

She glanced up when a breeze ruffled the window curtains—except there was no breeze. The windows were closed, and minimal air-conditioning kept the premises dry. Her skin prickled. Did she sense another presence?

Something crashed inside the closet. She shrieked, jumping in alarm. "What's that? Is anyone there?"

Her heart pounding, she approached, only to give a sigh of relief. A plastic hanger had broken, its pieces strewn beneath the dress bag. *Fool, you're imagining ghosts again.* If there were any spooks around, it was Polly trying to help her.

Stooping forward, Marla unzipped the garment bag and pried open its edges. Her jaw dropped as she eyed the contents. It held a two-piece ivory suit: a ruffled jacket with seed pearls and rhinestones and a lined satin skirt. The size eight looked as though it would fit her perfectly. *This has to be a wedding outfit,* Marla concluded, adding the silk negligee to her equation. Did Anita know about this? Maybe viewing the bridal ensemble would jar her mother's memories.

Of all her aunt's possessions, these were the only things Marla would have liked to keep for herself, partially out of honor to her aunt, but also because she didn't want such beautiful clothes to go to waste. People used to preserve evening gowns in trunks to pass on to the next generation. Polly's suit and nightgown were almost new, and Marla's pride wouldn't be lessened if she wore them. She'd consider them her legacy.

Something brushed her cheek in a gentle caress. Marla jerked back with a gasp. A strong impression filtered into her mind that she wasn't alone. Squeezing her eyes shut, she saw a brief image of Polly, whose smiling face glowed with health.

Mumbling a quick prayer for her aunt, she blinked. The musty atmosphere must be getting to her. Suddenly eager to leave, she snatched the silk gown and fitted it on a hanger. If she hung the negligee with the suit, she'd remember to retrieve the items later. But as she jostled the nightgown inside the confined space, its trailing hem snagged on a cardboard insert at the bottom of the dress bag.

"We don't need that," she said aloud, tossing the piece of cardboard aside.

Her eyes widened.

At the very bottom of the garment bag lay a banded packet of letters.

Chapter
Fourteen

Marla found Vail chomping on an apple when she arrived at the beach. He reclined on a chaise lounge, part of a double set separated by a slatted wooden shelf. An umbrella provided shade, which helped cool the two gaily decorated lunch cartons propped on the divider. Laughter from other beachgoers receded into the background as she kicked off her sandals. Her feet sank into the warm sand.

Tossing her beach bag to the foot of her chair, she shaded her eyes from the water sparkling on the ocean. A briny breeze blew her way. Like many fellow Floridians, she rarely went to the shore when home, and even now she felt restless. Maybe it just wasn't her nature to be idle.

"You're late," Vail said between bites, his expression hidden behind dark sunglasses.

Removing her terry cloth robe, Marla sank onto the chair and dragged her bag closer. Nestled under her towel were the valuable papers she had discovered. She'd have been stupid to leave Polly's letters in their room. "That's because I made an important find. How come you weren't worried about me?" Forty-five minutes had passed since his phone call.

"I was busy talking to Champagne." Lifting his shades, he regarded her clearly. His gray eyes were thoughtful. "She told me some interesting things. What did you learn?"

Marla's stomach growled, and she realized how ravenous she was. "You first," she said, bursting to tell him her news but needing sustenance first. She opened her box and examined the contents: cold fried chicken, containers of coleslaw and potato salad, chips, a shiny red apple, and a giant chocolate chip cookie. Ordinary, but welcome. "What's to drink?"

Vail reached behind his chair for a large sack. While she munched on a chicken wing, he placed two wine goblets on the platform between their chairs and opened a half bottle of chardonnay. "We're on vacation," he explained, grinning.

"I need to keep my wits about me," Marla protested, taking a sip nonetheless. The fruity liquid slid down her throat.

"Don't worry. If you become sloshed, I'll carry you back to our room." He leaned closer, lowering his voice. "Do you know where George Butler worked before he took this position?"

Marla spotted her mother strolling with Aunt Selma and waved, hoping they wouldn't come over. "No. Where?"

"He helped create behind-the-scenes special effects at an Orlando theme park and slipped into hotel management by accident. The consortium that owns this resort was looking for an applicant with experience in the hospitality field but also someone who could utilize its rich history to draw guests. Butler had an engineering degree, but he'd minored in hospitality."

Crunching on a potato chip, Marla raised an eyebrow. "He used to be an Imagineer? That could explain why some of these ghostly experiences seem so real."

She reflected on the rides at Walt Disney World, in particular the one in Tomorrowland where visitors felt as though a vicious alien creature scurried behind their backs. She'd actually felt a crawling sensation along her spine. Then there was the aroma of burning wood in the scene showing the fall of ancient Rome on Spaceship Earth. Were they dealing with something similar here? "Do you think the weird incidents are all faked? If so, why would Butler hire Spector's team?"

"To show that he believed the tales were true."

"But Dr. Spector says he's found evidence of spirits."

"His claims could reflect what he's been paid to say." Vail swallowed a big gulp of wine, then put his glass back on the wood platform. "Consider this: accidents plague the labor force, who are a superstitious lot. Blaming the problems on spooks takes the heat off the real cause."

Licking the salty residue on her lips, Marla regarded him. "And that is?"

He shrugged. She'd been trying to ignore his physique, but that gesture drew her gaze to his bare chest and wide shoulders. She drank in the sight of his contoured muscles before her attention wandered to his black swim trunks. Was the wine affecting her, or did merely looking at him have the power to stir her blood?

"Something odd is going on around here," Vail replied, snapping her back to mental acuity. "I have a hunch your Aunt Polly found out about it."

"Speaking of my aunt, I discovered her—"

"How are you, dearies?" sang out Wanda Beake. The large woman blocked the afternoon sun as she rooted herself in front of Marla's lounge chair. A whiff of coconut oil drifted from her presence. Seagulls flirted with one another in the distance, their raucous cries drowned out by the giggling of a crowd of teenagers.

Squinting, Marla wished she'd brought a hat. Wanda wore a wide-brimmed straw creation decorated with a persimmon ribbon. Her Hawaiian muumuu stretched over her generous bosom. "This lunch just hit the spot," Marla said. "My Aunt Polly would have enjoyed it. I feel bad that she isn't here to join us."

"Such a pity. I heard how the old lady organized this reunion. She'd want you to have a good time, you know. I'll bet you don't see your family members all that often, do you?"

"Not everyone."

"I noticed one of your cousins talking to the chef. They seem to be quite friendly. I hope Brownie isn't filling his head with wild stories. Ha ha." Her snicker seemed as false as her smile.

"You must mean Jeffrey. We're related by marriage. His wife, Lori, is my first cousin."

"The man gets around. I saw him in close conversation with Donna Albright earlier. It seems he has an eye for the ladies. You should tell your cousin to rein him in."

"Yes, I'll do that." What was he talking about with the city councilwoman? And why was Wanda keeping watch on him? "Come to think of it, I don't see Lori around." Scanning the beach, she identified people from her clan, but couldn't locate Joan and Julia's sister.

"Maybe she's out shelling. We're offering a prize for the person who brings in the largest whelk, but it has to be completely intact. There's a chart by the rental booth if you don't know what to look for. Check in at the cabana by three o'clock and you'll have a chance to enter."

"That's a good idea. We'll look for Lori while we're searching for shells. Where did you see Jeff last?" Marla would just as soon take a walk, then broil in the sun.

Wanda gestured down the beach to one side. The opposite end stopped at a cluster of mangroves that bordered the nature center. "I ran into him on that trail through the Australian pines. You know, the path that leads from the cisterns and old sugar mill to the shore. Go past the rental booth and banana boats and you'll find it."

"The volleyball court is in that direction," Vail interrupted. "Isn't there a game this afternoon?"

"At two o'clock." Glancing at her watch, Wanda raised her eyebrows. "Actually, it should be starting shortly, luv. Oh look, I see a roseate spoonbill. Will you look at that!" Raising the pair of binoculars hanging from her neck to her eyes, she hastened off.

After Marla finished her meal and they'd disposed of their trash, she and Vail headed south. Marla kept her sandals on, the sand being too hot for her bare feet. She'd slung her bag over her shoulder while Vail used his towel to protect his back from the rays. Her shoes sank into the sand as they marched forward.

"Have you gotten the results on Polly's autopsy yet?"

"It's a holiday weekend. I don't know if their lab is open. I thought I'd call later, but we may not know anything until next week."

"Ma can't plan a memorial service until the body is released."

"I know. Didn't you have something to tell me?"

She patted her beach bag. "I found Polly's letters. Would you believe they were at the bottom of a garment bag in her closet on the twelfth floor? And you'll never guess what was inside on a hanger: a bridal outfit. I can't wait to read these to see what they say, but I didn't want to be late in meeting you. Silly me, I thought you might get worried."

His eyes gleamed as he removed his sunglasses. "If you hadn't shown up, I would have come after you. This place isn't as idyllic as we'd imagined."

"No kidding." She kicked at a patch of dead seaweed. "It seems as though we can't go anywhere without something bad happening."

"I'll make sure nothing disrupts our honeymoon. And when will that be?"

Now wasn't the time to analyze why the mention of nuptials threw her into a panic. "We'll check our calendars when we get home," she hedged.

"Fine, but I intend to pin you to a date." His brow wrinkled. "Where did you say you found Polly's letters?"

Tilting her head, she pointed toward the surf. "Later. Lori and Jeff are down by the water."

Her cousins were engaged in conversation as she and Vail approached from their rear. Lori wore a one-piece black swimsuit with iridescent diagonal stripes. Jeff's swim trunks barely covered his essentials.

"I should've known you couldn't do anything right," Jeff was saying, testing his feet in the ocean.

"I'm just not as enthralled by this treasure hunt as you are," his wife retorted. Copper highlights glinted in her hair, wind-tossed into an unruly bob.

"I told you the floors don't add up. I've ridden the tower elevator four times now, and each time my measurements of the intervals are the same. It takes longer to go from the twelfth to the fourteenth floor than between any other levels."

"Isn't the penthouse closed to visitors?" Lori said.

"Oleander Hall is off-limits due to safety reasons, but no one is restricted from the tower. The rooms aren't available to guests, although I don't know why. They're still furnished."

"Probably renovations are needed to modernize the plumbing and so forth. What makes you think the treasure might be hidden there? That wasn't our assigned spot to look."

"Are you always such a Girl Scout, to follow the rules? It's logical that she'd hide something valuable in her former suite."

"She? You mean Andrew. Ruth never found the source of his wealth or the family would know about it."

"Oh, right." Jeff snorted. "I just wish they'd rip the whole place down so they could restore the original plantation buildings. Then we wouldn't have to worry about certain . . . past events."

Blatantly eavesdropping behind their backs, Marla stared at Vail. Was Jeff advocating the demolishment of the hotel in favor of a theme park? She'd thought he supported remodeling the place.

"You're getting enough money from your mother," Lori said in a scathing tone. "After all, you and your sister are heirs to her fortune. I don't understand why you're so intent on searching for valuables that you don't need and that may not exist. You're wasting our time."

"Let me be the judge of what I'm doing. *You* should spend more hours in the gym. Get rid of those extra pounds you're accumulating. Didn't I tell you to lay off the desserts? You can't even wear a two-piece swimsuit any more. Look at you," he said, making a disdainful gesture.

Lori turned away, coming face-to-face with Marla.

"Hi," Marla said weakly, warm embarrassment flooding her. "We didn't mean to intrude."

Her cousin's lower lip trembled. "Walk with me, please."

Marla flashed Vail a signal, then fell into place beside her cousin, who began trudging back toward the crowded beachfront.

"Is your husband always such a miserable lout?" Marla couldn't help asking. "I hope you don't believe those things he just said."

Lori bent her head. "I've offered to give him a divorce, but he won't cooperate. I don't know why, when he's so unhappy with me." A single tear trickled down her cheek.

"Is it true that he's rich?"

"His mother's family comes from wealth. He'll inherit his portion someday. That doesn't give him the excuse to act like God's gift to womankind."

Marla veered around a bluish blob that looked suspiciously like a dead jellyfish. Hot sand scrunched between her toes. "Why don't you leave him?"

"It isn't so simple. This resort . . . We've been here before. I think he's looking for something other than Andrew's precious gems."

Like Polly's letters, or the documents detailing the hotel sale? Did Jeff hope his wife would inherit property? That could give him a reason for not getting a divorce, except it didn't make sense if he had enough money of his own. No, there had to be another reason why he hung around and had enlisted Brownie on his side.

Those letters could hold the answers to many of her questions. She had to get away to read them. With that in mind, Marla murmured some encouraging words to her cousin before venturing off on her own. Since they hadn't signed up for the shopping trip to St. Armand's Circle in Sarasota that afternoon, she figured she should have some uninterrupted free time as long as Vail kept himself occupied.

Heading for the formal garden by the conservatory, Marla decided she didn't trust their bedroom, where doors unlocked by themselves and possessions shifted places in her absence. She'd rather remain outdoors in the fresh sea air.

Spying a stone bench bordered by tall hedges that would hide her from view, she donned a T-shirt from her bag. Her skin felt gritty with sweat and sand, but the shady location and light breeze should bring a measure of comfort. She draped her towel over the hard seat before sinking down. Withdrawing the packet from her bag, she grimaced when its elastic band crumbled into bits upon touch. Carefully, she fingered the brown edges of the envelopes in her lap. Postmark dates were still visible. She picked the earliest, dated May 1943, and opened it.

> *My Darling Vincent,*
>   *I am hoping that you will find it in your heart to forgive me. It was a terrible thing I did, making accusations without giving you a chance to explain. But you must understand how it looked to me, especially when you ran off so hastily. I'm sure you didn't mean those harsh words about Papa. We can talk about it if you'll only come home. I ache for your return and count the hours until we are together again.*
>   *Loving you always,*
>   *Polly*

Marla frowned. Who the devil was Vincent? Obviously, he'd had some kind of relationship with Polly until something happened that resulted in his departure. Maybe he'd worked on the plantation for her father. That would account for his words against Andrew. Did he leave around the time of Andrew's death?

Too bad the town records went up in smoke. She could have seen if the name Vincent popped up anywhere in the family books.

Carefully folding the letter back into its envelope, Marla selected the next on the pile, noting they were in chronological order. This cache of letters might be the only means of learning the truth about what happened to her family back then.

> *Dearest Vincent,*
>   *I sent my previous letter to your solicitor, but it came back address unknown. I am writing this now in the hopes that I can locate you again. Poor Agnes will not talk about that*

night, nor will she go near her room again. Mama has decided to move us all to the twelfth floor. I love you so much that I will forgive you anything. I'm sure there has to be a reason for what you did. Was I so inadequate as your wife?

Marla's eyes bulged. Polly had been *married?*

Of course. It would explain her wedding dress and the ivory silk nightgown in her upstairs bedchamber. But, then, why had Anita never mentioned this important event in her sister's past? She supposed her mother might have been too young at the time to remember Polly's wedding, but Uncles Moishe and William must have met the guy. Had their marriage been so brief that her family considered it inconsequential? Or had Anita in fact mentioned it before, but Marla hadn't paid attention?

Evidently, Polly and Vincent had never reconciled, because Polly had reverted to her maiden name. According to her letters, though, she'd never given up her infatuation for the man.

Marla's cell phone rang, breaking her reverie. She reached inside her beach bag, hoping it was Vail so she could share this information with him.

"Marla?" Joanne Cater's squeaky voice said.

"Is everything all right at the salon?" Marla's pulse accelerated. Their shampoo assistant hardly ever called.

"It's fine. Nicole said I should call you directly. I know this is bad timing, and I'm sorry to bother you during your vacation, but I got this job and it starts on Monday."

"Wait a minute." Leaning forward, she clutched the device to her ear. "You're going to work for another salon?"

"No, for an accounting firm. You know I've only been doing this temporarily until I could find a position."

Joanne had recently graduated from Nova Southeastern University, but Marla had hoped a permanent job might still permit her to work weekends.

She swallowed. "I'm happy for you. Really."

"I may still be able to come on Saturdays," Joanne said in an apologetic tone, "at least until you find someone else."

"That's okay. You can let me know next week. We'll miss you."

"Me too. Hey, keep me in mind if you want someone to take over your bookkeeping. I know it takes a big chunk out of your time now, but if you ever decide to add spa services like you've talked about, you may need extra help."

"Sure, you'd be the first one I'd call. How does your sister feel about it?" Jennifer was one of her stylists.

"My sister loves working with you, but she knows the salon isn't the place for me."

"Well, good luck with the new job. We don't even have time to give you a going-away party."

"Don't worry about it." Marla heard mumbling in the background. Then Joanne said, "Nicole wants to know if you're having fun?"

"Oh joy. Tell her Aunt Polly is dead, someone pushed me into a rock-lined pit, a ghost is guarding a haunted tower, and people are mysteriously disappearing. The resort is overrun with paranormal groupies looking for spooks, and I don't mean my dog. My relatives are searching for a trove of hidden jewels, while I'm uncovering family secrets buried for decades. I'd rather be at work."

She hung up with a smile on her lips. Sunlight glanced off a nearby window, making her blink. Beyond a cluster of scarlet crotons rose the conservatory, its domed roof dominating the 1920s structure with multipaned windows and white paint in need of a fresh coat. A figure moved inside behind one of the ceiling-high panes. A nature lover, she surmised. The greenhouse was open to the public, although she had yet to explore the interior. Too many other things to do.

Wondering where Vail had gone, she dialed his number.

"I'm in the arboretum by the cycad garden," he stated curtly. "Are you done with your cousin?"

"Sorry I left you so abruptly." She repeated the gist of her conversation with Lori. "Did you get anything else out of Jeff?"

"He was eager to skedaddle. I don't have a good feeling about him. He's up to something, if you ask me."

"I agree. What are you doing back in the Nature Center? Did we leave there too soon this morning? I know how you like to look at trees—"

"Marla, it's not that. Meet me here on the trail. Take your first right by the hackberry tree. Be careful where the path edges a sinkhole. You'll come to a yellow birdhouse on a post. Cross over on the grass, and you'll see me by a fresh pile of compost."

"I'm in my swimsuit. Can you wait until I get changed? The insects will have a feast on me otherwise."

"The insects have something else to nibble on. I think I've found Seto Mulch."

Chapter
Fifteen

Marla's stomach heaved when she saw limp fingers sticking from the pile of compost in the arboretum. She glanced at Vail, who stood sweating in the afternoon sun, his T-shirt stained with perspiration. Dirt splattered his swim trunks and blackened his hands.

"How did you know?" she said in a raspy voice.

"I remembered passing by here earlier. This heap looked fresh. Thought I'd take a look. Then there were the wheelbarrow marks and stains on the shovel at the work shed behind Mulch's house." He noticed the expression on her face. "You don't have to stay. I might be here a while."

"Maybe this time the cops will take things seriously."

"I've already called it in. The local boys should be here any time now."

"Who's going to tell the staff?"

"Nothing is confirmed until they dig him out. I don't think you'll want to be here."

She clutched her midsection. "What an awful weekend."

He stepped closer, lifting her chin with a finger. "I'll have to admit, things are never boring when you're around."

"Gee, thanks." She avoided his probing gaze. "What happens next?"

His hand rested on her shoulder. "The staff will be questioned. And some guests. It's apt to get tense around here, and we'll need to stick close by. An early departure is out of our hands."

"I got a chance to glance at Polly's letters. She was married to a man named Vincent. Her ramblings weren't so far off base after all."

His smoky eyes sparked with interest. "Your spinster aunt, married? I don't believe it. Wait, where did you say you found those letters?"

"At the bottom of a dress bag in her closet on the twelfth floor."

His brows drew together. "You went there without me? Not a smart move, hon. Don't go snooping by yourself again."

"I just went to take a quick look before we met for lunch. I'd been with Spector in Oleander Hall and noticed the fireplace in the parlor was similar to the one in Polly's room. I got to thinking that it might open to the secret passages. I felt *directed* to go to her former suite, and I met Jeffrey on his way out." She said that all in one breath, so now she paused to inhale some humus-scented air.

"Whoa, slow down." Footsteps crunched in their direction. "Dammit, I want to hear more about this." His mouth tightened in a grim line when he spied a uniformed officer marching their way.

"Detective Vail?" the burly fellow asked.

"You got that right." They shook hands. "This is Marla Shore, my fiancée."

"I'm Sergeant Hamilton. Crime-scene unit is on the way. I understand you been seeing some action this weekend. Where's the stiff?"

Marla winced. Perhaps it was time for her to depart.

When Vail pointed, the officer took out his notepad and pen. "Oh, I'm supposed to tell you that the preliminary autopsy report has come in on the old lady. We don't have the toxicology findings yet, but the presumed cause of death at this point is asphyxiation."

"What?" Marla said, feeling her heart skip a beat. "Aunt Polly didn't die from heart failure or an overdose of morphine?"

The sergeant turned his sharp gaze on her. "No ma'am."

"I thought she had the telltale signs," Vail said smugly. At Marla's shocked look, he added, "Well, it would've been easy to put a pillow over her face if she was zonked out on the drug. At first glance, it would appear to be simple respiratory failure."

"I've been given that case as well as this one," Hamilton said. "And I understand there's some question about a painter who fell off his ladder?"

"Thank God they've assigned someone competent," Vail mumbled. "If you don't mind my input, I have a few observations I'd like to share."

Sergeant Hamilton glanced over his shoulder. "Here come my techs. You can stay and watch if you want, but the lady might prefer to wait for us elsewhere. This will be a messy affair, from the looks of it."

Marla realized she'd lost Vail to the forensics team. So much for their plan to explore the secret passages. She'd just have to proceed on her own. "Where can we meet?" she asked him. "Oh gosh, wait until I tell my cousins about this."

"Don't say anything yet," he ordered, his steely gaze capturing hers, then softening. "Why don't you find your mother and ask her about this Vincent character?"

"Good idea." She purposefully didn't say when she might get around to it. Finding someplace quiet where she could read more of Polly's letters took priority.

"Rochelle is supposed to keep an eye out for Butler. Give me a call when he's returned," Vail said.

Oh, like the teenager had nothing better to do than watch for the manager? "Of course. What if I run into Champagne? She knows we were looking for Seto." She remembered something else. "I saw Donna Albright earlier. She told me that Mulch had a message for her regarding the hotel property. He never showed up for their meeting at eleven o'clock."

"My guess is the old guy was killed sometime between when you saw him yesterday and this morning," Vail replied, "but we'll know more later."

Her muddled brain couldn't think of anything else relevant to tell him right at that moment, so she left. She heard him conferring with the specialists as she stumbled back onto the guided path. A flash of white near a spreading banyan tree caught her eye, but when she turned her head, nothing was there. Her neck prickled with the sensation that she was being watched.

Bolstering her nerves, she hastened toward the main hotel. Wait. Who had told her that Mulch liked to hang out at the sugar mill ruins? Was something there that attracted his interest?

Remembering what had befallen her the last time she'd explored the crumbling stones on her own, she resolved to keep strictly to her route.

Exiting from the arboretum, she faced the hotel. On her far right stretched the seashore. Straight ahead, water glistened in the pool, with the Grand Terrace beyond. The westward wings of the hotel jutted past the conservatory on her left. Making a quick decision, she swung by the condemned hall. If an outside entry offered a route into the secret passage, it would most likely be there.

Strolling along a paved walkway parallel to Oleander Hall's beach frontage, she watched for any signs of a passage, but the crumbling exterior made it difficult to detect irregularities. She'd have to search for the portal from inside. When she changed direction, her glance fell on the shoreline over a rise of dunes.

Hmm, interesting idea. People could come by boat via the coastline, breach the hotel by means of the secret entrance, and make their way to the presumed speakeasy on the thirteenth floor. Was that how it had worked? Wondering if Polly's letters alluded to the Prohibition era, Marla hastened through a side entrance toward Hibiscus Hall. She needed some time alone to sort through Polly's missives.

Preferring comfort to security, she headed for her room, where she washed and changed into a navy slacks set before hopping on the bed with Polly's packet. Hoping she wouldn't be disturbed, Marla opened the next envelope in the pile.

My Dearest Husband,

I don't know if you will receive my letters because you never left a forwarding address. I am hoping my attorney will locate you. My dear friend, Seto Mulch, whom you may remember as our chief of maintenance, has offered to deliver these in the event you are found. I'm sure we've had a simple misunderstanding that can be easily cleared up. Let me share with you my perception of events. If this doesn't agree with yours, then we'll meet to talk things out. Love such as ours shouldn't be tossed away over a mere disagreement.

Suppose we start with my father's confession since that seemed to upset you so much. I don't know why, when I was proud of what he did. I will say that I was as shocked as my sister and brothers when Papa told us the truth about his origins.

Born in 1900, Papa was a descendant of Grand Duke Mihail Nikolaevich, youngest son of Emperor Nikolai 1st of Russia. Papa said his real name was Andrey Mihalovna.

Marla looked up. Andrew's real name? Moishe had said it was Andrzej Markowski, and he was from Poland. Could this be possible?

Heart rate soaring, her eyes devoured the ensuing words with growing amazement:

As one of the Emperor's great-grandchildren and a member of the Russian royal house of Romanov, Andrey's life was threatened by the revolution in 1917. He escaped by stealing the identity papers of a Polish Jew, Andrzej Markowski, killed in an accident while driving a cart on the family estate.

Omigosh. Andrew had never been born in Poland. He'd stolen another man's identity. That meant everything she knew about her grandfather had been false. It also meant she and her mother's family were related to Russian royalty. What about Andrew's marriage to Ruth?

Under his assumed name, Andrey applied as a student to the University of Warsaw where he studied architecture. In 1921, he emigrated to the United States where he changed his name to Andrew Marks. Two years later, he met and married Ruth.

Okay, so they got married. That meant things were legitimate, right? Or did the fact that he entered the country under a false name invalidate their marriage certificate? Holy highlights, then she and all her cousins would be illegitimate offspring. Folding her legs Indian-style on the bed, Marla switched to the next sheet of brown-edged stationery.

Before she could read the continuing saga, the phone rang. Cursing, Marla debated letting it go, but the possibility that it might be Vail made her snatch the receiver.

"Miss Shore? This is Dr. Angus, the resort doctor. I have some information for you regarding your aunt. Would you be able to come to my office?"

She winced. "Is this something you can tell me over the telephone?"

"I'd rather not. It's mighty delicate, you see. We'll have to discuss who else you should tell." His gruff voice seemed to have an edge to it as though he also had something else to say.

"All right." She sighed and lifted a hand to her hair. Yuck, it felt sticky. She needed a good shampoo-and-conditioner treatment. Glancing at her watch, she calculated how much time she had left before she needed to get ready for the evening's poolside luau. Or would the event be canceled once the staff learned of Mulch's death?

"Where can I find you?" she asked the doctor.

"I'm over at the fitness complex. Good place to be, ha ha, in case a guest works out too vigorously on the sports equipment."

"See you there in fifteen minutes." Hitting the flash button, she dialed Vail's cell phone. "Are you still in the nature center?" she said when he came online. "I'm going to talk to Dr. Angus. He has some news for me."

"I'll be wrapping it up here shortly," he said, his deep voice causing her nerve endings to thrum.

"Anything you can share?"

"Mulch's head impacted with a blunt instrument. Likely his body has been here since yesterday. Hamilton will be rounding up the hotel staff for questioning. Has Butler returned? The sergeant called his house, but no one answered."

"I haven't seen him, but I've been in our room. Dalton, you won't believe what—"

She heard mumbling in the background. "Later," he cut in. "I've got to go."

"What about the events we have planned? Shouldn't the hotel be closed down, considering all that's been happening?" Now that Mulch had been murdered and Polly's death shown to be due to other than natural causes, maybe they'd look into the laborers' mishaps also. But Marla didn't want to leave. Not when she was just learning about her family history.

"We'll see. Let's meet back in the room at six."

"But what about the passage? We were supposed to explore it today."

"I don't know how that matters anymore. These two homicides take priority."

"It's not your case, Dalton."

"Gotta go, hon." *Click.*

Marla slammed down the receiver. Some vacation. Next time, they'd better fly to a tropical island where nothing could interfere. Thinking of the travel brochures on her desk at home, she gave a cynical laugh. Forget Bora Bora and Hawaii. She'd be lucky to get to Key West.

Outside, the thunk of balls hitting rackets accompanied by

shouts and laughter met her ears as she strolled past the tennis courts toward the spa building beyond. Activities seemed to be proceeding normally, as evidenced by the happy chatter coming from the beach and from couples sauntering by holding hands. It was a perfect afternoon, blue sky with sun shining overhead, jasmine scenting the air, waves rolling ashore. A perfect afternoon marred by death.

A blur materialized and collided into her shoulder, sending her stumbling forward. It was her sensitive shoulder, too. Now her arm ached all over again. Ready to lash into the idiot who hadn't watched where they were going, she whirled to face one of Spector's teammates, a young lady with a long braid down her back.

"Oh, I'm so sorry," said the woman in a contrite tone. Her eyes bright with excitement, she carried a digital camera in her hand and had a bulging backpack strapped to her torso.

"What's the hurry?" Marla demanded.

"I just caught a vortex on film. I've got to show Dr. Spector."

Her curiosity perked. "What's a vortex?"

"A swirling vertical column. Look." She showed Marla the replay of her last digital photo, taken at the old sugar mill. Marla recognized the chimney stack along with the crumbling stone edifices. Sure enough, a twisting spiral of white light rose directly from the gap in its base.

"So what does this mean?" Marla asked.

"We have to do more readings, of course, but it could be an entity. I was lucky I wasn't aiming in that direction."

"How so?"

"Normally, you don't take photos in front of you. You may take pictures over your shoulder or snap a photo in the opposite direction from where you're looking. I took a regular shot, but I don't know if my thirty-five-millimeter caught the anomaly."

"If this was a ghost," Marla said, thinking of Seto Mulch, "how can you tell who it is?"

"Sometimes by the history of a place. Residual hauntings, for example, are like recordings. They reflect events that occurred at a particular location. Think in terms of an energy residue that keeps repeating itself. Footsteps going up and down stairs, soldiers fighting on battlefields, people walking down hallways; these are experienced in the same place over time, like the apparition in St. Augustine who's always seen doing her laundry. By doing the same action repeatedly, she's left an impression on the place. It's just a replay of the scene, like a traumatic event that has stamped its imprint on the locale."

"So actual ghosts aren't present?" Marla asked, wondering about the sounds coming from the thirteenth floor of people laughing and glasses clinking. Remnants of the Prohibition era, perhaps?

"You got it. This type of haunting is simply a recording of an event in time. Then we have intelligent ghosts who will try to get your attention, you know, by rattling doorknobs, creating odors, moving furniture, making noises."

"I see. Well, thanks for the information," Marla said, ready to move on.

"Then there are the anniversary ghosts." On a roll, the young woman continued. "They only appear on the anniversary of a significant event, although that could be another type of residual haunting. We also have the poltergeist that you're probably more familiar with from movies. They really don't intend to hurt people, but their high energy level can make them dangerous. They want people to know they're around."

"Do you think that's why you captured this vortex on film? It wanted to be seen?" Like Seto Mulch, trying to tell them something?

"Could be."

One fine point needed explanation. "What's the difference between an orb, apparition, vortex, and ectoplasm?" she asked.

"They're just different forms of spiritual energy. I'd better go show our boss what I got on camera. Sorry for keeping you." The ghost hunter bustled off while Marla turned toward the fitness center.

In his private office, Dr. Angus pushed aside his swivel chair to greet her after she knocked on his open door.

"Come in, come in," he said, his jowls quivering as he waved her inside before shutting the door in her wake. "Please, take a seat." He indicated a chair opposite his desk. Stacks of files littered his desktop, counter space, and floor. Marla tried to read the folder heading on his desk, but she couldn't decipher the upside-down lettering.

"What is it about my aunt you wanted to tell me?" she asked, smoothing her pants after she dropped into a chair. Her eyes skimmed his accessories, items you could pick up at Office Depot. What would make him stay here instead of maintaining a lucrative private practice elsewhere? Maybe he was paid well but had modest tastes. Or else he liked the food. His girth certainly attested to his appetite, and from his empty ring finger, she surmised the good doctor was single.

Folding his hands on the desk, Dr. Angus leaned forward. "I called the pharmacy given on your aunt's prescription bottle. They gave me the physician's phone number when I said she needed a refill. The man was shocked when I told him Polly had, er, passed away."

He searched her face for a reaction, but when Marla didn't move a muscle, he continued. Was he concerned about her sensibilities or wondering what she knew? "He told me his patient suffered from cancer."

Marla's head jerked up. "Cancer? That's impossible. She would have told us."

Dr. Angus's demeanor turned sympathetic. "She didn't want her family to know. Apparently, it started in the breast, and she refused treatment. At her age, Miz Polly decided to let nature take its course rather than submit to debilitating surgery and chemotherapy. It would have made her a burden, she said."

Marla felt like she'd been kicked in the gut. So that's why Polly had lost so much weight and didn't look well. "Was she in much pain?" she asked, thinking of the morphine sulfate solution.

"Not until recently. She told her doctor that you were helping her at home, but he wasn't fully aware of her circumstances."

"Like being alone at night, I presume. She would've needed additional care as time went on."

The doctor cleared his throat. "I don't know what you'll want to tell your family, but this may ease their concerns. If your aunt knew she was dying, and she helped herself to a bit too much of her pain medication, it may have been her wish to spare anyone the necessity of looking after her."

"She didn't die from an overdose." Marla met his gaze squarely. "Or from natural causes. She was murdered."

"What?" Angus half-lifted from his chair.

"My fiancé talked to the cops. Were you aware he's a homicide investigator back home? Preliminary autopsy reports say my aunt died from asphyxiation. She was smothered."

The doctor shrank back down into his seat. "No . . ."

"You were very hasty to ascribe her death to natural causes, just as you were quick to say the painter's fall from a ladder was an accident. How can you be so sure? Or is that what you're paid to do?"

He leaped up. "How dare you."

"Seto Mulch was just found dead in the arboretum. The old guy knew something about this resort that he was about to reveal. I think you'd better tell me what you know. Otherwise, you're likely to be implicated in their deaths."

Chapter
Sixteen

Angus's jowls quivered. "I've just been doing my duty. I can't help it if later findings show things that don't turn up initially. Don't blame me."

"Nobody would know the cause of death is different from what you certify unless you order autopsies, and the local troop is just as glad to look aside. They can't do that anymore, not with Seto's murder. They'll come up with some trace evidence eventually. Dalton will make sure about that."

Angus passed a hand over his pallid face. "The idiot should've kept his mouth shut."

"About what, Doctor? What's going on around here?"

"I'm the wrong person to ask." Facing her, he spread his arms. "Seto hinted at things, but I didn't believe him. About all those workers on the property. He knew more about it than me, being their supposed supervisor."

"What do you mean by *supposed*?" Rising, she flexed her arms. This had been a long day so far.

"Butler calls the shots. He's the real one in charge, along with . . ."

"Yes?"

Angus shook his head.

"Is the dessert chef involved? Someone searched through my

aunt's drawers. I smelled lilac fragrance in her room, and I know Brownie favors that scent." When Angus clamped his teeth shut, Marla persisted. "Then there's the bird-watcher. Isn't it interesting how she is large-boned like the nurse's aide who took care of my aunt the night she died?"

"I called the nursing service," the doctor offered. "They didn't send anyone to the hotel."

"You see? Then Wanda shows up conveniently the next day."

"You leave her out of this! She's nothing but Butler's flunky." His eyes widened, as though he realized he'd said something he shouldn't have.

"Oh, so she's following Butler's orders, too?"

"We all are, for heaven's sake. We're employees here, and he's our manager. You're trying to make a mountain out of a molehill."

She put her hands on her hips. "Am I?"

Convinced she could coax him to reveal more, Marla knitted her brows in annoyance when someone interrupted by knocking on the door and pushing it open.

"Angus, dearie," Wanda Beake said, sweeping into the doctor's office. Her binoculars hung lopsided on her neck, and her face appeared flushed. She breathed in rapid, shallow spurts. "The most dreadful thing has happened."

He hastened over to pat her shoulder. "Yes, I know, lassie. This lady has been telling me. I presume you're speaking of our late groundskeeper."

Sniffling, Wanda leaned into his embrace. "Aye, it's horrible. They've sent for poor Mr. Butler, but he's on his errand of mercy."

"What's that?" Marla demanded, not taken in by the woman's act. Those were crocodile tears, not real ones, but Angus seemed smitten. His hands were all over the large woman, patting and coddling.

"Why, he takes those workmen home to their families. They have no means of transportation, you understand, being so needy. It's most kind of him to create jobs to provide for them."

"Oh, so his motives are purely altruistic?" Marla didn't believe that for one minute. Where the manager had gone with his van-load of laborers was up for conjecture.

"I'm just sick over Seto," the bird-watcher whined, sagging against the doctor, who embraced her with a raptured look.

Marla watched their interplay with disgust, wondering if she could prove Wanda Beake was the same person who'd entered Polly's room the night she'd died. How had the nurse's aide left without anyone spotting her?

The fireplace. If the health care worker, along with Butler, knew about the secret passages, she could have exited from Polly's place and hidden out at the complex until late Thursday, when she drove to the airport and left her car, only to be picked up by Harvey Lyle after dark. Had she driven herself, or gotten a ride? Butler could've taken her, ostensibly going home for the evening. That meant on Thanksgiving morning, the aide—or Wanda—was still on the resort property. She could have easily entered Polly's room again through the fireplace panel and called for the meal tray. Had her aunt already been lying there dead, or was it at this time that the deed was done? Sergeant Hamilton hadn't mentioned the time of death.

Marla still wanted to follow the passage to find an outside exit from the hotel, but that could wait. The manager had absented the premises. If she could get into his office, she'd search for the hotel blueprints and any documents pertaining to its sale. Maybe she'd find other evidence as well.

"Please excuse me," she said to the duo, who appeared oblivi-ous to her presence. "I've got to meet my fiancé."

"Why, dearie," Wanda stated, breaking away from the doctor's groping fingers, "Is that gorgeous hunk helping the police?"

Halfway to the door, Marla paused. "He's a detective, so, yes, he's offering his input."

Wanda's blue eyes rounded. "Oh my, how dreadful that his va-cation is being disrupted. I don't suppose he's come across any-thing significant?"

You'd like to know, wouldn't you? Marla gave a smug smile. "We don't discuss business," she lied. "Besides, I'm just as glad he's occupied. I've been investigating my family history. Can you tell me why the two top levels of the tower are unoccupied? Those are the floors my grandparents lived in. Are these rooms not rented because they're haunted?"

"I dare say there have been reports of strange incidents."

"Yet the staff isn't afraid to go there. The place has been kept clean. So what's the real reason?"

Wanda exchanged a glance with the doctor. "Perhaps it's the guests who are shy of ghosts."

"Or perhaps the hotel is not free to rent those rooms."

The bird-watcher raked a hand through her ash-blond curls. "You'd best speak to Mr. Butler about your concerns."

"I intend to. Why do you come here so regularly?"

"As I said before, it's my favorite resort. Leading the tours helps me earn extra income. I'm saving for my island, you know. A place where I can be alone with my birds."

"Alone?" Angus blustered. "You said I'd come with you."

"Well, of course." Wanda smiled at him in a manner that reminded Marla of a hawk rather than a nightingale. "I meant the two of us." She turned to Marla. "Any luck discovering the old man's loot?"

"You mean Andrew's source of wealth? I'm beginning to believe it's a legend, nothing more. How do you know about it?"

"It's no secret, dearie. I've been looking for years. Finders keepers, isn't that the rule? There is this private island, you see, that I've had my eye on for my own. All I need is a few hundred thousand more. But I'm getting tired of putting myself at risk by—" She cut herself off.

Marla waited for Wanda to conclude her sentence, but the woman's expression changed to one of thoughtful speculation.

"I'll accompany you to the manager's office," Wanda suggested in a silky tone. "That is, if you want to ask him about the ghosts. He's the one who hired those silly spook chasers."

"Thanks, but I'll look for him later."

Exiting by the open office door, Marla halted upon confronting Brownie Butterworth, who'd obviously been eavesdropping. The pastry chef, caught unawares, jerked upright with a cry of dismay, whirled around, and ran outside.

Wanda, muttering an expletive, lurched after the chef's retreating figure.

Sensing this distraction would give her the opportunity she sought, Marla headed toward the manager's office in the main hotel building. Rochelle was nowhere to be seen. So much for the teen's compliance in watching for Butler's return. She'd probably left to go sunbathing with her friends. Teens didn't listen to warnings about skin cancer, a habit that would keep dermatologists busy in years to come, Marla reflected ruefully.

The administrative section was relatively quiet. Marla trod down a carpeted hallway, zipping past Champagne's suite in hopes that no one would notice her. Farther along, she reached a door labeled with Butler's name. After knocking gently, she twisted the knob when he didn't answer. It opened easily, which surprised her. If he had anything to hide, it seemed strange that he didn't secure his private domain very well.

Inside the room, she surveyed furnishings that might have remained the same since Andrew Marks had used them. A rolltop desk and swivel chair took up one entire corner. Facing the fireplace was a comfortable seating arrangement: a sofa, love seat, and armchair centered around a driftwood coffee table. Several more period pieces completed the ensemble.

Her gaze scanned the room for a computer and file cabinets, but these items were conspicuously absent. *That's odd*, she thought. Surely Butler used modern conveniences. Where was his telephone, or even a clock? This room appeared too much like a museum tableau, right down to the old-fashioned pen with an inkwell. Stacks of papers didn't even clutter his desk. Maybe he did his paperwork elsewhere, and this room was primarily for show. That meant she wouldn't find anything of significance here. No, he had to use another office, but could he access it from this one?

Roaming her critical eye along the walls, she stopped at the faint outline of a seam in the wood paneling. Was that a natural groove like the rest, or did it look like a door? Tracing her fingers around the rough edges, she failed to find a hidden lock mechanism similar to the one in Polly's room.

Wait a minute.

Dashing to the fireplace in Butler's office, she pushed aside the protective grating. A pile of logs took up space on the hearth, but ashes didn't darken the floor, and the rear panel looked much the same as it did in her aunt's room. Yes! Groping along the brick arch with shaking fingers, she discovered the expected hump and gave it a twist. Her ears picked up the sound of the latching mechanism as it clicked into the unlocked position, and she was able to push open the panel quite easily.

After a quick glance over her shoulder to make sure no one was approaching, even though she'd closed the office door, she scrambled through the opening into the passage beyond. A cool, musty odor tickled her nostrils. The walls felt damp, and she shivered as she heard a nearby scrabbling noise.

Retrieving a penlight from her purse, she shone it ahead into the tunnel. Spending her weekend in the dark wasn't how she'd envisioned this getaway with Vail, but the thrill of the hunt drove her forward. If Andrew had in fact occupied Butler's office, then this passage could lead to a significant find. After a few paces, the tunnel narrowed where a supporting beam sagged, and she had to crawl on her hands and knees, grimacing as her skin contacted sludge. She'd look a mess after this excursion.

After a few feet, the opening widened and branched into two directions. One seemed to lead back toward the main hotel. The other went the opposite way. Since the space was big enough for her to stand, she chose the latter and had just turned a corner when she tripped on a prominence and tumbled into a depression. No, not a depression—it was a flight of steps carved from limestone and leading downward. Recovering her balance, fortunately unhurt, she directed her light on the damp walls, which had a slick coating of mildew.

It wasn't long before she reached bottom. The space wasn't very deep, but a quick search and the alcohol-infused air told her its purpose. This had likely served as the main storeroom for Andrew's bootlegging operation. From the rows of bottles and kegs still unopened, she gathered that she'd found one of his stashes. Were these highly valued, like vintage bottles of wine? Open jugs lay about, their contents drained or long evaporated. The air smelled of rum, not wine or whiskey. But had they made this stuff on-site, or brought it in by boat? Because if the latter was true, there would have to be an exit to the outside nearby.

Clattering footsteps sounded on the stairs. Her gaze flew about looking for a hiding place, but it was too late. Harvey Lyle stumbled down the steps, catching her in the bright glare of his lantern.

"Well, lookee who we caught trying to plunder our treasure. This be mine, Missy. The boss said so hisself. Ya ain't supposed to be here." He swaggered toward her, his yellowish teeth gleaming.

"I'm your friend, remember?" she said, backing away. The steward stood between her and the stairs.

"Oh, so ya came to give ole Harvey what he's been after, eh? Let's see ya get nekked, then. Har, har." Snatching a bottle from a wood-plank shelf, he tipped its open end to his mouth and took a deep draft.

So this is where he gets his liquor, Marla thought, watching him smack his lips with glee. Switching off her penlight, she stuck it in her purse strapped to her shoulder. Her long metal nail file might come in handy, she figured, but not yet. Maybe she could talk her way out of this sticky situation.

"You can't blame me for searching for my grandfather's wealth. It's my legacy as his granddaughter. Or perhaps you've already found it. Are these bottles valuable?"

"Only to me. The boss lets me drink my fill. Couldn't get no job anywhere else, ya know. So I do what he tells me and he turns the other eye to my helpin' myself."

Butler probably encourages you so as to keep you in his pocket. "Seto Mulch was found dead. Did you have anything to do with his murder, or my aunt's?" Hoping to provoke him, she waited to gauge his reaction. Either he was a drunken flunky or an un-scrupulous killer. Sidling toward a rack of dusty bottles, she maneuvered herself to face forward while her hand snaked back to grasp one of the glass necks.

"I ain't no brute. Dunno who did the dirty work on old man Mulch, but I heard he'd been mouthing off in the wrong place. Mebbe one of the boys got to him. This is where Butler brings 'em in, ya know. Through that door there."

Marla glanced toward the dark corner.

"Don't ya be thinking about runnin' out on me." He leered at her. "Door only works to let folks in. Butler don't want none of the fellows gettin' away, ya understand. Now take off yer clothes, because I don't have all day. We'll do it real quick-like, then you'll stay here till I get off duty."

"I don't understand. What do you mean about Butler's boys?" She grasped the bottle, wondering if she should bash Lyle's head now or later.

"None of that coy stuff, Missy. I ain't no fool."

"You're right, but it's awfully damp in here," she said. "We could be a lot more comfortable in Butler's office on the couch. He's not around, so I doubt anyone would disturb us." She sashayed closer, tickling him under the chin with her free hand. "It'll be easier for me to please you that way. Look," she held up the bottle, "we can drink this together. I'll bet he has glassware somewhere in his office."

Ducking, she scooted past Harvey and scrambled up the stairs with him panting heavily behind her. At least this gave her a chance to escape without resorting to violence.

Once inside Butler's cozy domain, she pointed to the outline on the wall that traced the grooves in the wood paneling. "Is that an entrance? I don't see a computer or any storage space in this room."

Harvey unbuttoned his maroon staff jacket, underneath which he wore a sweat-stained undershirt. "Ain't no computer in there, honey buns. Watch this." Tossing his jacket onto the love seat, he tottered toward a bookshelf and shifted one of the volumes. The entire console rotated, exposing a computer station, fully stocked bar, and collection of CDs.

"Wow, I'm impressed." As though eager to proceed with their liaison, she gave Harvey a sly smile and loosened her shirt from her waistband. Her other hand still clutched the dusty rum bottle. "I still don't see any file cabinets."

"He keeps that stuff in the boardroom. That's what I call his private cellar. Can't barely make out the door, can ya?" Patting his pocket, he grinned. "I got me own key. Boring things, those walking sticks he collects. The boss gets his kicks from 'em, though. That's why he runs this little show. It's right weird, if ya ask me."

"What walking sticks?"

"Fancy canes, like gents used to carry."

They were playing a circle dance now, Harvey edging closer, Marla sliding sideways. She had to get access to that inner office. Harvey had just discarded his T-shirt, and Marla got a quick glimpse of his scrawny chest and wasted muscles.

Swallowing the bile rising in her throat, she approached him and ran her fingers up his arm. "Want to show me?"

"Ain't no business of yers what's in there, but this is."

As he slanted his mouth over hers, Marla grabbed a strand of his buckskin-colored hair and yanked his head back. "Wrong answer," she said, swinging the bottle at his head. Wincing at the impact, she was both mortified and grateful when he crumpled to the ground.

He might not be out for long. Kneeling, she fumbled in his pocket until she felt the cool touch of a key ring. That was only half the battle. Where could the keyhole be hidden? Before turning to that task, however, she needed to guard her rear. Crossing to the liquor bar, she opened a decanter and poured some whiskey onto the steward's chest, arranging props so it appeared as though he'd fallen in a drunken stupor.

Satisfied that if anyone walked into the room unexpectedly, they'd jump to false conclusions, Marla attacked the wall. She could lock the office door behind them, but Butler had left it unlocked, and she'd rather complete her business, get out, and leave things as they were. Her probing fingers found a gap in the paneling that was evident on close examination. Sorting through the key ring, she found a key with the appropriate shape, inserted it, and was gratified to hear a clicking noise. She pushed the door open easily and entered a windowless space with a single light switch.

File cabinets lined the entire opposite wall, but that wasn't what caught her eye. Glass cases extended from floor to ceiling on either of two sides, and in them was a collection of the most unusual walking sticks she'd ever seen. Not that she'd seen many, but these took her breath away. Each one bore a label giving its origin, description, and price. Marla's eyes bulged at the numbers. That silver-handled German cane made in 1890 sold for $7,500. Next to it rested an ebony shaft topped with a carved ivory dog's head for $5,500. A jeweled cane with enamel cloisonné from Russia listed its price as $6,000. Exotic wood, horn, bronze, silver, and gold decorated intricately carved handles, some from rare materials such as tortoiseshell.

She scanned cases containing walking sticks with amber knobs, with silver collars on ebony shafts, with rams-horn crooks and painted porcelain handles. Did Butler keep more of these things at home? If so, his collection would be worth a considerable amount. And he'd need extra income just to make new purchases.

Hey, this couldn't be Andrew's treasure trove, could it?

She peered into a case containing antique canes that concealed a variety of items: syringes and blood-drawing needles, attack blades that shot out from handles, painter's brushes, barber's razors, full-length swords, inkstands, and even a ruler. Some of the more recent models made her conclude this was Butler's stash, not Grandfather's.

Discovering the manager's private collection wasn't her purpose in coming here, however. She had to look through his papers. Reluctantly, she headed to the wall of file cabinets and debated which drawer to open first. A few random attempts left her frustrated when she found nothing relating to the property sale nor the blueprints.

Wait a minute. If he really wanted to hide something from sight, wouldn't he secure it inside one of those hollow shafts? Surely some of the antique canes had been used to transmit vital information. The display cases were locked, though, so it didn't appear as though searching his walking sticks was a viable plan. Instead, she began a methodical search through the files, growing excited when she came to a section holding legal records.

Oh yes. A chill crawled up her spine when she spied a folder labeled DEED. Inside were copies of documents pertaining to the transfer of property. Quickly scanning through the sheaf of papers, she didn't come across anything singling out the penthouse levels. It appeared to be a clear and undisputed transfer of property from Ruth Marks to the current hotel owners. Her grandmother's signature looked smudged, but there it was, clear as day.

Disappointed, she rustled through the rest of the documents until her glance caught on a brown-edged, well-worn stack of drawings at the bottom. Finally, she'd struck pay dirt. Her gaze widened as she unfolded a construction plan for the hotel. The secret passages were outlined just as blatantly as the public rooms, and so was the actual thirteenth floor.

So. Butler definitely had access to Andrew's former speakeasy. Had he already found her grandfather's loot? Was that how he could afford all those expensive antique walking sticks?

Rumbling voices from the corridor made her quickly stuff the papers back in the drawer and shut the file cabinet. She rushed to exit the inner sanctum, barely having time to close its door and leap behind the sofa before George Butler barged inside his office.

Chapter Seventeen

"I have work to do," George Butler announced. Crouched behind the sofa, Marla heard him thunk down a stack of papers on his desk. "I can't be bothered with this right now. Take it up with Miss Glass."

"She's not in her office."

Marla's pulse leapt into her throat. That whiny voice belonged to her irksome cousin, Rochelle.

"Ask the front desk to locate her," the manager ordered.

"Aren't you worried about why the police want to question people? I mean, you'd think it would be bad for business."

"Young lady, may I suggest you enjoy your vacation and let me get on with my job?"

"I mean, like, it's bad enough that my great-aunt Polly kicked the bucket while staying at your hotel. I can't imagine what kind of publicity that will generate when word gets out. Stay at Sugar Crest and join the spirits? This place is spooky enough, if you ask me. Just take a ride in the tower elevator."

"People want to believe in ghosts, so they exaggerate events to make them more exciting. You'd be surprised how quickly stories spread."

"Oh yeah? I think it's so cool how you hired those ghostbusters. Watching them act, like, so serious makes this haunted-resort thing seem real, doesn't it? Very clever."

Marla had to give her cousin credit for this intelligent observation. While Rochelle was distracting the manager, she realized it gave her the opportunity to slip from his office unnoticed. Darting to the love seat, she merely had to round the armchair to reach the door, which had been left partially ajar.

"What's this?" the manager snarled. "I didn't leave my computer station open."

While his attention was diverted, Marla scampered out and into the hallway, hiding behind a near corner to continue eaves-dropping.

"Maybe one of your ghosts got in here," Rochelle offered. Then, "What's that smell? It's coming from over there. . . . Omigod, it's a dead man. The ghost is for real!" The teenager must have bolted for the door because soon Marla heard her streaking down the corridor. At the corner, Marla shot out a hand and grabbed her by the elbow, yanking her into a recess.

"Dammit," they heard Butler complain, "Lyle is drunk again, the idiot. He probably hit the switch for the turnstile accidentally. Look at that mess. I'll kill him myself."

"Rochelle," whispered Marla, "take a chill pill. Harvey isn't dead. I knocked him over the head with a bottle."

Her cousin's wide eyes took in Marla's disheveled state. "Marla, I saw you heading in this direction. When I spotted Mr. Butler in the parking lot, I tried to keep him away."

"You did well, cuz. You bought me enough time to escape." She'd done her cousin an injustice and now regarded her in a newly respectful light. Releasing the young woman's arm, which clinked with a tangle of silver bracelets, Marla surveyed her denim shorts, tank top, and sandals. Instead of playing at the beach, the girl had done her job as lookout.

"Where is Detective Vail?" Rochelle asked, tucking a strand of highlighted brown hair behind her ear. "We should tell him you're safe."

Marla gave her an affectionate smile, no longer considering

the teen competition for Vail's regard. "Let's go find him. Have you heard about Seto Mulch?" She told Rochelle the news.

"Oh no. You mean two people have been murdered?"

"That's right, since Polly didn't die from old age or illness. But I want you to promise that you won't say anything to our relatives. I'm not completely sure they're all innocent."

Rochelle's eyes rounded. "You suspect one of us?"

Leading the way outside, Marla hastened to reassure her. "Not necessarily, but the police will want to question everyone, and it's best not to reveal what we know."

"Oh, I get it. So if someone blurts how awful it is that Polly was done in, we'll know they're guilty."

"Something like that," Marla agreed.

As soon as they reached the main lobby, Marla dialed Vail's cell phone number.

"Are you free yet? I just discovered a storeroom behind the manager's office. Before I conked him on the head, Harvey told me that's where Butler brings his boys in. Wait, don't interrupt. I want to follow the tunnels to see if they lead there. Oh, and I found the papers for—"

"What tunnels?" Rochelle said, eagerly listening.

"Be quiet a minute, will you?" Over the phone, Vail's curt voice hushed Marla. "I followed up on what you said about Donna Albright. Let's meet, and I'll tell you about it."

"It's getting late, and we have to change before dinner. I'll see you back in our room. We were supposed to meet there at six anyway," she said, noting it was nearly five-thirty. "By the way, Rochelle's here, and she tipped me off that Butler had returned. I was in his office, so she saved me from being discovered. We owe her one."

"That's great. See ya." *Click.*

"What did he say?" Rochelle eagerly awaited Marla's answer.

Marla patted her arm. "He's very grateful for your help. I don't want to keep you from your friends any longer. They're probably waiting for you on the beach." Impatient to leave, she took a step backward.

Rochelle's face fell. "Can't I come with you?"

"Not now, honey. Dalton and I have a lot to discuss. It will be safer for you if you stay with your group. I'll look for you at the pool party later. Thanks again for everything."

Vail wasn't ready to talk when he pushed into their room an hour later. Marla had already taken a quick shower and blown out her hair. She sat in her underwear on their bed, Polly's stack of letters in her lap.

He glanced at her, his face flushed and sweaty. "I'm going into the bathroom. Be with you shortly." Dumping the contents of his pockets on the bureau, he tossed his perspiration-stained shirt and pants on the floor and marched into the lavatory. She noticed he hadn't removed the ankle holster he wore holding his spare weapon.

She had so much to tell him that for a moment, she considered skipping the family dinner. Biting her lower lip, she stared at the fireplace and wondered when they'd be able to explore the passages again. How did she know someone wasn't behind there now, ready to listen in on their conversation?

Jumping off her perch, she proceeded to the recess and twisted the stone that unlatched the panel. A quick glimpse inside the dank darkness showed her no one was present. Tempted to explore on her own, she held herself back when a chill curled around her neck like a beckoning tendril.

Pounding the stone, she watched with relief as the panel shut. The cold dissipated, but not her sense of unease. She spun around, heading for the closet to select an outfit for that evening. She chose a conservative pair of khaki slacks and a burgundy sweater. After dressing, she was approaching the bed when she noticed a paper lying on the floor. Had that been there earlier? Shaking her head, she decided it must have dropped from Polly's pile that she'd thrown aside in her haste to check the fireplace.

Hearing the shower turn off, she grabbed the paper and flopped onto the bed, where she could read in comfort. But this was no letter, she noticed, unfolding it with care. It was a promissory note indicating that the bearer owed Polly the sum of twenty-five thousand dollars.

"Dear Lord," she whispered, squinting at the signature. *Michael Shorstein.* Her brother had borrowed money from their aunt. So this was where he'd gotten his loan.

She felt ashamed at her next thought. Did he have to repay the loan now that Polly was dead?

Wondering if anything else of significance was stuffed between the letters, Marla fanned out the documents. Another item stood out, lacking the browned edges of Polly's letters. Marla slid this from the bundle and opened it slowly, her eyes widening as she scanned the contents.

Vail entered just as her jaw gaped in surprise. "What's the matter?" he said, pausing in the act of towel-drying his hair.

"You won't believe what I just found. Oh gosh, sit down." She flicked her glance at him, dressed only in his boxer shorts. "It's a copy of Polly's will. If this is valid, she leaves everything to me. It's fairly recent, too."

He reached her in two steps. "Let me see." He flipped through the document, several pages long. "Looks legit. It gives the lawyer's name if you want to look him up when we get home. He may have the original."

She gazed into his clear gray eyes. "Should I tell Ma?"

"If you think it would put her mind at ease. So these are Polly's letters. Have you looked through them all?"

"Hardly. I keep getting interrupted." Her glance dropped to his chest. "Maybe you'd like to put a shirt on. I can't concentrate when you're half naked. Want me to blow out your hair?" She itched to run her fingers through his silken strands.

"No time," he said, rustling through the drawer where he'd laid his clothes. "Remember I said I spoke to the councilwoman? She admitted that Jeffrey Levine was one of her campaign donors."

Marla frowned, her hands bunching the bedspread. "Jeff said he thought the hotel should be restored to its former glory when I first met him on the grounds. This afternoon, he said it should be torn down. If he's supporting Albright, then he was lying initially." She shifted her position, watching Vail button his blue dress shirt.

"Why would he even care what happens to the resort?"

"That's a good question. Mulch accused Brownie of spying for someone. I think it was him. The old guy was talking to this person on the phone and said, 'I know who you are.' "

"How well do you know your cousin's husband?"

"He comes from a wealthy family. Heir to a toothpaste fortune, I believe, along with a sister."

"So money wouldn't be a motive. He must have another reason for wanting the place torn down."

"Maybe he hopes to invest in the theme park. It could be Jeff, and not Bruce, who's pushing his interest in the new venture."

"But you told me Cynthia's husband admitted he'd like to participate in a living-history experience."

Marla uncrossed her legs and stretched. "Why else would Jeff care what happens here?"

"Old secrets will remain buried if the hotel is destroyed."

"Or they'll be revealed," she said, thinking of skeletal remains. She filled him in on the letters she'd read so far.

"No kidding." His eyebrows lifted. "You're a descendent of Russian royalty?"

Her lips curled in a cynical smile. "Like it matters today. Do we have time to read more?" She'd already applied her makeup, so she just needed to put on her jewelry for the finishing touches.

"We can be a little late. Go on, what's next?" After belting his trousers, he settled on the bed, rubbing her neck.

Marla opened the next envelope in order of date and began reading:

Dearest Vincent,

Mama told me the most shocking news about Papa's death. She believed Aunt Esther and Uncles Joseph and George may have been responsible because they had been devastated by his disclosure. They feared he might soil our family name by revealing his true origins. Horror of horrors. What if he and Mama weren't truly married since he used a false name on their marriage certificate?

Uncle Joseph has been particularly incensed, calling Papa all sorts of names. Andrew wasn't even Jewish, for heaven's sake, but a royal Russian liar who'd stolen a poor peasant's identity. Uncle Joseph said our names would be dirt. Our family would be shamed and our businesses shunned. How could he pull such a deceit over our family?

She glanced up, studying Vail's reaction. He had a thoughtful look on his face.

"So Ruth suspected my great-aunt and great-uncles of hastening Andrew's death so he wouldn't disgrace the family name? Could that be what caused the rift between them?"

"That seems a lame reason, but, then, people have been known to commit murder for less. I suppose the truth could have stained your family's reputation. When did this happen?"

"In 1943. I would expect the war took precedence in those days. Hey, listen to this."

Mama explained to me how Papa's guilt about pretending to be a Jew led him to help the caravan that escaped from Hitler. He brought the boatload of Jews in through Mexico, hid the men in the former speakeasy, and transported them up north. It's likely he used the gems to fund the operation. I've long suspected those two men who came to see him were Nazi agents, not long-lost relatives of the Pole whose identity he'd stolen, nor Russians seeking to recover the alexandrite stones. They'd worn Cossack hats to fool him.

"Andrew helped Jews escape from Germany," Marla said in an awestruck tone. "That's amazing. He had his own version of the Underground Railroad. The secret passages were ideal. He wouldn't have wanted his neighbors to get wind of his activities. If word got out, his friends abroad would have been endangered. He had to have a network of people working with him. Maybe his friends were caught, and that's how the Nazi agents found Andrew. They came here to stop him, not to find the jewels."

"What jewels?"

She jabbed a finger at him excitedly. "Alexandrite stones. Aren't they extremely valuable? That's what Andrew brought to this country from Russia."

Vail rolled off the bed to pace the room in his bare feet. "I saw those gems once in a natural history museum. They fascinated me because alexandrite changes color. It looks grayish-brown in dim light, but in bright daylight, it turns green. And it's red under incandescent lighting. As I recall, red and green are the Russian royal colors, and the stones are named after Czar Alexander the Second. Mines in the Ural Mountains have long been closed, so gems from there are pretty rare today. Modern alexandrite comes from Brazil and elsewhere, but it's still expensive. One of the stones I saw in the museum was valued at eighty thousand dollars."

"I wonder if the gems belonged to my grandfather's family, or if he took them from the royal treasury."

"Who cares? I can see why people want to find them. Even one stone would be worth a great deal."

"Andrew may have spent them all, building the hotel and then helping those refugees escape."

"That must be why Polly returned here year after year. She hoped Andrew hadn't depleted his entire nest egg."

Marla nodded. "I gather Grandmother moved the family to the twelfth floor after some incident involving Vincent, but it's likely Polly believed any remaining gemstones lay hidden among her father's belongings. From Jasmine Hall she had easy access to the penthouse level."

"You said his furnishings were untouched?"

"Right." She wagged a finger. "I'll bet Ruth preserved everything because she was searching for the stones, and that's why Polly thought they must still exist. To my knowledge, no one's discovered Andrew's humidor yet. Maybe that's where he hid them."

A lock of hair tumbled across Vail's forehead, giving him a rakish look. Marla resisted the temptation to fix his unruly locks and instead unfolded the next sheet.

I don't know what Papa said to those men to make them leave, and Seto won't tell me. Aunt Esther guessed Papa might have given them the remainder of the stones as a bribe to chase them away, but I think Seto had a hand in it somehow. He didn't speak to me for days afterwards, and you know that's unlike him. You were always jealous of the attention the dear man showed me, but you need not have feared losing my devotion. I should have been afraid of losing yours, although not for the reasons Mama said. She accused you of marrying me because you expected me to inherit Papa's money, but when you realized Ruth had everything and the gemstones were gone, you lost interest. I know this isn't true, because we were so much in love. It's I who've hurt you. If I had satisfied your needs like a proper wife, you wouldn't have lusted after Agnes. When I heard her cries and caught you in her bedroom, I felt a terrible sense of guilt. You wouldn't have assaulted her if I'd been better in bed. My darling sister suffered from my failures. I should have realized it was my fault instead of screaming at you like I did. Will you ever forgive me? Please, please come back, and we'll make things right.

Your loving wife, Polly

"Sounds like Polly's husband was a skunk who hoped to become rich through their marriage, and when he saw that wouldn't happen, he assaulted her sister just for kicks." Vail's eyes smoldered.

"What an awful man. From her previous letters, I gather Vincent ran out on her afterward. Polly blamed herself, but I imagine she eventually got a divorce." Shuffling through the letters, Marla was gratified to spot a couple of other legal documents. One was Polly and Vincent's original marriage certificate. The other included a codicil to Polly's will.

"Oh my," Marla exclaimed upon reading the terms. Straightening her spine, she peered at Vail. "This cancels my brother's loan in the event of her death."

"What loan?"

She averted her gaze, studying the leafy pattern on the bedspread. "Michael lost money when the stock market plunged. He had to borrow to pay back his clients. I found the promissory note he'd made to Polly. He told me about it earlier, and he said he had a plan to fix things."

"You don't suppose—"

"No, Michael wouldn't. I'll bet he didn't even know Polly made this codicil. Let's go talk to him. He'll be at the luau."

"Better take those with you," Vail said, indicating the documents. "Someone has access to these rooms. Maybe it isn't Andrew's treasure they're looking for."

Marla slid off the bed and proceeded to the dresser, where she'd laid out her jewelry. Putting her diamond studs in her ears, she considered his suggestion. "Suppose somebody is looking for Polly's letters. Who else knows they exist?"

"Didn't you tell your family about them?"

"I can't remember. It might not be the letters they're after anyway."

"That leaves the will, codicil, and marriage certificate."

A startling idea crossed her mind. "What if Polly never divorced? Wouldn't Vincent be entitled to half her estate?"

"I don't think so. She could have made a case against him for abandonment. Besides, she clearly leaves everything to you in her will. Aren't her bank accounts in both your names?"

"That's right, but Polly has some additional assets that will fall under her estate."

"You can let the lawyers deal with it."

Marla was grateful he didn't ask how much Polly's estate was worth. She wasn't quite sure herself, when it all added up. She didn't want to think about that now. Losing her aunt was still a fresh wound. "I wonder if she ever found Vincent again. Maybe the rest of these letters will tell us."

"We don't have time right now." He gestured. "We're late already."

Gathering her purse, Marla stacked the papers together with a fresh rubber band and was about to stuff them deep inside her purse when she stopped. "You know, it might be safer to put these somewhere else."

On his way to the door, Vail halted to glance back at her. "Why?"

"No one will mess with your stuff. You take them."

He gave her a suspicious glare, as though pondering the different ways she might lose possession of her handbag. "There's always the hotel safe."

"Yeah, right. That would give George Butler carte blanche to acquire them."

"I can't imagine why he'd be interested in your aunt's papers," Vail said dryly in a tone that implied otherwise.

"Oh, I forgot to tell you. I had a look around his office while he was out. I found the sale documents for the resort property, and it appears Ruth sold the place outright, with no strings attached. So there goes my theory about my family retaining part ownership of the resort. Butler also has a set of blueprints that show the secret passages and thirteenth floor."

"Interesting." Vail took the bundle of Polly's letters. "We'll put these in my car." On the way to the elevator, he said, "You'd mentioned something about a storeroom?"

"Butler's office, which I suspect may have been Andrew's initially, has a secret entrance to the passages. It leads to a storeroom with an exit outside. I gather this was where the rum was stored during bootlegging days. Customers came by boat, were let inside, then followed the tunnels to the speakeasy. I suppose this is the same route Andrew used to smuggle in the Jewish refugees. They could have been transported across the Gulf from Mexico."

She pushed aside her thoughts as they approached the pool after detouring by Vail's car to lock the letters in his glove compartment. Sounds of laughter, clanging dishes, and steel-band music drifted her way as she padded along the crushed-shell path to the festive dinner. Party lights were strung among the lit globes, whose posts were decorated with colorful leis. Beyond a congregation of chattering guests, a long buffet table stretched, laden with filled steamer trays. Delicious smells permeated the air: barbecued chicken; roasted sweet potatoes; fried plantains; warm, buttery bread; and apple pie. Marla's mouth watered as she greeted her relatives, most of whom sat with plates in their laps and grease on their lips. Couples danced in a section of the pool deck cleared of lounge chairs. An open bar to the side was doing brisk business.

"Marla, where have you been?" Anita chided her, a bright smile on her face. Her white hair looked a bit limp, and Marla decided she could use a bit more layering. Again, the notion that a salon should be on-site rose to mind.

"We've been making some interesting discoveries," she told her mother in a low voice.

"Really? Tell me about them later. Aren't the kids adorable?" Anita waved at her grandchildren, Jacob and Rebecca.

Marla hastened over to greet Michael and Charlene. Anxious to confront her brother, she got caught in a swirl of cousins and didn't get the chance until everyone had mellowed from too many rum punches and bellies full of food.

Relaxing for the first time all day, Marla lay on a lounge chair next to Vail, letting the tropical drink potion erase all problems while a gardenia-scented breeze caressed her skin. Stars in the night sky twinkled at her as she peered toward the ocean, trying in vain to distinguish the horizon and wishing she could make sense out of recent events.

Rochelle skipped into view, giggling with her crowd of friends, and Marla signaled her over. "You should thank my cousin for keeping watch like you ordered this afternoon," she addressed Vail. "She helped me get out of Butler's office unnoticed."

The detective's angular face eased into a smile. "Remind me to pin you with a deputy's badge, young lady," he said. Reaching for Marla's hand, he squeezed her fingers.

She squeezed back, then let go. She'd just spotted her brother Michael alone for the first time that evening. After excusing herself, she sauntered to the bar, where he had just ordered another drink, one too many, in her opinion.

"Michael, can I have a word with you?" she said.

His brown eyes met hers quizzically. "Sure, what's up?"

He looked so carefree, she almost hated to ask him. "Were you aware Aunt Polly's death canceled your loan?"

Chapter Eighteen

"What do you mean?" Michael said, gripping his gin and tonic.

Marla ushered him away from the bar, where others might overhear their conversation. "You borrowed money from Aunt Polly. Was this how you repaid your clients?"

He glared at her. "What if it is? I mentioned to Polly that I had a problem, and she offered me the solution. It's not as though I asked her for a loan."

"Polly's dead. Murdered. And according to a codicil she wrote, you don't have to repay her."

His face contorted with astonishment. "She died in her sleep, and I don't know about any codicil. I sold some stuff on eBay, so I've started to send her monthly checks. I planned to repay her in full."

"Don't you see how this looks? Aunt Polly didn't die a peaceful death. Someone smothered her. And suddenly you don't have to come up with twenty-five thousand dollars anymore."

Michael took a large gulp of his drink. "Y-you know I wouldn't harm anyone. Tell me you believe me."

His earnest face erased her doubts. With sisterly affection, she patted his arm. "Of course I do, but I hope you have some sort of alibi." Had Vail mentioned the time of death? "Promise me you won't say anything about this. It's not common knowledge how Polly died, and we'd best keep things quiet for now. Since the groundskeeper turned up dead, the investigation will get more intense."

He tilted his head. "Why are you getting involved? You're supposed to be on vacation. I gather you and Dalton are helping the cops."

Marla shrugged. "I owe it to Aunt Polly. No one else cared enough about her, and we were just getting close. I feel like she'd want me to find out what's going on. We have a few leads, but not the links that tie them together."

"Well, let me know if I can help." He shuffled his feet, as though their sudden intimacy embarrassed him.

"I will." She winced at the sight of Anita bearing down on them. "Here comes Ma. You deal with her. I want to talk to Bruce about his interest in the theme-park development."

She didn't corner Cynthia's husband until later that evening. Distracted by her cousins, she got caught up in their discussion on water conservation while the hours flew by. After her relatives dispersed, she headed to the campfire in a clearing by the sugar mill ruins. *Perfect place for ghost stories*, she thought, waving at one of Spector's teammates in the distance. Remembering the report of a vortex by the chimney stack, she resolved to revisit the crumbling stones during daylight.

While Vail collected their skewers and allotted bag of marshmallows, Marla basked in the heat from the crackling fire. The aroma of rich humus mingled with pine to scent the cool air as she listened to the chitter of night creatures. In the background, the rhythmic music of waves kissing the beach created an ongoing symphony.

Unwilling to be lulled into tranquillity, she veered toward Bruce, who'd plopped onto a wooden bench, one of many set in a semicircle around the fire. "Hey, cuz," she yelled to Cynthia, who was already engaged in a heated dialogue with Joan and Julia. Marla looked for Lori, but didn't see her or Jeff anywhere.

Brow wrinkled in worry, she forced herself to focus on her task at hand.

"Bruce," she said to the tall man, whose height gave him a permanent stoop, "I wanted to ask you something. Have you reconsidered your position regarding the living-history experience?"

He ran stiff fingers through his black spiky hair. "I'm still in favor of the sale if the original plantation is restored properly, with care to preserving the environment. I think it would be valuable for our Florida heritage to rebuild the sugar mill complex."

"Do we really need another theme park, though?"

"A new attraction will bring jobs to the area."

"Oh, like there aren't enough construction workers here already?"

His eyes narrowed as he regarded her, as though wondering at her persistence. "Why do you care?"

"Butler wants the hotel restored to its former glory," she said, answering indirectly. "Cousin Jeff, on the other hand, favors tearing it down. He's been adding money to Albright's campaign coffers. Any idea what his angle might be?"

Bruce's winged eyebrows lifted. "That's news to me. Don't get me wrong, Marla. I love this place. Sugar Crest resonates with history, but Florida doesn't have a living-history museum where people can experience what it was like in the early plantation days. This is the ideal location."

"Have you been to St. Augustine? They didn't tear down the fort and rebuild it so people could experience fake battles. Work out a compromise. Isn't family history more important than your land development schemes? My grandfather owned this place. It's part of our heritage. Respect the hallowed ground on which it was built. Remodel the hotel, and open the top floors to the public."

Bruce grinned, his eyes reflecting the light from the shooting flames. "You present a mean argument. I'd forgotten about those Indian burial mounds. They may have archeological significance."

"So you haven't talked to Jeff about this at all?"

"Nope. He's got money, so maybe he's looking for a good investment. I understand he's due to inherit a fortune some day. He and Lori may want to retire to the Gulf Coast and look upon this as their haven. They vacation over here a lot."

"I'm not so sure that's why Jeff is endorsing the councilwoman's goals. Anyway, thanks for listening. I hope you'll consider what I said."

"I will." He nodded solemnly.

She spotted Vail waving to her. A few steps later and she was at his side. "What's up?" she asked, taking the bag from him and stuffing a marshmallow into her mouth.

He handed her the skewers. "I know you want to spend time with your family, but I'm really beat. Would you mind if I turned in early? Usually I can roll with the punches, but it must be all this sea air."

His eyes did look bleary, she noted, although his fatigue might be due to avoidance behavior rather than lagging energy. He'd probably had enough polite conversation for one day. "Go ahead," she said with an indulgent smile. "I'll be quiet when I enter the room."

He kissed her. "You're a peach."

She missed him when the evening swung into full gear with sing-alongs, charred, gooey marshmallows, and spooky tales that tickled the hairs on her nape. She glanced over toward the beach, where dancing lights caught her eye. Blinking, she looked again but this time saw nothing but yawning blackness.

Letting her curiosity lead her, she edged away from the crowd. Most likely, her imagination had been stimulated by tonight's stories and she'd discover nothing more than the pulsating tide and no-see-ums looking for warm-blooded food stock. Yet . . .

"Marla, you're not leaving, are you?" Champagne Glass's crystal voice rang out. The social director, in charge of their evening event, hobbled toward her in a pair of high-heeled sandals.

"I want to take a walk along the beach before I go to bed." Marla didn't slow her pace.

"I wouldn't advise going there tonight. The bugs are atrocious. You'll get eaten alive."

"I've sprayed myself with insect repellant. Don't worry about me. I won't be gone long."

Champagne's eyes glistened in the moonlight. "You won't be able to see the jellyfish in the sand. It isn't safe."

Is that the only reason you don't want me to go there? "All right," Marla lied, "I'll just head back to my room from this direction. Creatures of the night hold little appeal for me."

Crickets sang their ritual chorus as she plodded along a winding path toward the beach. Crossing through a brief stretch of pines that hid her from view of the campfire, she hoped it was true that bats ate mosquitoes and tried not to think of the possibility of the flying mammals using her hair as a landing site. Strange cries echoed through the hammock, and then she saw another waving light, this time coming from a window high in Oleander Hall. Underfoot, spongy pine needles gave way to firm sand as she neared the dunes.

A low murmur rose above the swell of the waves. Keeping well behind the mounds covered with sparse grass and sea oats, Marla let her ears guide her. As she continued on a route parallel to the ocean, she found herself nearing the condemned wing, where a babble of voices drifted on the wind.

Suddenly two forms dashed into sight directly in front of her. Ducking behind a dune, she watched each man topple to the ground in a limp heap. Someone else ran up, pointing an object in his hand. George Butler. Had he shot them? At his forceful gesture, several hefty fellows arrived and carried the pair away.

Marla's jaw dropped when she saw where they were heading: not to Oleander Hall, but to a door in the wing that could only lead to the storeroom behind Butler's office. Daring to peek over the rise, she felt her heart leap into her throat. Small boats lined up on the beach, spilling out dozens of men. She could barely discern the lights twinkling on a larger vessel farther out to sea.

Who were these guys, and what were they doing there? Where had that ship come from?

Wanting to learn more, she scuttled to the next dune. Her skin itched from insect bites, but she ignored the discomfort, wishing she had a pair of binoculars. The thought of binoculars reminded her of Wanda Beake. She hadn't seen the bird-watcher in a while. But that didn't mean Wanda wasn't involved in this operation, whatever it was.

Swatting away a bug that brushed her cheek, Marla licked dry lips. If only she had a camera that took pictures in the dark. Wait, Spector might be able to help her. Or was he part of this, acting to create a smoke screen under the manager's pay?

After each boat unloaded, its sole remaining crew steered the craft back toward the mother ship beyond the waves. Meanwhile, on shore, a brawny man waving an object in his hand ordered the disgorged passengers to fall into place. The scruffy individuals snaked toward the hidden entrance to the hotel, moving like silent wraiths through the shadows.

Another figure broke into a run and was quickly cut down. Two men quietly moved to cart him off.

Enough. Marla decided she'd learn what it all meant later. Right now she needed to get out of here before anyone spotted her.

She'd just sprung to her feet when a shout sounded from behind. A sharp sting burned her neck. She felt herself sliding to the ground but couldn't stop herself. Consciousness slipped away, and the last thing she felt was strong hands gripping her under the armpits and hauling her to oblivion.

Awareness seeped into her mind. She heard voices murmuring somewhere close. Her ears prickled as the sounds drew her to the surface. Feeling buoyant as a strand of seaweed, she floated toward the light, while a monotonous buzzing rose and fell like ocean waves.

She blinked her eyes open.

Darkness, interspersed by ghostly forms, surrounded her. Squinting, she made out draped furniture before her gaze fell on Wanda

Beake snoring beside her. They lay on a carpeted floor in what she surmised was Oleander Hall.

Dust tickled her nostrils. She wrinkled her nose, a sneeze threatening to erupt, but she managed to suppress it when heavy footsteps sounded nearby. A door crashed open. She snapped her eyes shut and regulated her breathing, her senses on alert.

"The woman still out. I give her another dart?" said a man with a heavy Hispanic accent.

"No, don't shoot her up yet." Butler's smooth answer sent chills up Marla's spine. "I'm not sure what I want to do with her. That cop boyfriend will get suspicious. We'll have to get rid of her soon, but in a manner that looks like an accident."

"He not be fooled, Senor. What about the other lady?"

"Wanda can stay here. Either she cooperates, or she's history. She knows the score, but I'll deal with her later. Let's get the boys processed."

"You want me to bind the women?"

"These windows are boarded. With the door locked, they can't go anywhere. Give our guest another half hour to come around, and then give her another dose. I don't want her too sedated. I'll think of some means of disposal before that wears off."

"Why not the water? It happens often."

"Hmm, a drowning at sea? We've had people go for a swim at night while underestimating the current. Yes, that's good. She'll even leave behind some clothing on the beach."

"You want me to do now? I will like removing this one's blouse. She have nice body."

"Later. Let's go."

Marla waited while the door slammed, the lock turned, and footsteps receded. Enough moonlight shone between the planks on the windows so that she could find her handbag when she shuffled around on all fours. She didn't find much else, certainly nothing she could use as a weapon. There weren't any lamps, heavy picture frames, or other loose objects.

Prodding Wanda, she hoped to rouse the woman enough to solicit her help. But the bird-watcher's snores merely increased in volume. Deciding to leave her behind wasn't easy, but Marla figured she could always bring assistance later.

She counted on Butler not being aware that she knew about the secret passages. Harvey Lyle wouldn't have wanted to incur his boss's displeasure by confessing Marla had seen the bootlegger's storeroom. So she approached the fireplace and inched her fingers along the cold stones supporting the arch, trying to focus her energy and squelch her nervous tremors at the thought of Butler's henchmen returning suddenly. One of the stones moved. Using the heel of her hand, she wedged it sideways.

Nothing happened.

No panel slid open, nor did she hear a latch clicking. Could she be wrong?

Her pulse throbbing in her throat, she pressed frantic thumbs on each stone to no avail. Then inspiration hit—she fumbled in her purse for her penlight. Thankfully, the contents of her purse remained untouched, and she found the penlight. Shining the small beam at an angle along the archway, she looked for protrusions. When that tactic failed to yield results, she turned the blue light to the back wall inside the fireplace. It was necessary to twist her body and turn her face upward to give it a full examination.

A crawly object fell on her cheek. With a sharp intake of breath, she brushed it away. Her body experienced a violent shudder. Losing balance, she tumbled sideways and hit the hearth, her sore shoulder connecting with something sharp on the way down.

"Ow," she cried, but her pain quickly receded when she heard a familiar clicking noise and the rear panel gave way. "Yes!" she muttered, tumbling into the tunnel. "At last, something is going right." Releasing the mechanism on the other side, she waited for the portal to close securely before illuminating the passage ahead. "Now, which way to go?"

Murmuring voices led her to a spiral staircase on her left. This wasn't the route she might have chosen, because her sense of direction told her the main hotel would be to the right. But another instinct told her to follow the sounds. Maybe her ghostly ancestors were drawing her that way, she thought.

Sparing a moment, she retrieved her cell phone from her handbag. Fortunately, it still had service, possibly because she stood near an outside wall. She dialed Vail's number.

He picked up on the first ring. "Where are you?" he demanded as though he'd been waiting by the phone.

"I'm in Oleander Hall. Do you want to meet me?"

He cursed, then: "Okay, how do I get inside?"

"Enter the tunnel from our room. Keep going down until you get to the lowest level, then pick a direction that takes you toward the main hotel. I'll join you around there."

"You're adding white hairs to my head, woman."

"We can fix that," she said, grinning in the near dark.

Five minutes later, she was creeping along the tunnel following louder, but real, voices on the third floor. *These passages must act like conduits to amplify sound,* she thought, pressing her ear against the wall. Spanish! She couldn't understand what the men were saying, but it didn't matter. Now she knew Butler used the condemned hall to house these guys who arrived by boat under cover of darkness.

This train of thought bore a germ of suspicion that erupted into conviction when she saw trailing wires and odd electronic devices.

"I get it," she murmured, almost tripping in her haste to reach Vail downstairs. She called him again to get a fix on his location. Using their cell phones like directional beacons, they met at an intersection on the ground floor.

"Dalton, there has to be a control room somewhere. I'll bet it's near Butler's office. This whole place is a fake."

His powerful form crouched in the narrow passage. "What are you talking about? And where's the exit?"

"Come with me. Remember I said there's a storeroom behind Butler's office that used to be where the bootleggers stashed

their rum? It has an outside door, and I'll bet we can reach it from
this end. Oleander Hall must have a way out, too, but we don't
want to risk running into Butler's gang there."

She told him how she'd ended up in the condemned section.

"Christ, Marla, you'll be the death of me yet. I can't leave you
alone for one minute before you get into trouble."

"Yeah, well, I don't look for it. It kinda finds me. Look at all
these wires fixed along the wall. We didn't notice them before."
She followed the cables until they reached a branch with a stairway curving upward to an apparent dead end.

"Now what?" Vail asked, pressing a hand to the small of her
back. "If my guess is right, going straight ahead will take us to
the administrative wing."

"That'll bring us to the storeroom. I'd hoped we could find
Butler's command station. He must have created the whole
show: sound effects, holographic images, and other tricks. Hiring
Spector's team was just a ruse. Don't you see? He's already created a theme park."

"Huh?" Vail looked at her as though she'd loosened a few
mental screws.

"The ghost stories, the sightings, even the bell ringing out by
the old sugar mill—Butler designed it all." Never mind the part
of her soul that wanted to believe in ghosts. Here was concrete
evidence that things were not as they seemed.

Vail touched her arm. "For what purpose? To increase business, because he thinks a haunted hotel would draw more
guests?"

"Partially. I also think it's a way of keeping people away from
the old wing. He scares them off with ghoulish tales and warnings that the building is unsafe. Truthfully, it doesn't look much
different than the rest of the place. No wonder he doesn't want it
torn down. That's the real source of his income, and he needs
extra money so he can add to his expensive walking stick collection, along with his retirement funds, I suspect."

She started up the unfinished staircase, with Vail in her wake.
"Explain," he ordered.

"During the war, Andrew smuggled in Jewish refugees, hid them on the resort property, then dispersed them up north. Assuming Butler knew the history of the place, I figure he converted this scheme to his own purposes. Instead of persecution victims, he boats in illegal aliens across the Gulf of Mexico. I heard the men speak Spanish, so that clinches it in my mind, along with the way they're treated."

She paused for a breath. "Butler houses them in Oleander Hall until he can sneak them off the grounds in the guise of construction workers. I'll bet he uses some of the guys as maintenance men at the resort and sends the others to labor camps. It could be quite a lucrative deal for him."

Vail's eyes gleamed. "I think you're onto something. And if he's running a smuggling operation, I'll bet your Aunt Polly found out about it."

Chapter
Nineteen

"We need more evidence," Vail said when they'd returned to their room for a strategy session. Their attempt to locate Butler's special-effects console had ended in defeat. "Did Butler kill Polly, or did that nurse's aide do the deed?"

"I think the aide was Wanda Beake in disguise," Marla said, lounging on the bed in her nightshirt. "She and Butler must have had a falling out."

"Do you think Wanda is in danger?"

"Not if she's smart and pretends to agree to Butler's plans. Maybe you can get her to turn witness."

"That may not be necessary. If we knew when those boats came in, we could set up a surveillance operation." Pacing the room, Vail plowed a hand through his peppery hair. "Or we can follow Butler when he takes those guys into town."

"Champagne said he gives the workmen a lift home, but that can't be true. He must transport them somewhere else. More people have to be involved."

Vail regarded her thoughtfully. "If you're right, we wouldn't want to tip their hand too soon. Approaching Wanda as a possible informant is a good move, but I'd also like to tail Butler when he leaves the next time."

"Why do you suppose the manager killed Seto? The old man

said he'd kept quiet out of respect for Polly. I'm not sure what he meant. Was Polly afraid it would ruin the hotel's reputation if they exposed Butler's scheme? Yet she tried to warn me that something was wrong." Her heart thudded into her throat. "You don't think . . . Polly was part of it?"

Her companion shook his head. "Nope. Your aunt might have had a loose socket, but I think she was guarding some other secret. We still have to figure that one out. Meanwhile, I'll notify the local boys about Butler when we have additional proof. All we've got at the moment are theories."

"How many staff members do you think are involved?"

"Could be all of them."

Marla tucked a strand of hair behind her ear. "I don't think Champagne understands the scope of things. She may keep herself ignorant on purpose to avoid getting sucked in. Dr. Angus, despite his claims to the contrary, probably gets paid to cover up the construction accidents as natural events."

She remembered the men who'd tried to run on the beach. They'd been shot down. Was death the punishment for attempting to escape? Or had they been hit by sleep darts like she'd been? But then what about the painter on his ladder?

She felt as though they were in over their heads when they followed George Butler in his van several hours into the morning. He'd loaded a crew of laborers to take into town. Except they didn't go into town; they headed off on a country road that led through orange groves into the boondocks.

"Where could he be taking them?" Marla asked, gripping her seat cushion as their car bumped over a rocky surface.

"We'll find out soon enough," Vail grated. He'd missed breakfast after catching only four hours' sleep. Butler had left at the crack of dawn, and the detective had been keeping watch. Recognizing his foul mood, Marla kept her thoughts to herself.

She had gotten dressed in time to observe the workmen filing into the manager's vehicle. They didn't appear to be the same ruffians who'd landed on the beach last night. Instead, she recognized some of the same guys she had seen before on the resort property. They must rotate, giving new arrivals time to get indoctrinated. Or to get their false identity papers ready. No wonder Sugar Crest had so many laborers.

Vail maintained a safe distance from the van in front that kicked up dust in its wake. They were heading east, judging from the sun on their windshield, although the rows of citrus trees on either side of the road blocked any perspective. A truck drove into view, coming straight at them, oranges piled high behind the cab. Vail veered out of its path, edging onto the shoulder, until it rattled past. Large tracts of land devoted to agriculture proved that urban development hadn't superseded Florida's rural origins. Plenty of space available for habitation remained. Marla hoped expansion wouldn't ever run the open range to ground.

"Look, he's turned into that driveway," Vail said. Passing by at a slow crawl, they read a sign for Parlay Farms. "This must be where he unloads his crew. I've never heard of the place, have you?" Without waiting for her reply, he pulled off the road beside a cluster of cabbage palms and cut the ignition. His stomach growled in the sudden silence.

"You must be hungry," Marla told him. "Want an apple? I stole one from the buffet yesterday. It'll give you some energy." Rummaging in her purse, she withdrew the piece of fruit along with a chocolate-chunk granola bar.

"We have to stop meeting like this," he said with a teasing grin as he accepted the snacks.

"Oh, I don't know. All this excitement turns on my engine."

"Yeah? I thought that was my job."

She suppressed a flare of desire. "Let's wrap up this weekend so we can go home already. What do you suppose Butler is doing? We can't just parade down there in the open. He'll spot us, and we don't have any backup."

Vail spoke between bites. "We'll leave the car parked out here, if you don't mind the hike. I'm not sure how far that driveway goes." He demolished his quick breakfast, dumping the apple core into the empty wrapper and storing it for later disposal.

Reaching into the backseat, he retrieved a 35mm camera. Then he pushed open his car door and got out.

Marla followed suit. "At least it isn't too hot yet," she said, listening to birds twittering in the still morning air.

"Don't talk too loudly out here. Our voices may carry," Vail warned.

They tramped along the cracked asphalt on the tree-lined drive. The cool temperature made her glad she'd worn a scoop-neck sweater with her jeans and canvas shoes.

As they proceeded toward a cluster of buildings, smells of bacon and toast reached her nostrils. Saliva pooled under her tongue. Their walk had already used up the calories she'd consumed from her nutrient bar earlier that morning. Careful to watch her footing, she trudged along the side of the road, remaining under cover of live oaks laced with Spanish moss. Gray tangles tickled her nose.

"Do you think the workers live here in some kind of dormitory?" she asked, figuring them for a migrant labor force.

"That depends on whether this is just a holding station or their final destination."

Marla didn't like that word, *final*. What happened to these people after the growing season ended? As they neared the farmhouse, her eyes widened. "Are those men holding guns?"

Vail's arm shot out, bringing her to a halt. "Get back."

She stood frozen, gawking at one of the workmen being dragged from the van, then beaten. Standing nonchalantly nearby, Butler conferred with a mustachioed man who muttered into a cell phone. When the fellow finished his call, the manager said something the other man appeared to dislike, gesturing wildly, spouting words Marla couldn't hear. Vaguely aware that Vail had extended his telephoto lens and was snapping photos, she craned her neck for a better view.

Butler accepted an envelope that the man thrust at him. More laborers filed from the van, lining up docilely for inspection by gun-toting foremen. All wore hats that shaded their faces, so Marla couldn't see their expressions, but their grungy clothes over muscular bodies made them look dangerous.

"Let's get out of here," she whispered. "Did you get enough pictures?"

"I think so. In any event, Butler is liable to return soon. He'll spot us on the road. We'd better cut through that cornfield."

Sawlike leaves hacked at her clothing as they retreated past the oaks to a dirt-packed trail lined with tall cornstalks. They'd walked for about five minutes when Marla noticed the direction of the sun had changed.

Wiping perspiration from her brow, she shaded her face to scan the path ahead. She couldn't see beyond the plants. "I don't think we're heading back to the road." Her skin itched, and her parched throat longed for a drink. A dunk in the ocean now would bring welcome relief.

Vail withdrew a pair of sunglasses from his shirt pocket and plunked them on his nose. "You're right. Let's try this way," he said when they came to an intersection.

They charged ahead, and suddenly the cornfield ended. In front of them were rows of tomato plants that offered no cover. Laborers bent to harvest the green fruits, and mean-looking henchmen ranged among them.

"Uh oh, we don't want to be here." Vail tugged Marla back into the cornfield.

"What if Butler finds our car parked by the road?" she said, urgency riddling her voice. She was hot, hungry, and craved a glass of water. Lost in the maze, they might get stuck there for hours. Stumbling over a piece of coral, she yelped when her foot agitated an anthill.

An answering shout came from behind, followed by a crack and a rush of air.

"They're shooting at us." Vail grabbed her arm and yanked her forward.

They careened around a corner. After a series of turns, Marla gasped when they reached a dead end. A perpendicular row of stalks faced them without a break in sight.

"Hold on, I know a trick that will help," Vail said. "Ever use your watch as a compass?" He squinted at his wrist dial. "Point the hour hand at the sun. Midway between that point and twelve o'clock on your watch indicates a south heading. Here, this should be the right direction," he said, gesturing.

Following his lead, Marla trudged down an alley between towering plants until they finally emerged onto the main road. She breathed a sigh of relief. Vail's car stood unmolested where they'd left it.

After he unlocked the doors and checked for booby traps, she crumbled into her seat. Her eyes closed when he turned on the ignition and a whoosh of air-conditioning blasted her chest. She barely had the strength to fasten her seat belt. Too exhausted to speak, she sank back against the cushions while Vail made a U-turn and headed west.

She heard him dial a number on his cell phone, ask for Hamilton, and in terse sentences explain what they'd observed. After a brief exchange, he hung up. Marla gave him a questioning glance.

"It'll take him some time to get warrants. He says to sit tight. In the meantime, we'll mingle with your relatives. Butler still might not realize how much we know, and there's always safety in numbers."

"But he caught me last night, and he'll realize I've escaped. He won't want me providing information to the cops."

"He didn't kill you outright, so he must have some other purpose in mind for you. I'm betting it relates to your family."

"Why? Because he still hopes to find Grandfather's loot? Why would he think I know something more than anyone else?"

"Maybe you do." He tilted his head. "You never finished reading Polly's letters."

Marla stiffened. "Oh yeah. Let's see what they say." She opened his glove compartment and withdrew the stack they'd put there for safekeeping. Then her phone rang, so she stuffed the packet into her purse to examine later.

"Hi, Ma," she said upon hearing Anita's lilting tone.

"Aren't you going to the outlet mall with us today, angel? I thought you wanted to go shopping."

"I'm kinda tired, so I think I'll relax at the resort. What's scheduled for later?" She didn't like to be herded, although today was her last day with the family. Everyone would be leaving tomorrow.

"Tonight's the seafood buffet, followed by dancing under the stars," Anita said. "Dalton told me he particularly wants to rock-and-roll with you in the moonlight."

Marla laughed. "You must be kidding. I have to pull him onto the dance floor."

"Well, you'd better be there," her mother ordered. "Don't get into any trouble while we're gone this afternoon. And save some energy for your honeymoon." Chuckling, Anita clicked off.

Marla gave Vail a doleful glance. "Ma probably thinks we're still in our room. She can't know how unromantic this weekend has been. I'm sorry. Next time we go away together, I promise nothing will interfere."

His searing gaze boosted her hormones. "I'll hold you to that, sweetcakes."

Hamilton was waiting for them when they arrived back at the resort. He commandeered Vail for a tour of the tunnels and posted a couple of his officers to keep a lookout for Butler. The manager hadn't yet returned. Marla suggested he might have gone home.

"We have someone watching his house," Hamilton said. His brusque tone indicated his displeasure at spending his weekend on duty. Or maybe he was just frustrated by the lack of evidence surrounding his cases. All he needed was for one witness to crack, Marla thought.

"Do you want me to look for Wanda?" she asked Vail. "She might respond to me better than a police interview, and I'd like to know she's safe."

He laid a hand on her arm. "You can either go to our room and make sure *all* the exits are secure"—he winked meaningfully—"or stay by the pool where people can see you. Don't wander off by yourself."

"It'll be lunchtime soon. You've hardly eaten all morning. You need something to fill your stomach." Playing the nurturer made her feel more in control.

"I'll worry about what I need, but I don't want to worry about you. Understand?"

"I could go with you."

"Why don't you get cleaned up and have a bite to eat yourself? Let me just show John what we've found behind the scenes, and then I'll join you."

Marla acquiesced without further argument, because she wanted to read the rest of Polly's letters. She couldn't concentrate until she'd showered and ordered a meal from room service, however. She didn't feel like dining alone in any of the restaurants or at the pool snack bar. One of her relatives might snag her and then she'd never get to Polly's packet.

She couldn't stay secluded in her room either, though. It was too beautiful outside. After downing her lunch—a chicken Caesar salad—and changing into black slacks, a turquoise top, and sandals, she packed her valuables into a large straw bag and headed outdoors.

The beach drew her with its fresh sea air, soothing swoosh of the waves, and sunbaked sands. Having doused herself with coconut-scented sunscreen, she settled onto a lounge chair and withdrew the letters. Her spot was isolated enough to give her privacy, yet within screaming distance of other patrons in case a threat materialized. Though she didn't think it would, not with the police patroling the grounds and rooting out Butler's associates.

Let's see, she thought, unfolding one of the parchment-thin papers. The last couple of letters had pointed out how Ruth believed the two strangers visiting her husband may have been Nazi agents, seeking to end his operation of smuggling Jewish refugees to safety. Either Andrew had bribed the men to get them to leave, or Seto had helped him dispose of them. Andrew had used the secret passages and former speakeasy as the hiding place for his persecuted friends.

Somehow, possibly through the original hotel blueprints,

George Butler had learned about Andrew's operation and used the idea to create a modern smuggling scheme. Where did Polly's involvement come in?

She scanned a couple of the previous letters to refresh her memory. Ruth suspected her siblings of hastening Andrew's death so he wouldn't ruin the family reputation. And this was because? Marla racked her brain while watching a pelican swoop after its prey. Oh yeah, Andrew had married Ruth under a false name. He'd stolen the identity of a Polish peasant and fled Russia during the Revolution. The alexandrite stones he'd brought with him had either belonged to his own royal family or been stolen.

Shortly before the two visitors wearing Cossack hats had shown up, Polly married Vincent. He'd been a fortune hunter who, disappointed when she didn't inherit riches from her father, had sought consolation with her younger sister. Caught in the act, he'd fled, never to return. Nor had Polly inherited a share in the plantation, according to the sale papers in Butler's office.

Her lips puckered. There wouldn't be any way of telling if Butler's document was a true copy of the original or not. If this wasn't what concerned Polly, what else had she been guarding so diligently?

Marla read the letter in her hand.

Vincent,

No dearest or darling, Marla noted, and this letter was dated months after the last.

I realize now that too much time has passed for us to mend things easily. I despair of finding you and have set the task upon Seto's shoulders to locate you. This he willingly does for me even though I know it pains him. Sometimes I feel like Alyssa must have felt, forbidden to love a man considered beneath her station. I might have looked toward Seto were he not one of our hired hands. But you captured my heart instead. Know this, Vincent. While I

*keep these letters for you, I have hired a private investiga-
tor. He will inform Seto of what he learns, who will in turn
tell me. I need to use him as intermediary so Mama doesn't
find out what I am about, or she'd cut off my allowance. I
am praying that you mean to return and are only waiting
for word from me to come flying back into my arms.*

Marla glanced up, squinting at the horizon through a pair of
dark sunshades. So Alyssa's tale had been real, not a figment of
Butler's imagination. Interesting, but irrelevant.

After skimming through several pages of brown-edged stationery wherein Polly never gave up hope of being reunited with
her only love, Marla withdrew a sheet dated years after Vincent
had disappeared.

In it Seto reported that the detective had found Vincent,
who'd died of pneumonia in the interim.

Heartbroken, Polly had continued to write to Vincent as
though he were still alive.

Wait . . . Seto had told Polly about Vincent's death. But what if
he'd lied to the woman he loved, who could never give him her
heart? Or at the very least, omitted part of the PI's report?

Someone at Sugar Crest felt threatened by Mulch, who'd said
over the phone, "I know who you are." Brownie spied for this
person. Who could it be, unless . . . ?

Connecting the links led her directly to the one individual
whose motives still eluded her.

Clang . . . clang. The hairs on her nape rose. Wasn't that the
slave bell by the old sugar mill? Twisting her neck, she glanced at
the other sunbathers, but no one seemed to notice the sound except her. *Don't be stupid, Marla. You can't go alone to the ruins again.
Remember what happened the last time?*

She'd stuffed her beach bag and was on her way before she
dialed Vail on her cell phone. "Where are you?" she demanded
when he answered on the second ring.

"I'm in Oleander Hall. We found Miss Beake, drugged but
quite unharmed. I think she'll sing like a bird once she's more

fully awake. We found a lot of other interesting stuff, too, up on the fourth floor." His jaunty tone showed his pleasure.

"Can you leave it for the local cops to handle? I'm heading over to the sugar mill. Meet me there. I think Mulch used to hang out with Alyssa's ghost for a reason." She cut him off before hearing his protest.

If she was right, she'd soon find the answers to most of her questions. Marla only hoped the wrong person hadn't gotten to them first.

Chapter Twenty

Marla followed the sound of the tolling bell toward the crumbling stone walls set among creeping vines and veils of Spanish moss. She veered around a long dried-up well, now a pit coated with slime-covered chunks of rock and holding layers of dead leaves instead of water. Past the cistern that collected rainwater, she saw a stone arch disappearing beneath a strangler fig. An adjacent archway seemed to lead somewhere, so she stepped through and found herself surrounded by walls that stretched toward the trees. Their canopy cut through the sunlight, enhancing shadows that played with her imagination. The smell of rotting vegetation permeated air that seemed charged with images of times past.

Her sandals crunched over dry twigs as she crossed the grassy plateau to a stone slab. Beyond, on a higher level, rose the thirty-foot-high chimney stack. Spector's team member had captured the vortex at its base.

She skirted a live oak, stumbling over its roots, on her way to a carved stone staircase protected by an overgrowth of needle palms. Careful not to touch the palms' stiff spines, she edged past through a swarm of tiny insects, around a saw palmetto, and into a clearing.

She stopped to listen—and frowned. The bell had gone silent.

She heard only the whistling of wind through the branches. In the shade, her skin felt cooler, or was it the presence of spirits that chilled the air?

Something rustled off to her left. She spun in that direction but saw nothing except derelict copper kettles and vines swinging in the breeze.

A chorus of voices rose from the ruins, dissipating when she strained to hear them. They seemed to come from ahead, where the chimney reached for the sky. It stood as a lone sentinel, guarding the site from intruders. Watching her footing, Marla picked her way forward, careful not to wrench an ankle on the jagged stones in her path.

A flicker of white registered in the corner of her eye, but when she glanced over, it vanished into thin air. Her heart lurched, and her fingertips grew icy. Someone, or something, was nearby. The voices came again, drawing together into a confluence, emerging as a single sound, a high-pitched wailing. Marla couldn't make out if it was a natural result of the wind passing through the ruined hollows or not. Her flesh crawled. *Finish what you have to do and then get out of here.*

Reaching the chimney, she crouched. The opening at its base looked wide enough for a small person to squeeze inside. With a grimace of distaste, she stretched out to her full length on the ground. So much for her clean clothes.

Now for a light source.

Before proceeding further, she withdrew the penlight from her purse and shined it into the interior. A cascade of dust blew onto her face, coating her lips and making her sputter. Wishing she had a handkerchief to use as a mask, she hoped germs weren't hibernating in the rubble. Stale air made her breathing rapid and shallow, or maybe it was the combination of fear and excitement that pumped her pulse and made her movements jerky. A sense of dread grew within her, making the air seem to thicken and swirl around her head.

She couldn't see much from where she was, just soot lining the floor. She'd have to get farther inside. Leaving her bag behind, she dragged herself forward until just her feet stuck out of the opening.

Her hair hung across her face, and she spared a moment to tuck it behind her ears. When she did so, she was thrown off balance and flung her arm forward to steady herself. Her fingers touched . . . metal?

Carefully, she slid the object toward her, feeling its edges. The spade-shaped scoop seemed to be attached to a small wooden handle. "Ouch," she cried when a splinter pierced her skin. Cursing under her breath, she examined the small shovel. The metal didn't appear to be rusted.

Gripping its handle, Marla felt her palm grow warm. The thing almost seemed to vibrate in her grasp. Without thinking about it, she plunged it into the earth. A compulsion took hold of her, and she continued to dig deeper with each shovelful of dirt until the spade struck a solid surface.

Gritting her teeth against the pain cramping her muscles, she dug a big enough hole to extract a metal container. After brushing dirt off its top, she pried open the rusted lock and gasped at her find: Andrew's humidor.

Andrew must have hidden it himself, or else his trusted caretaker had done so at his bequest. *Open it. . . . Open it.* The litany rang in her head. Or was it the bell pealing outside with its own—what? Sound of celebration? Warning?

Ignoring the goose bumps prickling her skin and her throbbing finger where the splinter had penetrated, she removed the top of the humidor. Nestled inside was a waterproof pouch. Joy rose in her heart. It must hold something important. But she needed more light to see it properly.

Suddenly there was a hard grip on her ankles. Startled, she cried out. Before she could berate herself for letting her guard down, someone dragged her outside.

"You!" she rasped when she caught sight of who hovered above her. Even as she snapped upright to her defense, he pushed her down, rolled her onto her stomach, and forced her arms behind her back. Duct tape quickly bound her wrists and ankles. Her mouth tasted dirt, but she spat out the words: "You'll never get away with this, Jeffrey."

Her cousin's husband snickered. "Oh, but I will. I knew if I followed you, you'd lead me to Andrew's treasure. Let's see what's in here."

Digging a knee into her spine to restrain her, he grabbed the pouch from her fingers. Marla bent her neck so she could see. He withdrew a small leather sack and packet of bound documents.

"Dear me, which shall I open first?" Pulling apart the drawstrings on the smaller receptacle, he peeked inside and yelped in horror. "There's nothing here. Witch, what did you do with the gems?" Bending forward, he patted her body along intimate contours. She bucked in resistance.

"I didn't take anything. Whoever buried this box must've emptied the pouch. What do you need money for, anyway? Aren't you rich from your inheritance?"

Squirming against his groping fingers, she struggled to loosen the tape binding her wrists. It slid over the slime covering her skin. Twisting onto her back, she scooted away from him against the cold stone wall of the chimney.

He regarded her with a leer. "My mother is the toothpaste heiress. After she dies, my sister and I will inherit, unless our cousin convinces Mother otherwise. His family was always suspicious of dear old Daddy."

Marla bent her knees to give herself more leverage. "I don't understand," she said, hoping to keep him talking until Vail arrived. If she screamed, Jeff might gag her and then she'd lose her chance to alert Vail.

"Polly didn't tell you? She never divorced Vincent. After he ran off, he assumed another identity and ended up marrying my mother. He died of pneumonia before my sister's second birthday. I found out who he was years later when a detective came around."

"That detective looked for Vincent for ages."

Jeff's eyes hardened. "I realized my sister and I might lose our inheritance if the truth got out. So I paid the detective to tell Polly that Vincent had died, without mentioning us."

"Why did you marry Lori, then?"

He swiped a hand over his face as though he could erase years of uncertainty. "I didn't know what the detective's report said, so I courted Lori to get close to your aunt. When I met Polly, we got to talking about traumatic past events. She mentioned letters she had written to a man she'd once loved. She'd hidden them at the resort. I determined to find them, because if my cousin ever hired an investigator, those letters would destroy my father's reputation."

Marla kept working the bonds behind her back. "So you've been searching for them during your visits to the hotel. I presume you employed Brownie to spy for you. Does she know who you are?"

"Not at all. I convinced her that Polly had hidden something valuable on the property. Dearest Brittany easily succumbs to flattery. She's an easy mark, unlike you," he sneered.

"Did she search my room?" Marla inserted hastily, to distract him from evil thoughts. "I smelled lilacs, and I know she likes that scent."

"Brownie looked in your room as well as your aunt's, because I didn't know how much the old lady had told you. I was afraid Polly would use this reunion to air old grievances. Time to get rid of her to end the threat."

Marla pushed herself upright. "You mean Wanda Beake didn't pretend to be a nurse's aide in order to kill her?"

"I don't know anything about that. Brownie told me about the secret passages. She'd seen Butler use them. It was easy for me to get into Polly's bedroom that night. She couldn't see me well enough in the dim light. I pretended I was you, giving her a drink of water. Brownie had noticed the medicine bottle, so I added a bit to her glass. A pillow over her face did the rest."

He picked up the spade, weighing it in his hand. Marla didn't like the gleam in his eyes.

"So you murdered Polly. What about the groundskeeper?" Seto had been killed with a blunt instrument. It looked as though Jeff had the same thing in mind for her. While they talked, she'd loosened her binding enough to slip a hand free. Scrabbling around in the dirt, her fingers closed around a sizable rock.

"Mulch recognized me the first time I showed up at the resort. He said I resembled my father. I convinced him that telling Polly would only hurt her."

"So why did you decide to do away with him?"

"After she died, Seto had no reason to keep silent. He became a liability. You see, the detective fully reported on my father's second family, and the report came to Mulch. It was Mulch's decision to tell Polly only that Vincent had died. He saw no reason to deepen her wounds. Now you're the only threat left. I figured Polly had confided in you, and that you might lead me to her letters." He lifted the document pouch from the humidor. "Guess I was right, huh?"

Marla didn't contradict him. Her glance slid to her purse lying a short distance away. "Did you push me into the boiling pit?"

He nodded. "I'd hoped to scare you off from asking so many annoying questions. Now you've forced me to take more drastic measures."

He lifted the tool, but before he could swing his arm in a downward arc, Marla shoved her feet into his stomach. Grunting, he fell backward. She threw the rock at his head, making contact, then scrambled to her feet. But her bound ankles made it impossible to hobble far.

An insistent tune played from within a bunch of crotons. Her cell phone. Vail must be trying to reach her.

Marla screamed as Jeff jerked her ankles out from under her, causing her to tumble to the ground. She scratched his face, which only enraged him. Straddling her, he caught her wrists with one hand and raised her arms above her head. With a snarl, he reached for her throat with his other hand.

She tried to twist her neck away, but his fingers gouged into her flesh, pressing deeply, cutting off her air.

Spots flew in front of her eyes.

Her lungs burned, but she couldn't drag in a breath.

Strength bled from her limbs while her vision tunneled.

Barely aware, she caught sight of an apparition, perhaps an angel coming to claim her. The woman wore a long white dress and stood, sort of floating, beyond Jeff's shoulder. Light radiated around her golden hair.

Jeff glanced up, startled, as though he'd seen it also. His grip loosened.

Marla jabbed her knee into his groin. He howled in agony and released her.

Rolling to her side, she managed to crawl a few paces before Jeff shot out his hand to impede her.

Shouts reached her ears, one of them achingly familiar.

"You'd better let me go," she said in a raspy voice. "Dalton won't take kindly to seeing your hands on me. He won't be alone, either. You'll be outnumbered."

They stared at each other for a brief instant, then Jeff nodded. Wincing as he straightened his lanky form, he pivoted and raced toward the stone archway.

Marla watched his retreating figure while she gasped for breath and her heart slowed to a steady beat. Through the over-hanging branches, she saw the sun expand. Or was it the sun? The bright light contracted sharply, coalescing into a ball sus-pended directly in Jeff's path. He gave a bloodcurdling shriek and disappeared behind the trees.

The air crackled with energy. Marla felt a chill envelop her. Something brushed her cheek, and then the moment passed. The birdsong that had hushed rang out again, and Vail was sud-denly crouching beside her, while the forest erupted with uni-formed police.

"I can't believe Jeff fell into the well and was killed." Marla stood beside Vail on the pool deck, where a band was gearing up for the evening dance party. Surrounded by her relatives along with members of the ghost-hunting team, they were bringing everyone up-to-date on recent events. "I'd been by there earlier, and it had a barrier around it."

"Rotten wood," Vail said. "Maybe you dislodged a section when you passed the area and didn't realize it."

"Tell me again about the orb you saw," Spector said, his eyes round like the globes that lit the grounds at night.

Marla glanced at the eager faces turned their way. "Alyssa saved me. I saw her before she lured Jeff away." *And I think Polly was present as well, making sure I was safe.*

She lowered her head, moisture tipping her lashes. Poor Polly had no children to mourn her. Her aunt's smiling face popped into her mind, gazing fondly at Marla. Somehow that image brought comfort to her heart. It also brought a startling revelation. Maybe Polly had joined Seto at his favorite haunt, her spirit finally accepting his love.

The past merged with the present, and she sensed that Alyssa's ghost had also been appeased. Perhaps now that Polly had found her true love, her ancestor could rest as well?

"I thought you didn't believe in spooks." Vail grasped her hand. He'd been hovering close ever since he'd found her that afternoon. Some things were more precious than treasure, she thought, squeezing his palm.

"Let's just say I'm willing to believe in things that are not readily explained," she said, smiling. "I don't think the spirits will bother people anymore. We've exposed Andrew's secrets and ended Butler's abuse of the resort. Now the ghosts can go to their rest."

"Butler has been taken into custody for running a smuggling operation, but not for murder," Vail told the crowd. "Too bad no one can prove anything about the work-related incidents."

"You said the manager had been boating in illegal aliens that he hid on the thirteenth floor?" Cynthia asked.

"No, he secured them in Oleander Hall," Marla replied to her cousin. "I gather he was too spooked by the ghosts in Andrew's domain. Dalton and I took a peek at the speakeasy. There's a beautiful bar up there. It'll make a great lounge once the hotel is refurbished."

"I can't believe Grandfather was a bootlegger."

Marla didn't tell them about the sounds of clinking glasses and laughter emanating from the Prohibition-era hideout. Residual hauntings weren't harmful, and the creepiness would only add to the resort's ambience. She'd still like to thoroughly examine the hidden level, but it would be difficult until proper lighting was restored.

"Butler was quite clever," Vail said. Marla gave him an indulgent smile. The cop in him just couldn't help commenting on the criminal mind. "He'd learned about the passages from the original blueprints and converted the tunnels to his own use. The manager was involved in more than transporting illegal aliens, however. He'll also have a charge of human trafficking brought against him."

"What's that?" Cynthia asked, her eyes wide with curiosity.

Letting go of Marla's hand, Vail hunched his shoulders. "Traffickers bring in thousands of people to the States each year, and Florida is one of the top three destinations, thanks to all our waterways. These foreigners are forced to work on farms, in factories and brothels. Runaways and the homeless are potential victims, too. It's a form of modern-day slave labor."

"Tell them about debt bondage," Marla suggested, knowing Vail got his kicks from discussing bad guys.

"Butler's men were charged one thousand dollars each for transportation. This debt supposedly is deducted from their weekly pay, along with food, housing, and supplies. Meanwhile, they live in substandard dormitories, have no medical care, and no access to the outside. They're kept under control with guns and physical force. Under these conditions, it takes the workers years to get free."

"What did Butler do with a continual influx of people, then?" Cynthia persisted. "I know you followed him to some farm, but he couldn't use all those workers at just one place."

"They got shipped to other citrus groves, strawberry farms, or labor camps up north. We've uprooted the entire network."

"I'll bet you didn't expect such excitement at our family reunion," Marla said. "I'm just sorry Aunt Polly had to die."

"May she rest in peace," Anita added. "We need to say kaddish for her. When will we be able to . . . plan the memorial service?" Marla's mother addressed her question to Vail.

"It'll probably be a few more days yet until the toxicology report comes back."

"I can start cleaning out her apartment," Marla said. Sadness tinged her voice. "You know, I think she had a premonition. Aunt Polly wanted to find the treasure so she could buy back the resort and leave it as her legacy."

She'd already explained to her family about Polly's marriage to Vincent and about finding her wedding dress, letters, and will. No one begrudged her being the woman's heir. She'd been more like a daughter to her than a niece, after all.

"Aunt Polly kept returning to Sugar Crest to search for the alexandrite stones," Marla went on. "She made Seto promise not to expose the manager's operation when she found out about it. She'd planned to right his wrongs when she bought the place."

"Marla suspected at one point that your family might retain part ownership of the upper floors," Vail offered. "That would have prevented a sale to the theme-park developers. It seemed a viable motive to get Polly out of the way, assuming she was the only one who knew about it."

"That didn't turn out to be the case," Marla said, sniffing the jasmine-scented breeze.

Anita addressed her. "I don't understand why Papa's possessions are still in the tower. How come Mama didn't sell his stuff? And after she died, why didn't the hotel owners clean out those rooms?"

"Well, now, you know the documents that were in the humidor? Ruth's will left her personal goods, including the furniture, to Polly. According to a copy of the *real* bill of sale that we found for the resort property, the family doesn't own the two top floors, but Ruth and her surviving children have the right to reside there as long as they live."

"Remember," Vail said, "Butler would not have needed to dispose of Polly for this reason, even if she was the only one who knew about that provision. He was in favor of the hotel being restored, so he could continue his smuggling operation. When Polly got wind of his activities, that's when she became a threat. But she didn't want to ruin the resort's reputation before she could afford to buy it back, so she kept silent."

"It was Jeffrey who funded Donna Albright's campaign for the living-history experience," Marla reminded them. "He wanted the hotel destroyed, along with Polly's letters and all evidence of his parents' illegal union. Greed and fear of exposure were his motivators."

Marla scanned the crowd but didn't see Lori. She felt sorry for her cousin, but at least Lori had been released from an unhappy marriage. Marla would find her later to express condolences and offer encouragement.

"Awesome," Rochelle said, sashaying into view, her young face aglow in the moonlight. A breeze lifted the hem of her floral skirt. Wearing a ruby tube top and strappy heels, she flaunted her assets in front of her young male cousins. "Andrew must have been happy you found his humidor, but it's a bummer the jewels were all gone."

"I think Seto buried the humidor. That's why he hung out at the ruins, so he could make sure it was safe," Marla said. She tightened the glittery shawl she wore around her black cocktail dress. "Besides Ruth's will and her sale agreement for Sugar Crest, we found the detective's report in the document pouch. Seto had enclosed a confession as well."

She paused while her relatives hung on her words. "Those two visitors who wore Cossack hats . . . It was a disguise meant to fool Andrew into believing they were from his home country. Once they were admitted to see him, they showed their true colors. They were Nazis spies."

"Oh, wow," Rochelle breathed, a dreamy look on her face.

"Here comes the best part. Seto and Andrew killed the men, bashing their heads in with those heavy candlesticks on the fireplace mantel. The stress of the event made Andrew ill, and he staggered out, after his trusted caretaker promised to dispose of their bodies. Mulch dragged them into the secret passage and later buried them under his flower beds."

"You're saying Papa was a murderer?" Anita said, gasping. Her shock was reflected on the faces of her siblings, who stood by with their families, glued to Marla's tale.

"Rumrunner, bootlegger, killer. Grandfather was a lot of things, but he wasn't done in by any of Ruth's siblings as she suspected. No, it was the stroke that got him. He died of natural causes. I think Polly figured it out and wanted to mend fences this weekend by bringing everyone together."

"What about that nurse's aide? Did you ever find out who hired her to take care of Polly the night she died?" Anita inquired.

"Yeah. Would you believe Polly hired the woman herself?" Marla's face split into a sheepish grin. "Here I was ready to accuse Wanda Beake, because of a resemblance between the two. When I looked through Polly's papers again this afternoon, I found a phone number for another nursing service. Polly didn't want anyone to know she needed help, so she hired the aide and instructed her to pretend she'd been sent as a gift. Apparently, this woman had worked for the other agency previously and still wore that name tag. That's why they said she wasn't in their employ when Dr. Angus called."

"Did you contact this person?" Anita said. "She would have been the last person to see Polly alive."

"I spoke to her briefly on the telephone. Polly was fine when she left, around eleven o'clock that night."

"So what's going to happen to the resort?"

Marla shrugged. "Champagne has been put in charge until a new manager is appointed. She wanted to fire the steward, but Harvey promised to go on the wagon if she'd keep him. Brownie will stay on as dessert chef until she finds another position. She really didn't do anything wrong, except to act as a snoop for Jeffrey."

"I thought the council already voted to sell the place," Cynthia said, smoothing her linen pants set.

Bruce smiled at his wife. "Another development company has made a better offer. They've got plans to explore the site's archaeological value, so the ruins will remain untouched. But they'll restore the grand hotel. It'll be a gold mine, with its legends, ghosts, scandals, and secret passages. This will be a true living-history experience with a glimpse into the past."

Marla's jaw dropped. "Bless my bones, is that your doing?"

Rubbing his hands together, Bruce nodded jovially. "It promises to be an exciting project. I think we'll leave Butler's special effects in Oleander Hall and charge extra for folks who want to stay in the haunted wing. The concierge level, of course, will move to the penthouse. And the speakeasy will make a great lounge, as you said." He made a slight bow.

Marla gave his shoulder an affectionate swat. "Leave it to Bruce to see that the hotel remains in the family."

She had one more piece of unfinished business. Spotting her brother chatting with one of their uncles, she waved. "Hey, pal, can I see you alone for a minute?" She glanced at Vail. "You won't mind, will you? I'll be right back."

He tilted his head. "Take your time. While I'm waiting, I'll hit the bar for a drink refill. This whole *megillah* has left my head spinning. Ma, can I get you anything?" he asked Anita.

Marla beamed with pride as she watched him fold Anita's arm into his own and stroll away. Her fiancé seemed much more comfortable with her family than when they'd first arrived. That had been her goal in bringing him along, after all. She felt a warm glow of satisfaction. Dalton would fit in just fine with her family.

"So tell me, bro," she said to Michael, "did you talk to Charlene about your problems?"

He regarded her warmly. "Yep, and you were right. She had some good ideas that will help us get off the ground."

"You may not owe Polly any more money, but you've lost your

savings." When they reached a darkened corner, she rummaged inside her purse and then withdrew her fist. "I'm giving these to you on one condition. You don't tell anyone about this exchange."

She opened her palm, and gleaming in the moonlight were three smoky stones.

Her brother's eyes widened. "You found the jewels. Where?" he choked out.

"They were under a false bottom in the humidor. I don't think even Seto knew they were there. He might have given them to Polly otherwise." She leaned forward. "Promise me you'll use these stones to clear your debts with any extra going into your retirement funds."

He didn't make a move to take them. "Are there more?"

"No, this is all that was left. Don't argue with me. I want you to have them." Marla chuckled. "In my mind, this isn't the real treasure. Would you believe we're all descended from Russian royalty? I found another document in the humidor: Andrew's true identity papers."

His face sobered. "We're all his heirs. Those stones belong to our parents: Ma and her brothers. They should sell them and divide up the money."

"Not really. Ruth may have put the proceeds from the hotel sale into her estate, but she left her personal possessions to Polly. That means these belong to me now. I'm giving them to you along with my blessing."

"But you—"

She shook her head, soft waves of hair brushing her face. "I don't need them. I'll get Andrew's furniture and paintings that I suspect will fetch a decent price, plus whatever Polly has in her accounts. I've been thinking of adding spa services to my salon. Maybe now we'll be able to expand."

If she had anything left after paying off her loan from Miriam, that is. She'd rather move the salon to a bigger space in a more upscale location. That wasn't her main reason for wanting a change. She couldn't stand dealing with her landlord any longer. They'd had too many run-ins for their continued association to remain pleasant. Getting away from him had become her new goal.

"Marla, I still feel bad about taking what's rightfully yours. How can I ever . . . ?" Michael's voice broke.

"Consider it an investment in my niece and nephew." She hugged him, patting his back.

After dropping the stones in his palm, she strode away.

Vail stood by the pool tapping his foot. The Jamaican steel band had kicked off the dance party with a fast beat, and a mass of jiggling bodies crowded the deck. Waitresses strolled among the seated observers, hawking tropical drinks with chunks of pineapple and party umbrellas while flaming torches added to the ambience. Fuel tainted the air with a chemical scent.

"I guess your good deed got accepted," Vail said when she accosted him with a kiss. "Let's get out of here." Grabbing her hand, he wormed through the throng toward an isolated section of beach, where they shed their shoes.

Marla's feet sank into sand as he led her along the shoreline. Edging closer to the water, she splashed into the sea foam, feeling the sting of salt water on her legs. The guitar music receded as they increased their distance, and soon she heard nothing except an occasional seagull taunting its prey with a shrill cry and the soothing swoosh of the ocean. Out to sea, moonbeams cut the crests into sprays of diamonds.

She gave Vail a sidelong glance. His impressive profile quickened her pulse. He looked handsome in a gray sweater, black trousers, and sport coat. His clothing highlighted the silver streaks in his hair.

His gaze darkened as he halted to face her. He said nothing, clearing his throat in an uncharacteristic manner.

Her toes sifted warm sand while she waited for him to speak. Would this be good news or bad? Her stomach muscles clenched.

"I'm glad I got to meet your family this weekend, despite the events that transpired. You'll get your chance to meet mine soon enough," he said, chuckling, while Marla considered an appropriate response.

"About the holidays," she began, but he cut her off.

"I've decided it's time to let go of certain things." He kicked at a seashell. "Like ghosts of the past. If I've learned nothing else from being here, it's that people's spirits deserve their rest. It hurts them for us to keep them here, and it doesn't do us any good, either."

He drew a deep breath and spurted out his next words. "So I propose that we look for a new house when we return home."

Stunned, Marla stared at him. "Are you sure?"

"I know you hate being in the same house that Pam and I shared. Brie can still keep what she wants from her mother's collections. Meanwhile, we can work out what we'll each contribute to our new home. You might even want to add some of Andrew's furniture." He stroked her chin. "Your mother made this suggestion to me a while back, but it's taken me this long to realize she's right. Could you accept me on these terms?"

Too choked with emotion to speak, Marla nodded. She never thought she'd get him to budge from the house he'd lived in with his late wife, but the fact that he could finally move on meant he was ready to let Pam go. Afraid her bubble might burst, she bit her lip and kept silent.

"There's one more thing," he said, taking a velvet box from his pocket. "I thought of hiding this inside a conch shell, but you've had enough treasure hunts for one trip. Open it."

Marla trembled as she raised the lid and spied the diamond solitaire nestled inside. "Oh, Dalton."

"Now it's official." His lips curved upward as he took the ring and slipped it on the third finger of her left hand.

It might have been Marla's imagination, but she thought she heard muffled cheers and applause wafting from the direction of the old sugar mill.

Author's Note

This was a great story to research. I used the *Haunt Hunter's Guide to Florida* by Joyce Elson Moore to read up on haunted sites in the state and then visited the Gamble Mansion in Ellenton, Florida. With its rich history as a sugar mill plantation and its location among moss-draped oaks by a river, it inspired my design for Sugar Crest Resort in *Dead Roots*. Reading the history of other grand resorts in Florida also provided information, as did the www.ghosttracker.com Web site for explanations of ghostly phenomena. And, of course, don't forget the Tower of Terror in Walt Disney World. If you get the chance, watch the film based on the attraction; it's a lot of fun.

Marla's family history is based on my own; my maternal grandmother had eight children, and my ancestors come from Russia and Poland. However, I cannot claim any royal lineage.

I love to hear from readers. Write to me at P.O. Box 17756, Plantation, FL 33318. Please enclose a self-addressed stamped #10 business-size envelope for a personal reply.

Email: nancy.j.cohen@comcast.net

Web site: www.nancyjcohen.com

HOOD COUNTY LIBRARY

HOOD COUNTY LIBRARY